Thisby Thestoop

AND THE

Black Mountain

Thisby Thestoop

AND THE

Black Mountain

By Zac Gorman

HARPER
An Imprint of HarperCollinsPublishers

Thisby Thestoop and the Black Mountain

Text copyright © 2018 by Zac Gorman

Illustrations copyright © 2018 by Sam Bosma

All rights reserved. Printed in the United States of America.

No part of this book may be used or reproduced in any manner whatsoever without written
permission except in the case of brief quotations embodied in critical articles and reviews. For
information address HarperCollins Children's Books, a division of HarperCollins
Publishers, 195 Broadway, New York, NY 10007.

www.harpercollinschildrens.com

Library of Congress Control Number: 2017934813

ISBN 978-0-06-249568-6

Typography by Joe Merkel

19 20 21 22 23   CG/BRR   10 9 8 7 6 5 4 3 2 1

❖

First paperback edition, 2019

FOR SUZY

PROLOGUE

Far below, a torch flickered in the darkness. Its bright orange flame bobbed along like a buoy adrift on a blackened sea, swaying rhythmically as it went and casting strange, nervous shadows amid the ruins. The light followed an irregular path, weaving between pillars engraved with long-forgotten languages, ducking beneath barely-held-together arches, and ambling through doorways leading to yet more doorways through an endless labyrinth of rooms, until it arrived at last at a passageway, where it paused.

Attached to the end of the torch—the nonburning end, of course—was a man, clad in full plate armor, upon whose shoulders rested the fate of an entire village. He held the torch out at arm's length and waited for something, for anything to give him a reason to turn around. But nothing came. There was no noise, no movement. Nothing but a chamber of impressive darkness. Darkness so impressive that it took on physical characteristics. It had a weight, a texture, a smell. This particular darkness smelled something like an old root cellar after a thunderstorm.

The man stood at the doorway for some time considering his options, but finally, seeing no better alternatives, stepped forward into the dark.

We call him "the man" here because his name does not matter. His name does not matter because this man did not succeed in his quest, and therefore his name did not need to be remembered for songs or epic poems or history books. No parents proudly named their children after this man. No sculptors needed to know how his name was spelled when they were engraving their statues of him.

No, this man died. Just like all the adventurers who came before him to this horrid place seeking treasure, whether for their own selfish gains or for noble reasons such as saving their village from a terrible plague by returning with a vial of magic elixir. The reason didn't matter. It never did. Neither did it matter that this man was handsome, or brave, or skilled with a sword. There are certain traps that cannot be escaped once entered.

The man heard a noise behind him and spun around, but only darkness stared back. If he was a coward, he'd have run.

It wouldn't have helped.

He held up his torch and turned to watch the shadow play on the wall. His own puppet, the shadow he cast, was as high as the rough-hewn cavern, stretched out like a grotesque giant. For a moment, he thought he saw something move behind it. Another shadow, perhaps, just beyond the periphery of his vision. He heard the noise again, closer now. He drew his sword. The familiar *shhiiiiiiiinng!* of his steel blade against its hilt rang out like a challenge to the darkness. This far below in the dungeon, however, the darkness always won.

With a gust of cold air that sounded a bit like a cruel laugh, his torch was extinguished. The darkness washed over him, as thick as mud, and the only solace he was offered was that he never saw the creature bearing down on him.

CHAPTER 1

Thisby Thestoop wiggled her toes in her boots, carefully placing her pinky toe over the toe-which-comes-next-to-the-pinky-toe. It had become a bit of a nervous habit, you might say; but if Thisby was nervous, you'd never have known it from her businesslike demeanor or the tuneless song she hummed mindlessly as she went. This was especially interesting considering that Thisby was currently inching along a damp rock wall in complete darkness, an arm's length away from a sleeping troll.

It probably goes without saying, but most people do not hum around sleeping trolls. Thisby, however, knew that trolls were notoriously hard to wake with noise but alarmingly easy to rouse with smells, particularly the scent of meat. Which was why in all of the many, many pockets in the overlarge backpack she always wore, each serving of meat—and there were many—was dutifully wrapped in heavy butcher's paper, and several bundles of sweetgrass were tied to the outside of her pack to mask the smell. Thisby knew to do this because it was her job to know these things, and she was quite good at her job.

Thisby was quite good at most things, as a matter of fact, but not for the reasons most people might assume. She wasn't born particularly clever or brave. She couldn't move like a shadow or shoot an arrow through the eye of a needle. And she most definitely wasn't predestined to greatness through some divine prophecy or "Chosen One" hooey. No, Thisby Thestoop was astoundingly average in every way, save one—a trick she'd learned when she was quite young and had made into a habit through sheer force of will, first as a means of survival and later as a way to slake her endless curiosity: Thisby took diligent notes.

The troll mumbled something in its sleep. Its voice sounded like a bunch of rocks rolling around inside a cast-iron pot. Thisby crouched low to let the bottom of her backpack touch the cold cave floor before squeezing together her shoulder blades and wriggling free. The bag stood upright on its own as she got onto her tippy toes to dig around inside the main compartment.

A quiet voice whispered in her ear, "He wants to crunch on your bones."

Thisby continued digging.

"It's what he said. In Trollish," the voice continued.

"You don't have to whisper, Mingus," said Thisby.

She unhooked her lantern and whirled it around the backpack gracefully, illuminating the fastidiously buttoned pouches, which she promptly set about opening. As the little jelly inside the lantern slid to and fro in his smooth glass enclosure, his glow changed from a warm, golden yellow to a sickly chartreuse.

"BE CAREFUL! YOU MIGHT CRACK MY JAR!" shrieked Mingus.

Thisby ignored him.

She dunked the lantern inside the bag's main compartment. It was followed shortly thereafter by her entire head, well past her shoulders. The inside of the backpack was exactly as organized as Thisby's notes—which is to say, not very well—although that, perhaps, depended upon who was looking. Thisby always seemed to know exactly where to find what she was searching for in the maze of boxes, bags, jars, and oddly shaped containers. Despite being crammed full of goods, the backpack was still large enough for Thisby to crawl inside and take a nap—not that she usually had time for naps, but if, on a rare slow workday down in the dungeon, you came across a large, snoring backpack, well then, mystery solved.

"Brighter, please," said Thisby.

"It's rather cold in here today. I wish I had a sweater. But I suppose I'd need arms to wear a sweater. Perhaps a scarf? But I suppose that would require a neck," said Mingus. The jelly glowed ever more brightly as he spoke, illuminating the inside of the bag with a pleasant ochre hue. He watched Thisby as she worked. At least, it appeared that way.

Back when they first met, Thisby had been kind enough to make him a pair of makeshift eyes out of painted buttons, so she knew where to look when they spoke. She'd taught him how to bend a crease to use for a sort of pretend mouth as well. He'd wiggle it open and closed when he was talking, despite the fact that the sound he produced actually just kind of vibrated out of his whole body. He'd even learned how to make some basic facial expressions by reshaping the jelly around his faux eyes to look nervous or surprised.

"Ouch!" Thisby exclaimed, sucking at her finger.

Mingus did his best disgusted face. "When's the last time you washed that finger?"

"It's fine!" she said, missing the point. "It's just a little pinprick. What do you want me to do? Let it bleed everywhere?"

"No, I—"

"Wait! Maybe you could use your mysterious slime healing magic to fix it!" she teased, waving her bloody finger toward his jar.

"Stop it! Cut it out!" he squealed.

It was an inside joke.

Once, on one of the rare occasions when Thisby had been forced to physically lift Mingus out of his jar—rare indeed because Mingus hated to be touched—a troublesome wart on her finger had miraculously vanished the next morning. Thisby found this quite amusing and never let the joke drop.

Thisby withdrew a large brown paper parcel from her backpack and tossed it to the ground several feet away. It landed with a wet *thud*. She checked an old, weathered notebook and muttered to herself.

"Drop off seven pounds of raw beef for the troll! Check! Oh! I almost forgot!"

Thisby reached into her backpack and withdrew a small burlap bag. From it, she pulled several branches of fragrant rosemary, which she tossed near the dripping brown paper parcel on the cave floor.

"Come on," she said.

"Please be careful with me this time . . . I think the structural integrity of my jar may be weakening."

"I could always take you out and have you sit on my shoulder. Like a parrot!" Thisby teased.

Mingus looked sicker than usual. "P-please, Thisby . . . don't say that . . ."

"Geez! I'm only joking!"

She hooked Mingus's lantern to its dedicated spot on her backpack and hoisted the monstrous bag onto her tiny shoulders. Thisby knew they had roughly four minutes

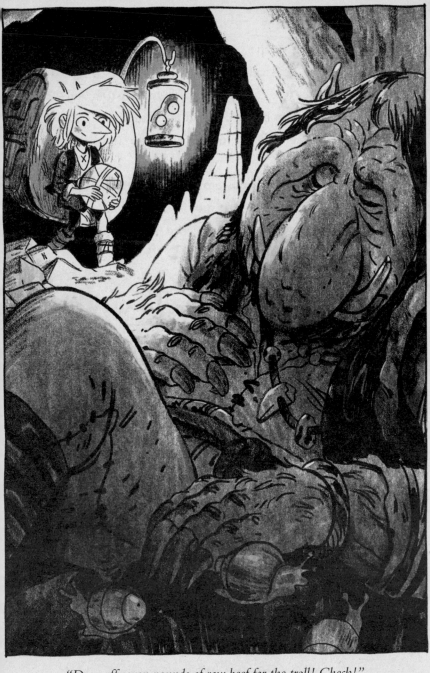

"Drop off seven pounds of raw beef for the troll! Check!"

before the smell of the raw meat would permeate the paper enough to rouse the troll from sleep. She also knew hungry trolls were most definitely not "morning people." She'd found that one out the hard way. It was just another in a seemingly endless list of potentially deadly quirks she'd come to understand during her tenure as gamekeeper.

She moved at a brisk trot farther down into the dungeon and blew into her hands to warm them. It was, in fact, unseasonably cold in the mountain today. Perhaps the ice wraiths had woken up from their hibernation early, she thought. Defrosting an ice wraith nest wasn't exactly something she was looking forward to, but it needed to be done and nobody else was going to do it. Thisby pulled a small notebook from her pocket and scribbled some notes as she walked.

BIG GREEN = 7 MOO (+RM)
SLUSHIES = ZZZZZ?

It was going to be another busy day.

Castle Grimstone had existed for as long as the people of Three Fingers could remember, which isn't really as impressive as it sounds. The villagers of Three Fingers rarely made it past the age of twenty-five, and the ones who did were too busy barely staying alive to remember things like when castles were built and all that other nonsense.

The castle stood atop a mountain, long ago corrupted by the vileness that dwelt within. Even moss would not dare grow on its craggy surface. The mountain was colloquially called the Black Mountain—its only name, actually, since nobody was brave enough to give it a formal one—and it was the biggest in all of Nth and quite possibly the entire world, though nobody but wizards had ever traveled far enough to see for themselves and nobody believed anything wizards had to say—and rightly so. But it was there, atop the mountain's highest pinnacle, that Castle Grimstone had stood for as long as the blighted, dirt-farming yokels could remember.

Grimstone looked as if an angry four-year-old had smashed a toy castle apart and her poor, exasperated mother had hastily put it back together all wrong. There were all the telltale signs of a castle but there seemed to be no logic as to its construction. An excess of towers jutted out at irregular angles and none of the parapet walks made any sense. A few of them even seemed to be upside down. Nearly every exterior surface was covered in black iron spikes, which stuck out in every imaginable direction, and where you could see through, there were only black stones, perpetually wet and slick like they'd just been covered in fresh oil.

It was on her zero-th birthday that Thisby had first come to the castle. Her parents, a particularly dull and cruel pair of Three Fingers yokels, had traded her for a bag of mostly unspoiled turnips that morning, and by that afternoon the wandering salesman on the other end of the bargain was already lamenting the haste with which he'd accepted the deal. When he returned to insist upon a refund, he found that her parents had already used the turnips to make a paste to ward off bad spirits, which they'd promptly smeared all over their bodies. After giving it some serious thought, he decided that a trade back seemed unwise. Disheartened, he dumped the baby at the foot of the Black Mountain and vowed to be more thoughtful about his business decisions in the future.

It was nearly midnight when a blackdoor in the mountain opened and a shadowy figure peered out into the night, glancing at first right over the tiny newborn baby on the doorstep. When the towering, hairy figure went to step forward, something beneath its massive hoof made a strange gurgling sound. It looked down to find what seemed to be a miraculously as yet uncrushed human infant. The creature picked up the baby and thought for a moment. But he'd had a big lunch that day, so he took the baby inside for later.

He quickly scrawled a note, which he laid down atop the baby, nearly covering it completely, before shuffling back out into the night. The note read:

> FOUND THIS BY THE STOOP.
> PLEASE KEEP FOR LATER.

Fortunately for the baby, minotaur penmanship is notoriously sloppy, and several hours later when the goblin maintenance staff were cleaning up the kitchen, they lifted the sheet of paper off the squirming newborn baby and read it as thus:

FOUND, THISBY THESTOOP.
PLEASE KEEP FOREVER.

And so they did.

CHAPTER 2

Thisby finished her rounds in the dungeon before heading up to bed for a few precious hours of sleep. As she darted between the shadowy crawl spaces and hidden passages that only she was privy to, Mingus read off the list of chores that she'd dropped into his jar that morning. It was a sort of fail-safe they did every day to make sure she hadn't missed anything. Mingus would read the name of the chores she'd completed one by one, and she'd respond with an audible "*Check.*"

She'd fed the troll, peeked in on the ice wraiths (which were thankfully still asleep), removed the bones from the ooze pit, watered the creeping death vines, baited the spike traps, reseeded the wereplant den, turned the hydra eggs, trimmed the griffin's toenails, uncrusted the rock imps, and stabled the nightmares. As she half listened to Mingus reading the list, she'd already begun to think ahead to the new chores that were waiting for her tomorrow: dousing the rogue fire elementals, unsalting the meat for the slughemoth, polishing the ifrit lamps . . . and so on and so on, she thought, until she'd nearly made it all the way back to her room at the top of the mountain. But just before her hand could reach the iron ring on her door, Mingus read off one last item.

"Pick up the herbs from Shabul."

"*Che*— Oh, no!"

Thisby raced back down the rickety ladder that led up to her room and darted across the wooden bridge that connected it to the castle cellar, her footsteps thumping against the makeshift boardwalk. She wasn't technically allowed inside the castle proper. The Master preferred to keep his dungeon separate from his castle, presumably because it was unsafe, but based on the kind of abhorrent creatures that freely roamed the castle halls with complete impunity, this seemed fairly unlikely. The far more likely scenario was that the Master simply preferred for his subjects to live in a constant state of fear and distrust. And just like every Master from every history of every world that has ever existed, he knew that the easiest way to achieve such a horrible state of fear and distrust was to separate his creatures into groups and arbitrarily tell one group that they were better or worse than the other groups. In the Black Mountain, there were a lot of groups.

As gamekeeper, Thisby was part of the staff and had more freedom than the enslaved monsters who lived in the dungeon. She had her own room as close to the top as one could hope to live while still residing in the mountain itself, and she was rarely beaten and usually had enough to eat. She didn't have the clout of the staff that worked inside the castle of course, but as long as she finished her chores, she was able to come and go as she pleased. The catch, of course, being that her chores were never finished.

"Watch where you're going!" hissed a voice from the darkness.

A mindworm the size of Thisby's forearm, with twelve magnificent glittering eyes and a shiny, ruby-hued body, shrank back into its hiding hole as she ran past. Thisby ignored its angry hissing and tried to shake the image of her own gruesome death from her imagination as the worm chided her telepathically.

She removed a piece of wood from the cave wall, revealing a hole just big enough to fit her and her cumbersome backpack. Deciding not to wake the now-sleeping Mingus, who dangled from his usual hook—he'd returned to his normal grayish color—she entered the darkened tunnel without the aid of his light and relegated herself to bumping her elbows and cutting her knees against the crude, unforgiving rock walls.

The tunnel ran just below the edge of the castle and was so tight that she had to remove her backpack and slither flat on her belly for the last few feet. At the far end of the tunnel was an opening just wide enough for her head and shoulders to push through and peek out into the cool night air. The wind whipped her short, sweaty hair over her face so that it was hard to see the darkened pines that dotted the smaller mountains to the south.

Being outside felt incredible. Like the first drink of ice-cold water after you've been running around in the heat all day. Only better. She closed her eyes for a moment and drank it in. Inside the mountain, the air was as old as the rocks themselves, but out here, it was new and wonderful and almost thirst quenching.

"Hey!" a voice rasped in that particularly unhelpful-to-anyone type of yelling whisper. "Girl! Girl! It's me!"

Below her, standing on a narrow cliff, was a sullen-looking old man.

"Girl! It's me! Shabul! With the herbs!"

Thisby thought it was strange that even after years of their arrangement, Shabul still thought it was necessary to introduce himself this way. Also, that he hadn't bothered to learn her name. Still, it was business, and Thisby didn't take it personally.

Shabul was the only person, as far as Thisby knew—and admittedly she knew very little of the world outside the dungeon—who dared come this far up the Black Mountain. He grew herbs near the foothills, down where things would still grow, and every few weeks he'd bring his herbs to Thisby in exchange for ingredients for his potions, which she collected around the dungeon. It was a mutually beneficial relationship. She had use for fresh herbs, and his magic potions appeared much more impressive to the locals when he infused them with exotic ingredients from the most dangerous place in the entire kingdom. He neglected to mention that he actually traded for them with a rather polite twelve-year-old girl.

As little as Thisby knew about the outside world, she knew even less about magic. And what she did know, she didn't exactly find encouraging. Most wizards, she assumed, were like Shabul, making so-called potions out of detritus. She found it absurd to think anybody could truly believe that bits of basilisk bone could cure jaundice, or behemoth dung could cure leprosy, but still, Shabul was nice enough to bring her herbs, so she didn't mind him personally.

"It's nice to see you again, Shabul!" she yelled before wriggling back through the small opening to grab Shabul's bag from her backpack. When she returned, she dropped it into a bucket on the end of a length of rope and lowered it down to him. "How're things at the store?" Thisby asked. Shabul wasn't much of a conversationalist, but Thisby had no other connection with the outside world, so she made do. Shabul was distractedly eyeing the bucket on its way down.

"You know. Same as always." he said. "I grow herbs. I make potions. Of course, next week will be busy, busy, busy!"

When Thisby stopped lowering the bucket, just out of

arm's reach of Shabul, he looked up at her, a bit irritated.

"I mean, when the royals come up mountain next week. For Inspection."

Thisby's heart sank. The Royal Inspection. She'd always known Inspection was a possibility, but somehow it'd never felt real before. According to some of the older staff around the dungeon, the royal family used to come around for Inspection every few years to check out the dungeon and make sure everything was in order, but she'd been here for twelve years and this was the first she'd heard of one actually happening.

"But why now?" Thisby blurted.

"Apparently, the Prince fancies himself a bit of an adventurer. Wants to see the biggest and baddest dungeon in all of Nth!" Shabul laughed, amusing himself. "You know what I think—" he started, but before he could even finish his sentence, the bucket clattered to his feet as Thisby ducked back through the tunnel, snatched her backpack, and was running full steam toward her chambers, her tiny feet slapping hard against the cold stone.

By the time she reached her room, she was sweating. Her mind was dizzy with thoughts of all the work that would be necessary to get ready for an Inspection. She already barely had time to sleep as it was.

When Thisby stepped through her darkened doorway she was so lost in thought that she didn't even notice the pale, gnarled man standing at the foot of her bed.

CHAPTER 3

"Keeper," grunted a gruff voice in the dark.

Thisby's heart tried to escape through her mouth before she realized who it was. But even that did very little to settle her nerves.

The figure shifted so the light shining through the crack in the door illuminated his pockmarked, stony face. Thisby knew her boss could see in the dark and that he liked to use this to his advantage to keep her on her toes. Anything to keep her scared and in her place. Thisby regained her composure as quickly as possible, but she could tell by his unusually smarmy grin that it was too late.

"Roquat," Thisby said coldly.

Roquat was a miserable old Dünkeldwarf whose family had lived in the mountain for generations. Like most Dünkeldwarves, he was as pale as moonlight and as thick as a tree trunk turned sideways. He had milky white eyes and a beard into which he'd woven little bits of every rock that he'd ever tasted, a teeth-shattering tradition among Dünkeldwarves that Thisby found particularly stupid. (Although, admittedly, she found certain aspects of their culture quite fascinating—like how they had no word for love but more than one hundred words for granite, or how their people had lived in the Black Mountain longer than anyone else, predating even the goblins. As far as Thisby knew, Roquat was the lone survivor.)

"Come now, Keeper. You'll call me Boss unless you desire a week of digging trenches in the Deep Down," he wolfishly mumbled through a mouthful of sharp, blackened teeth. Normally, her deliberate impudence would've resulted in an immediate punishment, but Roquat's pride in catching Thisby off guard had tempered his anger. For Roquat, this was as close to pleasant as he could manage.

"You know why I'm here, Keeper."

Thisby's mind raced while she tried her best to look collected.

It was possible that he knew about the Royal Inspection, but it was just as likely that he knew nothing. Roquat was Thisby's boss, and he served as liaison between the dungeon and the Master. But he was a long way down the ladder in the

"Roquat," Thisby said coldly.

grand scheme of things. The Master entrusted only a small group of people with privileged information, and Roquat— likely for good reason—wasn't one of them. Besides, the sooner Roquat found out about the Inspection, the sooner she'd be spending her nights cleaning the scum off the walls of the gnoll pits. Thisby wasn't new to this game, and she knew better than to volunteer information freely in the dungeon.

"I'm afraid I don't have your connections, Boss," she said with as much forced reverence as she could stomach.

Roquat moved into the light and stroked his beard thoughtfully.

"Hm. That you don't, whelp. That you don't." Roquat chuckled as he sat down in the chair at her desk. The legs creaked and splayed beneath his weight. "You didn't forget what tomorrow is, did you?"

Thisby's momentary relief vanished. Roquat recognized her look of revelation. He let out a throaty laugh that sounded like he was choking on a bagful of marbles.

"The Darkwell!" blurted Thisby.

"Your mind's been slippin' lately, Keeper! Maybe it's time you started writin' some of this stuff down!" Roquat was positively delighted.

"And what does an illiterate like you know about writing?" squeaked a voice from the doorway.

Thisby and Roquat looked over at the little old goblin standing in the doorway. Roquat bolted up to his feet, tipping over the chair. Even though he was easily ten times their size, something about goblins had always made Roquat uncomfortable. Thisby suspected it was their magic.

With a curt nod, Roquat excused himself from the room but couldn't resist one last parting shot.

"Better get to bed, Keeper. You've got a busy day tomorrow and you don't want to keep him waiting. It's a long walk to the Darkwell." Roquat let his ominous words hang in the air as he went. As he shoved past Thisby, his body odor stung her nostrils. It was terribly unpleasant, even worse than usual, and it caused her to gag. She almost said something mocking but decided to bite her tongue. As sweet as it may have been to get in the last word, the likelihood that it would've resulted in a beating was fairly high, and besides, even if it hadn't, there was nothing in the world worth having to deal with him for a second longer, anyway.

Thisby relaxed her shoulders. It wasn't until Roquat left her room that she realized they'd been pulled up around her ears the whole time.

"Never mind him! What was he doing in here anyway, don't you lock your door?" said the old goblin in a tone that Thisby could only describe as motherly—somehow both soothing and stern simultaneously.

"I thought I did," said Thisby.

"Well, never mind, never mind!"

She patted Thisby genially on the hip—which was about as high as she could reach—and crossed over to the desk. She gently picked up the chair that Roquat had tipped over and returned it to its proper spot, nodding contentedly as if erasing the memory of his presence.

"Thank you, Grunda. You're too kind," said Thisby.

Grunda pretended like she hadn't heard Thisby and continued to dutifully straighten up her room. Thisby knew goblins were notoriously bad at taking compliments but figured it was worth a shot anyway.

Thisby watched Grunda organizing her notebooks and tried to fight the uneasy feeling in the pit of her stomach. She trusted Grunda more than anybody else in the dungeon, but lately, she'd been feeling particularly careful about her belongings, her notebooks especially.

A week ago, Thisby had returned to her room to find several of her notebooks missing. The strangest part was that her room had been locked, and when she returned, it still was. Of course, she'd suspected Roquat, but he didn't have a key and he couldn't simply walk through walls. It was possible she'd left the door open, but had she really been getting that careless? She'd seemingly just done it again, so it was possible. Or maybe he did have a key. She'd have to look into it.

She hadn't suspected Grunda—after all, they were friends—but Thisby knew goblin magic was particularly adept at sneaking goblins into places where goblins didn't normally belong, and Grunda was far from the only goblin in the dungeon. She hated herself for even thinking such ugly little thoughts, but just like goblins couldn't help but get into mischief, humans couldn't help but mistrust. A nasty little disease of the human spirit to which even those as good-natured as Thisby weren't completely immune.

Thisby shook the thought from her head and smiled at her friend.

"He's right about one thing, though. You'd better get to bed," Grunda said as she blew some dust off a filthy old notebook in which Thisby had jotted her notes on the biology of carnivorous dungeon plants. "It's at least a day's trip to the Darkwell, and you know how cranky he gets when he's kept waiting."

CHAPTER 4

The scariest room in any house is almost always the basement. Sure, occasionally you might come across an especially spooky attic, or a creepy nursery, or a haunted broom closet, but nine times out of ten, the last place you want to be in a house on a stormy night is the basement. The Black Mountain was no exception. The lower you went, the scarier it got.

Near the top of the mountain, you had your basic goblins and imps. Small monsters who could be fairly vicious when riled but weren't enough to thwart most hardy adventurers who wandered into the dungeon in search of treasure. Below that were your zombies, ghouls and vampires. Undead creatures, that sort of thing. Below that you started getting into your bigger nasties: trolls, orcs, were-things, wyverns, dire this-and-thats. Of course, the lower you went, the better the treasure. That was sort of the whole appeal of the dungeon. Test yourself against the deadliest monsters on the planet and leave with a fistful of coins to show for it—if you leave at all. Most adventurers who tried their luck in the dungeon never made it any lower than the midway point, let alone to the bottom. They were lucky. Below the midway point was when you started to get into the really nasty stuff.

Thisby had seen it.

Thisby had been as low in the dungeon as any human had ever been, possibly lower, and she moved about it all with ease. She could traipse among vile, ooze-spitting giants and look into the eyes of a spectral ghoul without blinking. She could do this because she paid attention. She studied the behavior of the monsters. She knew their strengths and their weaknesses. Their patterns and their habits. She knew the tricks and the secrets of every inch of that dungeon, and somewhere, buried inside her notebooks, there was an answer to every problem the dungeon could throw at her. It's unbelievable what can be accomplished when a person pays attention and takes diligent notes, and nobody paid better attention or took better notes than Thisby Thestoop.

But even Thisby had her limits. There was somewhere in the dungeon that nobody had ever been. Not even the Master.

The basement.

★★★

Thisby stood on the rocky precipice that overlooked the Darkwell—the basement door. The only thing standing between her and the darkness at the bottom of the world. The Darkwell was the spot where the dungeon ended and the Deep Down began. A single, solitary gate protected the dungeon from whatever it was that lay beyond. She held a candle out at arm's length and strained her eyes to see if she could detect any movement. That she couldn't see a thing made her heart climb even farther up into her throat.

It was hard to see without the help of Mingus's brilliant light. This far down into the mountain, the darkness proved challenging even for someone as well adapted to it as Thisby. The dark down here wasn't like other darkness. Here it took on its own physical properties. It had weight. It moved. It pulled you in like quicksand and made it hard to run. She'd tucked Mingus safely away inside her backpack as per his request. If there was one thing in the Black Mountain Mingus hated more than anything else—and the list of things he hated was very, very long—it was a visit to the Darkwell. Periodically, she would hear him softly muttering comforting words to himself through the thick canvas walls of her bag, but she tried her best to tune him out.

She bounded from rock to rock down the steep ravine toward the Darkwell. The Darkwell was more than fifty feet in diameter with a short rim made of rough stone that seemed to jut up from the dusty earth like the pursed lips of a pouty child. Inside, covering the round opening, was a wrought-iron gate forged in an ancient method known as blackweave, the bars knitted together like cloth to form a nearly impenetrable tapestry of twisted metal. The bars were so tightly knit that not even the smallest creature in the Black Mountain could squeeze through. This was intentional. There was nothing from beyond the Darkwell that anybody in the rest of the Black Mountain wanted anything to do with.

What exactly was beyond there was impossible to know. The gate had stood for hundreds of years, and nobody who was around before that time cared to talk about it much. Perhaps the strangest feature for something commonly referred to as a gate was that the Darkwell didn't appear to have any latches or hinges. This was also intentional. There was no way in, and there was no way out of the Darkwell.

This should have made Thisby feel safe, but it didn't. It wasn't just the unknown horrors that lived beyond the gate of the Darkwell that made her uncomfortable, but the thing that stood watch at the gate as well.

Her candle created a thin bubble of light that seemed to be growing weaker under the oppressive weight of the encroaching darkness. She thought about Mingus hiding in her backpack. It would've been nice to have him out, if he weren't so scared. He could glow far brighter than any candle—and having some company, no matter how frightened that company may have been, wouldn't have hurt, either. She allowed herself a few seconds to imagine she was back in her tiny bedroom, pouring over the day's notes and lying snugly in bed, before a deep voice from across the well snapped her back to reality.

"Hello, Little Mouse."

She felt his breath like a warm breeze, reaching her on a delay as it traveled from half a room away.

"Tut, tut, tut!" he clucked derisively. "You came all this way and didn't bring me a treat?"

She watched the shadows move just beyond the lip of the well, shapes swimming in darkness like oil dropped into a bottle of ink. The creature was coming her way.

As he moved closer, she could make out some of his features in the dim candle glow. First his large, shining, saucerlike eyes. Then his sharp teeth, pearly white against the black velvet shadows. Finally, his gigantic body slunk out in front of her in its entirety. He revealed himself in exactly the order he intended, maximizing his dramatic impact.

The Sentinel of the Darkwell climbed up onto the grate and began to pace slowly. His toes were the size of wooden barrels, yet his footfalls were completely silent. The only sound he made was the occasional scraping of his claws against the blackweave gate, a noise like a kitchen knife being sharpened against a whetstone. It was unsettling, to say the least. Thisby knew it was intentional. If he'd wanted to, she knew that he could tap dance on sheet metal without waking a sleeping baby in the next room. The noise was a threat.

As he moved closer, she could make out some of his features
in the dim candle glow.

As someone who'd spent her entire life in the company of monsters, Thisby had never seen a normal cat. She'd seen pictures of them, of course, but after meeting the Sentinel, she could never quite understand why any rational human would want a miniature version of such a horrible monster as a pet. What could be the purpose of such an obviously deceitful creature, so predisposed to violence and mayhem, and why would anybody want to keep one around?

"Next time, Catface," said Thisby.

The Sentinel bristled.

"Did you come here to mock me, Little Mouse? Or do you have other business? Bringing me dinner, perhaps?"

Another veiled threat. They both knew Thisby wasn't there to deliver food. The Sentinel didn't need to be fed. He hunted his own dinner in the Black Mountain, and every creature in the dungeon knew to stay out of his way when he was on the prowl.

Thisby stiffened her resolve and tried not to think about the cat, large enough to easily swallow her whole, pacing in front of her as if she were his next meal.

"I need the count," she said as calmly as possible.

This was her monthly duty, and she hated it with all her heart. On the last day of every month, Thisby would come down to the Darkwell and meet with Catface to receive the count. And every month, Catface would taunt her and torment her until he'd had his fill, and then he'd reply with the same exact thing: ze—

"One," said Catface.

Thisby froze.

"You mean, 'Zero,'" she said.

Catface stopped pacing.

"Do I strike you as a creature who says things they don't mean, Little Mouse?"

"No, but . . ."

"ONE," he said again, this time making effort to add verbal punctuation.

Thisby couldn't believe her ears. Never in all her years had anything passed through the Darkwell. The room felt suddenly colder.

"W-what? What could have gotten through? H-how?" she stammered. At any other time, Thisby would have been embarrassed by her voice cracking in front of him, but not when it came to the Deep Down. Not when it came to the place beyond the Darkwell. This was the place where monsters feared to go. This was the basement of the world.

"You were supposed to be guarding it," Thisby muttered automatically. The moment the words left her mouth, she realized the offense. But the repercussions never came.

"I don't know . . . ," he said, trailing off. His brow furrowed. "It must've been some type of magic," Catface concluded, mostly to himself. There was a sort of unspoken question mark dangling curiously at the end of the word *magic*.

"What happened?" Thisby asked, trying to regain her composure.

"I was hunting. When I returned, there it was. A creature from the Deep Down. A Deep Dweller. Standing right there. Right where you are now."

Thisby tried her best not to look behind her.

"I never got a good look at it. I ran after it, but it disappeared before I could pounce. Vanished. Magic, most likely. At first I thought it was just an imp that had gotten too brave for its own good, wandered too close to the Darkwell, but the scent of the creature lingered. Its scent was unmistakable. It came from the Deep Down. Somehow it passed through the Darkwell."

"But—but that's impossible!" blurted Thisby.

"It should be. But it happened."

When Thisby was little, Grunda had told her that not even magic could cross the barrier at the Darkwell. Thisby thought about it now and felt foolish. Maybe she'd just been naive. It was likely that Grunda had only told her that so she wouldn't have nightmares. It could have been a blackdoor, she supposed, but those were created by the Master himself. And how would someone from beyond the Darkwell get ahold of one in the first place?

"And now there is of course, the obvious question this all raises . . . ," said Catface, interrupting Thisby's train of thought before trailing off.

He didn't need to finish his thought. Thisby knew what the question was. If one creature could get through when Catface's back was turned, how many more could have come and gone? Once a way through the Darkwell had been exposed, what was left to stop dozens, maybe thousands, of creatures from coming through?

"I'VE GOT TO TELL THE MASTER!" Thisby realized aloud.

It wasn't a thought she was thrilled about. News this bad was bound to end up coming back to hurt her, despite her lack of involvement. The Master was a notoriously poor news-taker, and Roquat would delight in doling out any extra punishments that the Master himself would be too busy to administer, as he always was.

Catface's big yellow eyes locked on to Thisby.

"Do you think that's best?" he purred. "After all, with the Royal Inspection coming up, perhaps it's best that we keep this between you and me . . . at least until we have more information. No reason to stir up trouble."

It was no surprise to Thisby that Catface knew about the Inspection. Secrets didn't stay secret very long in the dungeon, and Catface was quite persuasive. She eyed him cautiously. He gave away very little, staring back at her with his big glowing eyes shining in the candlelight.

It was an interesting gambit. He knew that if she told the Master, her life would be unbearable, especially with the Inspection on the horizon. Of course, if she didn't tell the Master, then they were both in it together. Keeping a lie this size from the Master could very well result in something far, far worse than extra chores if it ever were to get out.

"Why tell me at all, then?" asked Thisby, unable to

restrain her curiosity.

A look flashed across the cat's face that she'd never seen before in all her trips to the Darkwell. It was one she immediately wished never to see again . . . fear.

"Because," he said, turning away from her, "if something were to happen to me, I can't be the only one who knows."

And with that he slunk back into the shadows, leaving Thisby standing alone in the room, standing much closer to the Darkwell than she'd realized.

When Thisby was little, she'd had a recurring dream.

In the middle of the night, she'd wake with a strange feeling in the pit of her stomach. She'd try to go back to sleep, but it was no use. The feeling wouldn't go away. It pulled her to get out of bed, to go out into the hall, like she'd swallowed a bunch of iron and somebody was standing just outside her doorway holding a gigantic lodestone. She was drawn to it; she had no choice. The feeling just wouldn't go away.

She would feel her bare feet press against the cold, uneven wood as she left her bedroom and walked out across the gangway. Her footfalls were the only noise, echoing softly off the walls of the cave like the sound of a distant drum. *Thump. Thump. Thump. Thump.* At the end of the gangway was a platform. At the end of the platform was a ladder. It was a familiar ladder. The ladder she'd climbed twice a day, every day, since she was four years old. Every morning she would climb down three hundred and four rungs into the Black Mountain to go to work, and every night she would climb back up three hundred and four rungs to the relative comfort of her bedroom. In her sleep, she walked to the edge of the platform and stared down.

The ladder descended into a darkened rough stone tunnel about the width of fishing pole, the bottom of which was impossible to see from the top. It reminded her of looking down the throat of a gigantic beast. The stones were its rib cage. The ladder was its tongue. The feeling in her stomach had now grown worse than ever. It was pulling her. Over the edge. Stronger.

"Jump," it said.

She stared into the abyss for as long as she could manage before the pulling became too much. *Jump. Jump. Jump. Jump.*

She hesitantly dangled one foot precariously over the edge and felt the cool breeze kiss the sole of her foot.

"More," the voice said.

The pulling grew stronger.

She lifted up her other heel from the dirty wooden planks.

It was only her toes touching the ground now.

So close.

She leaned forward.

And . . .

She woke up.

Thisby felt the same pulling in her stomach as she approached the very edge of the Darkwell. She didn't want to look into the darkness. She didn't want to see if there was something looking back at her from beyond the blackweave gate. She didn't want to see what was waiting on the other side of the abyss.

But the pulling was strong.

She stepped up to the edge and peered in through the razor-thin gaps between the bars.

Nothing moved. Nothing looked back. Beyond the bars was just . . . nothing. Horrible, silent, overwhelming nothing.

The trip back to her bedroom was a blur; she ran through the winding corridors and secret passages until her legs felt like they were about to give out. When she couldn't run she jogged, and when she couldn't jog, she walked. Hours passed. Outside the Black Mountain, night slowly surrendered to day and all the while Thisby never stopped moving and her mind never quit racing. The exhaustion of traveling for almost two days straight without rest didn't sink in until she'd crossed over gangways and climbed up the ladder—all three hundred and four rungs—all the way back. When she got there, she pushed her chair up against the door and flopped down on her bed, exhausted. She remembered that Mingus was still in her backpack and forced herself out of bed to get him out. He was sound asleep. She knew this because he'd put in his "sleeping eyes," little white buttons with lines drawn in a semicircle across them to indicate closed eyelids. The silliness of him putting in fake eyes specifically for sleep comforted her somewhat, but it wasn't enough.

That night, for the first time in years, the dream came back.

CHAPTER 5

The carriage came to a stop so abruptly that Iphigenia nearly spilled her sparkling hibiscus tea. The silk and lace decorative pillows that were once neatly arranged to optimize the energy flow of the carriage had been flung from the daybed in such a violent manner that it would take a team of professional carriage pillow stylists an entire afternoon of rearranging to make things livable again. It was more than any sane person could handle.

"Driver!" Iphigenia screeched.

There was no immediate answer from the driver, so she tried again. After three or four more screeches—each slightly shriller than the last—the carriage door slid open and her brother, Prince Ingo, smiled back at her pleasantly. He was as handsome as he thought he was—and that was saying something. He had raven black hair, like all members of the Larkspur royal family, and the kind of face you wouldn't realize you were staring at until it was too late and you had to fill the resulting awkward silence with a lot of "ums" and "uhs." Despite being only fifteen years old, Ingo already had received so many marriage proposals that the palace had to employ a full-time clerk to sort through them all.

Iphigenia followed him out of the coach. Her dress was a dark emerald color that intensified her olive skin and long black hair, which was currently pulled back into a series of elaborate interweaving braids. She took Ingo's hand as she delicately stepped through the mud.

"I hate it here. It's horrible," she said matter-of-factly.

She wasn't wrong. Everything about Castle Grimstone was indeed designed to be horrible. That was the whole point. Of the thirty-three architects who had overseen the construction of the castle, only two of them weren't criminally insane, and at least one of those two was just never caught in the act.

Ingo beamed at his sister.

"There's history in these walls!" he exclaimed, gesturing emphatically toward the rotting black walls of the castle.

Iphigenia screwed up her face.

"I think I can smell it," she said.

A trumpet that sounded as if it'd been stuffed full of wet socks tooted sadly from some distance, and at once a large wall composed of various skulls began to open. Apparently, this was the gate. From the gate, a company of armored ghouls riding monstrous battle boars rode toward the Larkspur twins, followed closely behind by four trolls carrying an ornate wheel-less carriage suspended by wooden poles. The ghouls parted and the trolls stepped through, coming to rest mere feet in front of Iphigenia and her brother. The trolls turned the carriage sideways ninety degrees with a prancing, well-rehearsed sidestep that didn't quite jibe with their brutish appearance. The door of the carriage creaked open.

Inside was only darkness, and for a moment, everything was quiet.

Princess Iphigenia yawned.

Then with a *whoosh*, a shower of yellow and green sparks exploded from inside the wheel-less carriage. Skulls made of prismatic smoke swirled around it, yowling at the pain of having been conjured into existence. All four of the trolls carrying the carriage unzipped, starting at the top of their heads and running all the way down to their toes, revealing each of them to be a swarm of locusts who'd been wearing troll-shaped costumes all along. The locusts then burst into the sky to form an undulating cloud above where the trolls had just stood, and from that cloud a lightning bolt struck down and split the carriage in two, leaving in its wake a cloud of unnatural, living smoke that crackled with magical energy.

Iphigenia smoothed out the folds of her dress.

When the smoke dissipated, standing in the spot where the lightning had struck was the castle's Master, a tiny old man in a black cloak, holding a gnarled staff of yew that on its crown held a glowing red gem. He was grinning from ear to ear, and it looked as if he perhaps had too many teeth. He also appeared to be a little out of breath.

Ingo applauded politely.

Iphigenia watched a moth that had landed on one of the castle's many protruding iron spikes. It flapped idly.

"Welcome . . . ," the Master said, pausing for effect and perhaps to catch his breath, ". . . to Castle Grimstone!"

The tour was taking forever. The Master was quite proud of his castle and the history it had seen, but Iphigenia had grown up in a castle. Lyra Castelis, the royal castle of Nth, to be precise. And needless to say, it was a much, much nicer one.

"And over here," the Master continued, "is where Anouk the Blade met her grisly fate at the hands of one of my many enchanted armors! She thought she could simply sneak in and take me hostage in order to extort the mountain's great treasure! Fah!" He snorted. "As if nobody had thought of that one before! If I gave up my dungeon's treasure to the first person who wandered in here and put a dagger to my throat, this whole place would've been out of business years ago!"

Iphigenia was getting the sense that this tour was more for the benefit of the Master than it was for her and her brother. He seemed to be enjoying recounting the tales of the many adventurers who'd perished in pursuit of the Black Mountain's legendary treasure, although it struck her as odd that he seemed reluctant to lead them down into the dungeon itself—the very reason they were there in the first place. In fact, the few times they'd passed entryways or stairwells that appeared to lead down, the Master had given them a particularly wide berth, avoiding even looking in their direction. It reminded Iphigenia of how her family would behave when they passed commoners on the street.

The Master prattled on. Iphigenia let out a loud sigh, which caught a polite look of disapproval from her brother. While it was hard for Iphigenia to hide her disdain, Ingo had no problem whatsoever. Nobody was as diplomatic as Ingo Larkspur.

Ingo could engage in scintillating conversation with royals and commoners alike. He could negotiate sensitive matters of court as easily as he could entertain a barroom of farmers with ribald tales. And when he spoke to you, you felt as if you were the most important person in the world. If anybody were ever born to be King, it was Ingo Larkspur. Unfortunately for Ingo, he wasn't.

While he and his twin sister, Iphigenia, were born only minutes apart, it was his impatient sister who'd managed to sneak out first, and thus, she was destined to wear the crown when her parents finally vacated the throne. It was a cruel twist of fate that would've torn a lesser man apart, but Ingo bore it all with good humor.

Iphigenia Larkspur could not have been more her brother's opposite. She was impatient and snotty and at times downright mean. She was intolerant of stupidity—and she saw stupidity everywhere. She saw it in the fat red faces of the stammering dukes who attempted to win the crown's loyalty through bribery and flattery. She saw it in the senseless violence of the commoners who were too busy fighting one another to build a better life for themselves or their families. And currently, she saw it in the tottering old man who wouldn't stop feeding his ego for long enough to get to the point of this whole stupid visit.

"With a castle this wonderful, I can only imagine the amazing sights in store for us in the dungeon!" said Ingo, sensing Iphigenia's pending outburst.

"Yes, yes! You'll see the dungeon, Your Highness. But first, there's one more thing that I must show you . . . ," said the Master.

He led them to a large pair of iron doors beneath a black stone archway. There was no handle anywhere to be seen, just a small golden trumpet attached to what looked like a jewelry box that clung to the wall beside the doors. The Master leaned over and mumbled something into the trumpet, and at once the doors began to open. The Master grinned at Iphigenia, proud of his own cleverness.

"It's a riddle," he said. "Only those who know True Magic can open it."

Iphigenia wanted to smack the smarmy grin off his stupid face.

They walked through a series of winding corridors. The walls were made of shiny dark stones that shone eerily in the faint green light illuminating the halls. Bizarre runes were engraved on them. Iphigenia struggled to make out a few of them before ultimately deciding they were complete nonsense.

At the end of the corridor they came to a door blocked by two skeleton warriors decked out from head to toe in spiked full-plate armor. The Master nodded to them and they silently stepped aside. He placed his hand on the ornate door, but before he pushed it open, he paused for dramatic effect. Iphigenia had never wanted to punch somebody in the mouth more than she did right then.

They walked into the room, and even Iphigenia—though she'd never admit it—was impressed by what she saw. The room was completely circular, with a system of moveable ladders and walkways that allowed one to access the higher levels. In the center of the room, an enormous golden contraption the size of several large elephants stacked directly atop one another spun and clicked mechanically, diligently performing its skillful, arcane choreography. Arms branched off it and rotated around in orbits of whirling golden arcs, buzzing as they went.

The walls of the room were lined with crystal balls that appeared cloudy until you came closer, and then strange images would appear: a troll eating its lunch, a fire drake sleeping, a scrawny little girl with an enormous backpack running around frantically.

"Amazing! With these you could watch the whole dungeon from one room!" shouted Ingo, delighted.

"Oh, but I can do far more than just that! Just you wait!"

Ingo picked up a crystal ball and gazed into it, his eyes wide with wonder. He was really laying it on thick.

"Brilliant," said Ingo.

The Master looked beyond pleased with himself as he poorly feigned humility with an awkward bow. Iphigenia thought his ego might burst through his skin and do a little jig on the carpet right there in front of them.

"You're too kind, Your Highness! But please allow me to show you how this machine really works!"

The Master scurried up a ladder with surprising agility and climbed into a little bucket seat attached to the side of the gigantic golden contraption. He pulled some levers and the machine bent to his will, rotating in jerky movements, its gears clanging. To the surprise of the royal twins, the walls of the room itself began to rotate, shuffling the crystal spheres like billiards balls until one of them reached a chute down which it slid. At the bottom it was loaded into the base of the strange contraption. The noise of the machinery grew so loud that Iphigenia couldn't even hear herself be unimpressed. The Master climbed back down the ladder, grinning his toothy, sharklike grin from ear to ear.

*They walked into the room, and even Iphigenia—though she'd
never admit it—was impressed by what she saw.*

"THOSE CRYSTAL BALLS, YOU SEE, ARE SIMPLY A POWER SOURCE!" he shouted over the din.

Unlike his sister, Ingo was watching the little red-faced man with rapt attention.

"THIS MACHINE IS THE GREATEST ACHIEVEMENT OF ALCHEMY AND MAGIC IN THE MODERN WORLD! COME! LOOK!"

He led them over to the opposite side of the room where an empty golden doorway, leading to nothing but more solid stone, was set up against the wall and tethered to the machine with several glass tubes. Iphigenia hadn't been able to see this from the opposite side of the room, as it was hidden by the machine. Despite her better judgement, she was starting to find her interest—well, not piqued maybe, but perhaps gently nudged. A strange black jelly filled the tubes, and suddenly the empty golden doorway was no longer empty.

Inside the doorway was a rocky stone cavern bathed in orange and yellow light. Through it ran several thin streams of red lava, erratically dividing up the cave floor like the veins on a witch's leg. Iphigenia could feel the heat radiating from that room, through the doorway and into the room in which she stood. She moved closer and stretched out her hand.

Carefully, slowly, she extended her hand through the doorway. It was like sticking her hand into a hot oven, the heat quickly becoming almost unbearable. She reached farther in, unable to resist the temptation, and prodded a nearby stalagmite with the tip of her finger.

"Ow!" she cried.

She sucked at her burnt finger as the Master came whirling around from where he was fiddling with more knobs.

"What are you doing!" he chided. "Of course it's hot!"

Suddenly, he remembered that it was the Crown Princess, the Heir to the Throne of Nth, who he was scolding as if she were a petulant child, and he quickly regained his composure.

"I mean, what shame it would bring to this dungeon if Her Majesty were to befall a tragic accident while under the supervision of such a lowly subject to the crown as myself?"

Iphigenia ignored him and looked at her finger. It was red and painful. Wherever that doorway led, it was no illusion. It was as real as the room in which they were standing.

"Wonderful," said Ingo, ignoring his sister's pain. "Just wonderful!"

The Master looked pleased that he was off the hook for yelling at the Princess and beamed back at Ingo.

"It's a blackdoor," said the Master. "And it's the secret to how I manage the entire dungeon! With this machine, I can create a doorway to anywhere in the mountain! All I have to do is call up the proper scrying sphere—the, ahem, crystal balls you see lining the walls of this room—and I can create a doorway that I can simply walk through to be in that location instantly! Not to mention that the scrying spheres are quite good for spying as well, you know."

Ingo was delighted, and his delight pleased the Master to no end.

"But what if you were down in the dungeon and had to get out?" said Ingo.

"I'm glad you asked! You see this?" said the Master, pointing to a small slot on the side of the machine. He turned a wheel above it and the doorway snapped shut. The lava-filled chamber that had just been on the other side was gone, and the doorway was once again filled with empty space. The inside of the machine banged and whirred.

Ingo watched closely as a small black bead tumbled out of the slot and onto a tray below.

"This," the Master said motioning to the bead, "is also a blackdoor. Only portable. I call them blackdoor beads. They're not quite as powerful as the real thing of course. They can only be used once and will only take you to one predetermined location. But still quite handy!"

"Wonderful! Wonderful! And it will go anywhere?" asked Ingo.

"Well, yes. Anywhere inside the Black Mountain, at least. There are limits. It can't go outside, or above, or, uhm, or below . . ." The Master seemed to choke a bit on that last word and turned away from the Prince.

Ingo changed the subject.

"You must keep such a brilliant invention under very tight guard!"

"Oh, um, yes! Yes, of course!" muttered the Master, who brightened again the instant the word *brilliant* was mentioned in reference to himself. "I strictly regulate the total number of beads produced as well as . . . hmm . . . It's probably easier if I just show you my bookkeeping methods. You see . . ."

Iphigenia had wandered off by this point. Partly to look for some cold water to run her burned finger underneath, and partly because she had no interest in this old man and his dumb parlor tricks. Behind her she could hear the machine clank and whir back to life. Ingo must've wanted more of a demonstration. Iphigenia sat down on a bench to sulk.

This was how things were and how they would always be. She loved her brother, but sometimes he drove her crazy. She hated how he pleaded for the approval of idiots, how he'd rather be popular than right. But she knew deep down that this was what it took to be a beloved King—it was what her father said it took, at least, and Ingo would've made a beloved King. Perhaps the most beloved of all time. But Iphigenia had been born first. Because she was impatient. Because she didn't have time to sit around in some stupid womb while the rest of the world passed her by.

Iphigenia smiled. Maybe it was Ingo they had wanted, but it was her they would get. And it served them right.

CHAPTER 6

Meanwhile, far below the castle, Thisby was rounding the corner on her forty-second straight hour without sleep. The poor, bedraggled gamekeeper's sleeplessness had nothing to do with nightmares or ominous warnings from giant cats. In fact, she hadn't even thought about what Catface had told her since the news of the Royal Inspection had first reached Roquat's nubbly, misshapen ears several days ago. With all the chores Roquat had her doing, there was simply no time for anything but work.

"The carriage should have arrived by now," said Mingus with a yawn. "A few hours ago, maybe. Depending on the weather."

"I don't need you to remind me," said Thisby. "Besides, they have the tour of the castle first. We should have plenty of time before the Inspection starts to get a little bit of that . . . thing? What's it called? You know what I'm talking about, right?"

"Sleep?" asked Mingus.

"Ah. Yeah. That's it. That's the one." Thisby grinned. "It's been so long, I forgot what it was called."

She slumped against the newly scrubbed wall of the gnoll den, her tunic soaked through with sweat, soap, and who knew what else. It'd taken her the better part of the morning to clean up after the gnolls, who had—just as they did in the wild—caked the walls of their den thick with mud and waste in order to mask their scent. It was hard for Thisby to believe this odor could possibly mask anything. In a stiff breeze she thought she probably would've been able to smell it from across the Nameless Sea.

The grotesque goblin-wolves known as gnolls returned, as she knew they would. One by one, they began sniffing around excitedly, first on all fours, and then walking bipedally when they spotted Thisby. The den leader approached her first, walking upright so that she towered over the diminutive gamekeeper, her shaggy fur bristling.

"How dare you defile our den, girl! That took us weeks!" the gnoll snarled in her face. Flecks of yellow spittle hit Thisby on her turned cheek. The gnoll leader bared her jagged teeth and produced a low, rumbling growl, while the rest of the pack paced back and forth menacingly behind her. It was quite the show.

Thisby took her notebook from her pocket without so much as looking up at the snarling, angry jaws that were mere inches from her face and began to jot some quick notes. The gnoll was incensed. Thisby did her best to ignore it, no matter how much it growled, and kept her eyes glued to her notes. When she was finished, she stuffed the notebook into her pocket and began to casually gather up her belongings. The gnoll chased after her as Thisby moved to exit the den, but the gnoll stopped hard at the edge of the cave as if blocked by an invisible force field.

Thisby yawned as she walked away.

"Come back here, human girl! Come back and fight!" the gnoll snarled. But Thisby was already gone. For several minutes after, the gnoll paced angrily at the edge of the cave before giving up and stalking back to its den to begin a long night of gathering more mud and making more waste.

Thisby crossed *DOG PIT* off the last line on her list of chores and had to blink several times before she could believe her tired eyes. She was done. Waves of relief washed over her, and she felt as if she might collapse. She closed her eyes and let out a deep sigh.

"How'd you know they wouldn't kill you?"

"Hm?" said Thisby, opening her eyes a crack.

"The gnolls," said Mingus.

"Oh. They won't attack another creature unless it directly provokes them. You gotta be careful, though. Even looking them in the eye might be considered provocation, so it's best to just keep your eyes down and walk away silently." Thisby paused. "Don't you read the notebooks I loan you?"

"I do!" said Mingus defensively. "Only sometimes your shorthand is hard to follow."

Thisby smirked.

"That's an old Grunda trick. When she was teaching me about the dungeon she used to say, 'Only write down what you want to share,' but that only works if you've got a good memory. Mine's just okay, I guess. When she realized that I had to write everything down, she thought I might as well make it hard to read."

The two went on their way ahead. Despite her exhaustion, Thisby felt lighter than she had in days. She hummed a mindless tune, as she often did, and thought about how nice it would be to finally get a few hours of sleep before the official Inspection began. She was so wrapped up in thinking about her bed that she was startled to look up and find a shaky, thin man pointing a sword directly at her throat.

"S-s-s-stay b-back! I'm warnin' you!" he choked out in a thick valley accent.

Thisby held up her hands in a playful mockery of defeat and eyed the nervous adventurer standing before her. He was probably in his early twenties, quite poor by the looks of his makeshift armor, which didn't fit him properly, and terribly filthy. Over his shoulder he'd slung a "shield" that appeared to have been crafted from an old barn door. Thisby wasn't sure his sword was sharp enough to cut her even if he tried. Thisby would've laughed, if she hadn't been overcome with pity.

"The dungeon's closed," she said politely. "Look, maybe if you come back next week I can move you to the front of the line or something."

The man stared at her, bug-eyed.

"Whatchoo mean, the dungeon's closed?" he asked.

Thisby was beginning to think this could take a while and potentially cut into her precious sleep time.

"The royal family of Nth is here tomorrow on a private tour, so I'm afraid we're not admitting any adventurers until after they've left. You know, the last thing they need is a bunch of corpses to trip over."

"But—but I'm here to fulfill my sacred mission!"

"Yeah, well, it'll have to wait. Sorry."

The man looked as if he were about to cry. He lowered his sword and wiped at his nose with his sleeve.

"What's your name?" Thisby asked.

"Gregory," he said, fighting back tears.

"Why are you here, Gregory?" asked Thisby. She'd seen so many adventurers die in the dungeon that she wasn't sure why anyone came down here, let alone a sad sack like Gregory.

"I'm here to f-find m-my fortune! To start my life as an adventurer!"

"GRE-GOR-Y?" said Thisby, hitting every syllable in his name like a school teacher reprimanding a child.

Gregory swallowed.

"I'm trying to impress a girl," he said, defeated.

"Hold on a second," said Thisby.

She set down her backpack and began digging through it. Gregory looked nervous and pointed his unsharpened sword in her direction. Thisby had seen more threatening mops.

"How do I know this isn't a trick?" he demanded.

Thisby continued to dig, ignoring him. He eventually gave up and sat down on a rock, leaning his sword against the wall as Thisby searched through her bag. Mingus watched him pick his nose for a few minutes before thinking that he should say something.

"You know, a girl who asks you to risk your life to get treasure from a dungeon probably isn't one you should be interested in," said Mingus.

Gregory watched him out of the corner of his eye.

"You a slime or somethin'?"

"Or somethin'," said Mingus.

"I seen some slimes earlier. Only they didn't talk."

"I'm special," said Mingus.

A noise that sounded like a bagful of jellybeans spilling over came from Thisby's backpack accompanied by some light, muffled cursing.

"What color were the slimes you saw? Green? Blue?"

"Green," said Gregory.

"Technically that was an ooze then. The blue ones are slimes. Neither one has conscious thought. Not really. At least, they're not intelligent like me or . . . well, they're not very smart. Let's just leave it at that."

"You ain't a slime, then? What are you?"

"Well . . ."

"Here!" exclaimed Thisby as she popped out from behind her backpack holding a bag.

She walked over to Gregory and told him to hold out his hands. Several small glittering stones fell into them.

"They're beautiful!" exclaimed Gregory.

"They're wyvern beads. Taken from the belly of slain wyvern who've swallowed them. They're extremely valuable and beautiful and best of all, they'll prove beyond the shadow of a doubt that you not only came into the dungeon but you slew dangerous beasts within. Take 'em back to your girl."

Gregory again looked as if he might start crying.

"Follow that tunnel behind you until you get to a door. Do not go through that door! Make a right instead and follow that to a fork in the road. Turn right. You'll eventually come to a ladder that will lead you up and out of the dungeon. Getting back down the mountain is up to you."

Gregory got up and hurried off, but stopped just at the edge of the tunnel and turned back with a look of deep consternation on his bright red face.

"How do I know this ain't some kinda trick?"

"Don't come back here, Gregory," said Thisby, and at that, he was gone.

Thisby and Mingus continued on toward her bedroom.

"Wyvern beads?" Mingus laughed after some time had passed. "Weren't those rock golem droppings?"

Thisby shrugged and the two of them laughed all the way back to her room.

Thisby awoke several hours later to a banging on her door that was loud enough to wake the dead—and probably did, considering the roomful of zombies sleeping only two floors below her. Before she had time to climb out of bed, her door burst open, and an angry Roquat stormed in, looking as if he'd run the entire way here. If she weren't so annoyed by his presence, Thisby would have burst out laughing.

Roquat was dressed in finery that underscored rather than hid the indignity of his true nature. He wore an all-white suit—the color of royalty for Dünkeldwarves—with intricate silver designs stitched into the fabric. His hair and beard were heavily oiled and pulled into a single braid that met below his chin. The suit had probably fit Roquat at some point, but that point had long since passed, and now it looked as if his body were trying to escape through the seams. He moved with an odd, stilted gait that made it appear that with every step, he was afraid his outfit might simply explode off his body.

It would have been hilarious indeed, had he not stormed

into Thisby's room and immediately begun to throw her stuff around.

"Get up, you rat! You're late!" he bellowed.

He grabbed Thisby by the wrist and dragged her out of bed.

"Hey!" squeaked Thisby.

"You're tryin' to make me look like a fool in front of the royals, is that it? You want to mess everything up, right? Right?"

He flung her to the floor roughly amid piles of notebooks from her overturned bookshelf and gave her a swift kick to the ribs with the toe of his massive boots, grunting something at her about being down there in five minutes or else. From her place on the floor, Thisby watched him tug his suit back into place from where it had shifted around his bulky frame and smooth down his black, greasy braid, collecting himself. When his eyes caught Thisby watching him preen, she suspected another violent outburst, but was pleasantly surprised when he instead lowered his gaze and hurried out of her room a bit abashed.

Thisby got dressed and made her way to the spot near the southeast entrance to the dungeon where she was told to wait for the royals to arrive. Unlike Roquat, Thisby was dressed in her usual old clothes—a worn black canvas tunic and leggings that she'd patched so many times it was hard to make out what material they'd been made from to begin with. It was fine, however, because if all went according to plan, Thisby would never be seen by the royals at all. She crouched there and waited. She waited until her thighs got sore, and she had to shift her weight back and forth to keep her feet from falling asleep.

Finally, she heard some mumbling getting louder. Roquat approached the entrance from the dungeon side with a band of armored ghouls marching in orderly formation behind him. He'd added a cape to his ensemble; it seemed to have been designed for a much taller dwarf, as it dragged on the ground behind him. He barked some orders at the ghouls and then cast an angry grimace toward Thisby, who was hiding in a rocky outcrop some twenty feet above them.

She fantasized about throwing a rock at his big dumb head.

The entrance to the dungeon opened, and Thisby caught her first glimpse of the royal family of Nth. The Larkspur twins stood side by side, flanked by a few royal guards who'd accompanied their carriage. The Master was nowhere to be seen.

The twins strolled elegantly into the dungeon and were immediately at odds with their surroundings. Their pristine clothing, their pretty faces, their natural grace, all clashed horribly with the filthy dungeon that up until a moment ago had seemed to Thisby to be pretty neat and tidy.

As they walked down the rough stone steps to greet Roquat and his men, for the first time in her life, Thisby suddenly wished she were better dressed. Or that maybe she'd washed her mousy brown hair so it didn't stick out all stringy and gross. Or that she'd patched the holes in her tunic. She even wished momentarily that her nose wasn't so long and pointy—she'd been told once by a particularly mean goblin that it resembled a draftsman's angle, and the image had stuck with her ever since. Somehow this all seemed to matter like it hadn't two minutes ago.

The silver lining was that she was completely hidden from their sight—and it was her job to remain that way. Thisby, like most of the staff of the dungeon and castle, was never intended to be seen by outsiders, as seeing what goes on behind the curtain might break the mystique of the experience. If adventurers had to stop and think about how the monsters that lived in the dungeon stayed fed, or why the more valuable treasure chests always seemed to be guarded by the more dangerous monsters, then they might realize this wasn't actually an "evil dungeon being kept alive with powerful, ancient magic," but more of a tourist attraction, a sort of day care for bored kids with swords—albeit one with a terribly high mortality rate.

Thisby stretched her legs a bit and then proceeded to walk along the ledge in a sort of crouched, stooping posture, following as close to the group as possible without arousing their notice. She peeked over the edge to watch.

"Your Highness Prince Ingo! My Lady Iphigenia!" Roquat blurted nervously.

"Actually, as the Crown Princess, I'm 'Your Highness,'" said Iphigenia.

Thisby watched Roquat come undone as he groveled for forgiveness, which Iphigenia seemed uninterested in providing. The twins walked farther into the dungeon.

"Let's get this over with," said Iphigenia coldly.

Thisby followed along with their tour, moving through secret passages, climbing along ledges, at times even walking directly behind the group very, very quietly so as to avoid detection. As they went, Thisby ensured that the Larkspur twins got the best show possible while staying as safe as she could manage.

She stoked the fire elementals to rouse their anger but only did so once the twins were safely behind the ice runes Grunda had cooked up and Thisby had carefully placed earlier that day. She set their course through the werewolf dens but only after she was certain the werewolves were too fat and bloated with horse meat to bother chasing after some scrawny humans. She even let herself act as bait to distract the creeping tendrils of the man-snare plants so the royals wouldn't fall victim to their poisonous vines of death. And she did it all without being seen.

The Royal Inspection had been created as a show of good faith between the Black Mountain and the people of Nth— more specifically, the royal family, who, at the time of the Inspection's creation, had become very concerned about the growing, potentially militaristic power of the dungeon. Over time, as the likelihood of a war between the Black Mountain and the kingdom of Nth decreased, the Inspection became more about spectacle than anything, with each Master trying desperately to outdo the last. So far, thanks to Thisby's hard work, it seemed to be going well enough.

The whole way through the dungeon, Ingo clapped with delight and asked Roquat questions that he was obviously unprepared to answer. Thisby knew the answers of course, or if she didn't, she at least knew where to find them in one of her many notebooks. Roquat, however, was the type of guy who preferred to solve his problems with brute force. By Thisby's estimation, he knew as much about the dungeon as the troll did, maybe less.

"Look out for the venom vine, Princess!" said Roquat, pointing at an old piece of rope covered in moss.

"Are we about done here?" asked Iphigenia.

Thisby was hoping that was the case as well. They'd been at it for hours, and all this sneaking around was beginning to get exhausting. Roquat, however, was starting to look nervous.

"B-b-but you haven't even seen the best part yet!" he blurted.

Iphigenia decided—for the first time all day—that she'd play along.

"Okay," she said, grinning. "So, what is it?"

Roquat glanced, panic stricken, at Ingo, as if he could somehow save him from the path he'd started down. But it was too late. Roquat was going to have to find a way to make good on what he'd promised . . . he was going to have to find the "best part."

Thisby didn't like the wild look in her boss's eyes. She began flipping through her notes. The whole tour was carefully planned in order to show the royals an exciting, yet safe, trip through the dungeon. Every step of their tour had been diligently organized to maximize excitement while minimizing danger, and going off script could have dire consequences. She tried to catch Roquat's eyes without alerting the royals. It was no use.

"Tell me, Princess, have you ever seen . . . a tarasque?" asked Roquat.

Thisby wasn't afraid of any creature in the dungeon this side of the Darkwell, save Catface, and even then it was more of a healthy caution rather than outright fear. After Catface, the tarasque was next on the list of creatures to be healthily cautious around. Roquat deciding to veer from the itinerary had put the royals' lives in immediate danger.

She zoomed through the tight-fitting tunnels on her way to the lower dungeon. Her backpack collided with the walls as she ran, knocking her around like a human pinball. She even banged her head once, opening a small cut on her forehead. The tunnels here weren't designed for running, but beating the royals to their destination was her only chance to prevent an outright disaster.

She cursed Roquat with every breath. He was going

to get the Prince and Princess killed, and then what? The dungeon would surely be sieged by the King of Nth. He'd have no choice. Would they be able to survive a war? The dungeon wasn't much of a home, but it was all Thisby had, all she'd ever known. The monsters she cared for were the closest things she had to friends. Now she'd have nothing. All thanks to Roquat.

Thisby arrived at her destination, sweat soaked and red faced. She unhooked Mingus from her backpack and held him out in front of her. He gazed nervously back in her direction. Thisby could tell he wanted to say something, but thought better of it. She followed the wall down, running her free hand along the smooth bricks, until she passed through a final doorway that emptied into an ancient, underground city—the City of Night.

CHAPTER 7

It was called the City of Night because—as the story went—
if you stood anywhere within the city's ruins, the cavern that
contained it was so large and so dark that it was impossible to
see the walls of the cave, giving the illusion that the city was
outside on a still, black night. Thisby thought you'd have to
be pretty stupid to fall for this, and that the lack of the wind
was a dead giveaway, but poetics were often lost on her. The
impact, however, was not.

By the time Thisby came to know it, the City of Night
was a city in name only. The ruined structures that lined its
long, winding streets had long since abandoned their primary
purpose and submitted to a life of form without function,

more like growths than buildings. They were scar tissue built up from some horrible tragedy, existing only as a stubborn refusal to be forgotten.

How the ruins of a city came to exist within the Black Mountain was uncertain, although everyone had their theories. The mountain itself was easily large enough to hold several cities stacked atop one another, but why this one had been built, as well as why it had been abandoned, remained a mystery. It was a puzzle that fascinated Thisby, as did most things, but in her twelve-year tenure in the Black Mountain, she'd never had the opportunity to spend much time studying the City of Night or the monsters that dwelt within it. Actually, her trips to that particular area of the dungeon had been so infrequent that she could count them all on one hand and still have a few fingers left over. It wasn't due to lack of interest. Instead, it was because the City of Night more or less regulated itself, and to put it simply, her time was better spent elsewhere. The City of Night was an ecosystem unto itself inside the dungeon, large enough to support an entire food chain of monsters large and small, which didn't depend on Thisby's interference to keep itself in balance. And at the very top of that food chain was the tarasque.

Thisby walked through the city with Mingus in hand. He'd reduced his glow to a faint blue light at Thisby's request. If she could've moved without any light, she'd have done so, but the noise of her tripping over loose stones and crumbled columns would've drawn more attention than it was worth. She shook her head when she thought of Roquat, bumbling along carelessly with the royal twins in tow, an entire entourage of outsiders, in fact, and how much noise they were inevitably going to make.

She'd already come across a pack of wolf moths, a slime mephit, and some kobold raiders out hunting for loot, but for the most part the city was quiet. It was early still, and the City of Night lived up to its namesake. Before long, though, Thisby knew the dangerous beasts would begin to appear, ready for another night's hunt.

The forum at the center of the city was a large stone building shaped like a bowl and had begun to crumble beneath its own weight many years ago. Its original purpose had been buried under centuries of neglect, but it was called the forum by the inhabitants of the city, so that was how Thisby had always known it. She'd been there only once in person, on her first time in the City of Night. She'd gotten lost on her way back up from the Darkwell—one of the only things of significance lower in the Black Mountain than the city—and was naturally drawn to the structure.

Even in ruin, the forum was a thing to behold. It was easy for her to imagine what it must've been like in its prime, bustling with people and activity. Of particular interest to her were the gates to the forum. Aside from the Darkwell, they were the only other instance of blackweave Thisby had ever come across in the mountain. In the shadow of the building, dwarfed by its size, she paused at the threshold, silently acknowledging the power of this place before steeling her reserve and heading in.

Inside the building it was pitch black, save for Mingus's soft blue light, which illuminated the hallways with its swaying glow, giving the distinct sensation of being deep underwater. It reminded Thisby of the mermaid coves she swam through once a year to check for red algae buildup, only here there were far fewer irate mermaids biting at her ankles. Right now, though, she thought angry mermaids would be preferable to whatever was waiting for her in the darkness.

Something rattled nearby. The noise echoed off the walls, which made its origin impossible to pinpoint, but it seemed close. For a moment Thisby stood still, wondering if she should draw a weapon, but decided against it. This was fortunate, as she didn't carry any. The Master never would've wanted her to use one. As far as he was concerned, a good monster was worth twenty gamekeepers. There was a small utility knife in her backpack, but it was barely sharp enough to cut hair—which she knew full well, as evidenced by the ragged ends left over from last week's hack job.

"Probably just rats," said Thisby.

"That's not much comfort, you know," said Mingus. "Down here, dire rats can grow to the size of a carriage."

"I know! I know! I meant it's probably a beetle or a salamander!"

"The beetles are even bigger than the rats! The salamanders breathe fire!"

"Would you just stop it already! Just calm down and be quiet!" shushed Thisby.

The last thing she needed was Mingus freaking out. When Mingus freaked out, his light was unreliable, and when his light was unreliable, well, she was likely to trip over any number of the loose fixtures and crumbled stones that blanketed the floors of the ruined forum. She often toyed with the idea carrying a regular old nonsentient lantern with her—just for backup—but she'd never followed through with it. She was too worried about hurting Mingus's feelings. Their friendship was more important than being able to see in the dark, anyhow.

Following years of neglect, the once simple layout of the forum had become a maze of blocked passages and accidental shortcuts through crumbling stone walls. She'd found a map of it several years ago, which she'd copied into her notebooks, but that book was sitting on a shelf in her bedroom back at the top of the mountain. Besides, she knew it wouldn't have done much good since new paths opened and old ones closed daily as the building shifted and settled.

Thisby resented the hurry she was in, thanks to Roquat. She'd never had a chance to properly take notes on the forum and was overwhelmed with fascinating new discoveries wherever she turned. She saw carvings of strange creatures doing battle in what looked like the center of the forum, detailed diagrams of the city center, even something that looked like a statue of Roquat—as confusing as *that* was.

She easily could've spent hours filling her notebooks with scribbles and drawings, but there was no time now; she'd have to come back when there wasn't so much impending doom.

Thisby stepped out through an archway at the top of a staircase that had about half its stairs intact. She looked around, straining her eyes against the darkness. There was still no sign of Roquat and the others.

She peered over the edge, leaning through a gap in the broken brass railing, and assessed her situation. She was some three dozen rows up from the ground level, just high enough to see over the back of the tarasque asleep in the center of the forum. As Thisby stared at the monster, which undoubtedly had bits of food larger than herself stuck between its teeth, an unpleasant thought creeped into her mind and didn't let go.

"Now what?" she mumbled.

At a loss for what to do next, Thisby did the one thing that came most naturally to her: she took some notes. She pulled out the first notebook she could find in her backpack and began to scribble down as much information as possible before the others arrived. She began with the most obvious thing in the room—the seventy-ton monster—and figured she'd work backward from there.

As far as Thisby knew, the tarasque was the largest creature in the dungeon. Her best guess put it at two hundred to two hundred fifty feet long from tail to nose. It had a heavily armored spiny shell on his back, like that of a snapping turtle, and six legs that looked as if they were designed for short bursts of tremendous speed, but probably not maneuverability. Its head was a massive jumble of horns and teeth, partially hidden beneath a mane of thick hair that wreathed its face and made it hard to distinguish individual features. It was impossible to get an accurate idea of its tooth length and jaw structure from the angle she was sitting, but Thisby figured that since it could probably open its mouth about as wide as a drawbridge, if it ever came to a direct confrontation, it was best to avoid its bite regardless.

The one thing Thisby found most interesting about the tarasque, however, wasn't its size or its jaw, but its tail. On the end of its long, plated tail was a jagged barb resembling a scorpion's stinger. It was shaped in such a way as to imply that it was indeed designed to deliver poison, but try as she might, Thisby couldn't figure out why something as massive as the tarasque would need poison. Poison was typically a weapon for small creatures. An evolutionary defense mechanism to ward off larger, more dominant predators. A chill went up her spine when her brain forced her to imagine the obvious answer she'd been avoiding.

There was something bigger than the tarasque.

Moments later, Roquat arrived looking the worse for wear. His fancy suit was unbuttoned and untucked, and his eyes darted back and forth between the buildings ahead. Behind him, the royal twins walked in the middle of a circle of guards who had their weapons drawn. It looked as if they'd encountered trouble along the way.

They made their way into the forum, entering low at ground level. Thisby winced when she saw them.

"You'd have to try to be that stupid!" chided Thisby in a hoarse, angry whisper.

"What do you mean?" asked Mingus.

"They came in low! The tarasque will feel their vibrations! It's like they're trying to get caught!"

She could hear hushed voices down below as the group moved in for a better look at the hulking behemoth. Thisby darted back into the building and headed down to get closer. Perhaps if she could get Roquat's attention, she could talk him out of whatever it was he was planning to do without alerting the royals. When she emerged from the floor just above them, she could hear Roquat anxiously explaining the tarasque to the still unimpressed Princess.

"It's big. I'll give you that," said Iphigenia as they walked by a claw the size of a horse. "Does it do anything besides sleep?"

Roquat stared at her blankly. All day he'd been pushed to his limit trying to please her, and all day he'd fallen short. The Princess stared back at him, daring him to make the next move. Much to her surprise, he burst into laughter.

"Does it do anything besides sleep?" Roquat wheezed, fighting back his uncontrollable laughing fit. He clasped one of her guards on the shoulder in order to prevent himself from doubling over with laughter and waved a hand toward the Princess. "Does it do anything besides *sleep*, she says!"

Iphigenia glowered at him as he stumbled around guffawing like an idiot, trying to catch his breath. The tarasque stirred in its sleep, and everyone but Roquat took a step back. Roquat slapped his knee and continued to roar with laughter. Iphigenia turned red.

"*Stop it!*" she commanded.

A switch flipped in Roquat's brain, and his expression dropped at once into an eerie blank stare. He walked toward the Princess, moving like a puppet being dragged across the stage by his strings. He got as close as her guards would allow, and they watched him with a nervous energy, their hands wrapped tightly around their weapons.

"Lemme tell you what it does besides sleep," he said. "It destroys. It destroys people. It destroys villages. It destroys kingdoms. You think you're safe in your little castle. Safe on your little throne. You think this whole place is some sort of game, because that's what it's been turned into. A tourist attraction for royals and idiots with swords who want to play adventurer, but you have no idea of the power that dwells within this mountain. Let alone below it. You have no idea what's coming, do you? Lemme ask you a question . . . Have you ever seen the Eyes in the Dark?"

"*Enough!*" shouted Ingo.

He stepped between Roquat and his sister. Roquat scanned him, his eyes darting back and forth across Ingo's face, waiting for his next move. Ingo nodded at him curtly and then turned to his sister.

"We should go, Iphigenia," he said.

Iphigenia nodded.

Before they could take more than two steps, a horrible screeching note emitted from Roquat's direction. Thisby looked down to see him blowing on some sort of strange flute until he was red in the face.

Everybody froze.

Everybody except the tarasque.

CHAPTER 8

With a terrible roar that shook the entire cavern, the tarasque awoke.

The forum trembled as the tarasque rose to its feet, the dust from its years-long slumber stirring up around it. Thisby looked down to see Iphigenia and her guards looking confused and panicked. Roquat and the Prince were nowhere to be found.

"He took him! He took him!" screamed Iphigenia.

In the middle of the forum, Iphigenia and her guards had begun to flee back the way they'd come. The tarasque whirled around. Its tail smashed into the side of the amphitheater, violently shaking the entire forum. Thisby regained her footing and ducked back the way she'd come as well, racing toward the exit, trying to outrun what she expected to be a rapidly collapsing building. Mingus slid back and forth wildly in his lantern as she ran.

A collapsing column barely missed them as Thisby and Mingus dashed through an exit and out into the city streets. Behind her, the tarasque was trying to exit the forum the hard way, smashing through the walls rather than climbing over them, and Thisby was thankful for the time it would buy her. A rush of fleeing monsters scurried past her as they scrambled to get out of the way of the angry tarasque, and Thisby caught her first break.

"Come on!" she shouted to Mingus—as if he had a choice—and followed after them.

Following the monsters seemed to be the only logical choice. For one, they definitely knew the city better than she did, and also, it didn't hurt to have a lot of moving targets around in the likely scenario that the tarasque caught up with them and decided he wanted a snack.

Iphigenia and her crew had a different idea. Thisby watched as the Princess and her guards ducked into a building to hide, and she let out a frustrated groan.

Thisby had never claimed to know everything. She was the first one to admit that. But she knew enough to realize that hiding in a building directly in the path of a rampaging monster capable of stepping on buildings and turning them into dust . . . well, wasn't a great idea.

With a terrible roar that shook the entire cavern, the tarasque awoke.

"Princess?" Thisby called as she rushed into the darkened building.

"We need to keep moving!" yelled Mingus.

"I can't leave here without her!" snapped Thisby.

Despite not being capable of crying, Mingus sounded as if he were on the verge of tears, "What good is it if we die, too, Thisby?"

Thisby ignored him. The dungeon belonged to the Master, but the lives of the creatures inside it were her responsibility. All of them. From the lowliest mindworm to the adventurers who came in search of treasure to the Crown Princess herself, the moment something set foot inside the dungeon, it was her job to make certain it was cared for to the best of her ability. If anything happened to any of the inhabitants of the dungeon, it was her fault—and that much she was certain even the Master would be quick to agree to.

Thisby ran through the building until she heard voices from the next room.

"Princess?" she called again, running toward them.

Iphigenia watched as a mousy little girl wearing a backpack at least three time her size stepped out from the shadows. They stared at each other. The two of them couldn't have been more different: Thisby in her ragged canvas tunic and patchwork leggings, with her dirty chin-length hair that stuck straight out to the sides, and Iphigenia with her resplendent emerald dress and her tightly woven braids. Where Iphigenia's face was soft, Thisby's was sharp, and vice versa. They were only a few years apart in age, born in the same kingdom, and yet they could've been from two different planets.

THOOOOOM!

The room shook as the tarasque let out a tremendous roar.

"We need to go!" Thisby shouted.

Iphigenia's nostrils flared.

"Who are you to speak to me like that!" she screeched.

THOOOOOM! The building shook violently again.

"I'm the only person here who's going to keep you alive," replied the gamekeeper, reaching an outstretched hand toward the Princess. The guards who'd been pointing their swords in the girl's general direction—on the off chance that this was some sort of extraordinarily circuitous assassination attempt—lowered their swords and muttered among themselves.

KRAKA-THOOOOOOOM!

The forum wall gave way at the exact same moment as Iphigenia's dignity. She grabbed the girl's filthy, outstretched hand and the two of them were off and running, the guards following close behind.

They spilled out onto the city streets in time to see the last remains of the forum crumbling to the earth. A cloud of dust rose in its wake and swept toward them, expanding through the darkened cavern like a tidal wave. Through the yellow-gray dust they could barely see the towering silhouette of the tarasque as it trumpeted its victory loud enough for the entire dungeon to hear.

Before the girls could even find their footing, the tarasque charged.

No matter how fast they ran, Iphigenia knew it wouldn't be fast enough. The tarasque's legs were so long that it would overtake them in mere strides. Just as it was about to reach them, the strange girl screamed, "TURN!"

Only Iphigenia was quick enough. Her guards vanished with an awful squishing sound in a storm of footsteps. The next thing Iphigenia knew, the mousy girl, now freshly coated with powdery, gray dust, was helping her to her feet and they were running again. They ducked and hid behind buildings, Iphigenia following as best she could. She took the girl's hand when it was offered. Everything around them blurred with dust that made it impossible to take a deep breath without choking.

The world was chaos. In the darkness, buildings fell around her. She could no longer hear anything but distant ringing, but she didn't need to hear to know the tarasque was near. With each step the monster took, the entire cavern quaked.

Occasionally, in the darkness and the dust, Iphigenia encountered other creatures fleeing from the tarasque. She nearly stepped on a family of rats who'd fled their nest in the confusion, and once a ghostly white bat the size of an eagle flew so low she could feel the beating of its wings. She even saw several injured kobolds limping along, who locked eyes with her for a moment before hurrying on. When things got too hectic, Iphigenia looked for the glow of the girl's lantern. At times it was the only thing she could see.

The last thing Iphigenia could recall with any certainty from that night was the strange girl standing over her, asking if she was okay. Moments later, she succumbed to exhaustion and collapsed from the waking world.

CHAPTER 9

The Princess awoke, surprised to find she wasn't in her usual bed. Her pillow wasn't nearly as soft as it should've been, either. She rolled over onto her side, annoyed that she had to call for her personal pillow servants this early in the morning, and found herself face to face with a long scaly snout and two beady black eyes.

"*Kopi*," it said.

Iphigenia sat upright and assessed her situation. Then reassessed it. She was in the middle of re-reassessing it when a small, filthy girl with a giant backpack walked in and everything from last night came flooding back. None of this, however, explained why she was sharing a bed with a kobold.

"I see you two've met!" said Thisby brightly.

"What—" started Iphigenia.

"Oh! Well, we had to stay the night here because you weren't in any state to head back, and quite frankly, you're heavier than you look or else I would've carried you."

"EXCUSE ME?" said the Princess.

"It wouldn't have been a problem most of the way, sure, it's just getting up the ladders and stuff like that. That would've been next to impossible!"

The Princess stood up and began to indignantly smooth out the folds of her dress. Her mind reeled as she tried to figure out which thing happening to her was the most insulting.

Thisby continued, "And of course, Ralk here would've helped, too, if he didn't have a bum leg! Which is why he's here, of course! I was helping fix him up while we waited. Figured you two wouldn't mind sharing a cot."

BINGO.

"OF COURSE I MIND!" screeched Iphigenia, loud enough that all the air was sucked out of the room. It was a talent she'd honed to perfection over the years.

Thisby and Ralk stared blankly at the Princess.

"DO YOU KNOW WHO I AM?" she continued. "I am Princess Iphigenia Larkspur, Heir to the Throne of Nth, and you will treat me with the dignity of my position or I will personally see to it that you are banished from my realm under penalty of death!

"My brother, Prince Ingo Larkspur, Second-in-Line,

has been taken captive by one of your men, and if he is not returned immediately, my father will march his entire army on this horrid place and burn it to the ground with every one of you still inside. Now, if you have any hope of getting out of this situation alive, you will do exactly as I say. You will reunite me with my brother this instant, you will escort us out of this godforsaken dungeon, and you will pray for our mercy . . . which I cannot guarantee!"

Thisby knew what the Princess said was true, even though she didn't particularly care for the way in which she'd said it. All night, Thisby had been going over in her mind why Roquat would possibly do something so stupid as awaken the tarasque, but had he really taken Ingo, too? Thisby had lost track of them in the dust, so anything was possible, but it was hard to imagine why Roquat would do such a thing—not that he was incapable of it.

"Are you sure Roquat took your bro— the Prince?" she corrected herself.

"I'm quite sure! I saw him take my brother by the arm and then they vanished!"

Thisby considered it. But why would he kidnap the Prince? Thisby had seen him awaken the tarasque intentionally, so she agreed that whatever was going on, Roquat was definitely involved. The problem was that Roquat had always struck her as too stupid to plan something this elaborate by himself. If she could get to the Master, maybe Thisby could get some answers. Unless, of course, the Master was behind the whole thing, although that didn't seem to add up, either. The Master had a reputation for being cruel, not stupid. Roquat, on the other hand, was certainly both.

The answer wouldn't come. There were too many pieces still missing from the puzzle. In the meantime, Thisby knew it was her job to keep the Princess safe at all costs. The only thing worse than one royal dying in your dungeon was two royals dying in your dungeon.[1]

"Look—uh—Your Highness?" Thisby wasn't quite familiar with the protocols of addressing royalty. "We need to get your brother, His Highness, back safely, and we need to get you both, Your Highnesses, out of here, but right now we have no way of knowing where your brother is, or if—"

"The blackdoor machine thingy," said Iphigenia, sounding awfully confident for someone who had just said the word *thingy*. "It had crystal balls that your Master uses to spy on his dungeon. We can use them to find my brother."

Thisby was frankly shocked she hadn't thought of it first. The Princess was cleverer than she looked.

"That's a great idea, Princess! Shoot! I mean, Your Highness! Sorry!" said Thisby, catching herself. She hated coming off rude, despite the fact that the Princess had just threatened to burn her alive. Most people would take offense to something like that, but it was nothing compared to the threats Thisby heard every day in the Black Mountain for

1 Three royals dying in your dungeon *would* be worse than that even. Or four. The only thing worse than one royal dying in your dungeon would be $y = x + 1$, where $x \geq 1$ and $y =$ something worse than the number of royals dying in your dungeon.

far more minor transgressions. Just last week, a bugbear had threatened to "use her liver as a sock puppet" because she'd accidentally served him horse meat instead of his usual donkey.

Iphigenia seemed taken aback by the compliment.

"Yes, well. We should go," said Iphigenia.

Thisby leaned over and helped the injured kobold to his feet. He looked like a cross between a lizard and a greyhound, with long, ratlike whiskers protruding off his snout. He was only a few inches taller than Thisby, who handed him a walking stick as he braced himself on her shoulder.

"Take it easy for a few days," said Thisby.

The kobold dug around in his pocket for a moment until he produced a nubby little candle. He thrust it toward her. Thisby refused at first, but the kobold persisted until she took it. She rolled it over in her hand, not exactly sure what to make of it. For all intents and purposes, it looked like a regular candle. She vaguely remembered Grunda once telling her something about kobold magic and candles—but she'd have to look it up later. She smiled at him.

"*Mara'wak kombeh*," he said, smiling back.

The kobold nodded and gave an awkward little bow and hobbled off, back toward the City of Night. The devastation seemed to be done for the time being. The tarasque had returned to its place of rest in the ruins of the forum—what little of it still remained—and life had begun to trickle back into the city after the long night of destruction.

Thisby thought of all the monsters that suffered due to the tarasque's rampage. She couldn't make sense of what Roquat was up to, but she knew what she had seen. Waking the tarasque was clearly intentional, even planned. And if he'd really taken Ingo . . .

Nothing about it felt right.

"I suppose . . . ," said Iphigenia, letting her words hang in the air until she had Thisby's full, undivided attention.

Thisby turned toward the Princess, who looked as if she were holding something bitter and unpleasant in her mouth.

". . . I should learn your name. If you cross me, I'd like to know who to execute," she finished.

"Thisby Thestoop, Your Highness. I'm the gamekeeper here in the Black Mountain."

"Very well, Thisby. I will allow you to guide me back to Castle Grimstone. Please be quick about it. I don't intend to spend another night in this wretched place."

Thisby scratched her head idly. "Uh, well, Your Highness, about that . . . I was just out scouting the area, and, well, the main passages around here, they've all, um, collapsed."

"And?" asked Iphigenia sourly.

"And what should be a day's journey up through the mountain from here to the castle could easily take us three or four. We're gonna have to kinda zigzag, you see?"

Iphigenia's arms were crossed so tightly that she began to lose circulation to them.

"On the plus side," added Thisby, "you'll get to see some

pretty neat stuff along the scenic route!"

Iphigenia sighed. This was just her luck. She hadn't even wanted to come on this stupid Inspection to begin with, but her brother had insisted on it. He'd practically begged her father to let them go, and of course, whatever Ingo wanted, Ingo got. It was always that way with her father. Now here she was, the future Queen of Nth, being dragged around a dungeon by some filthy girl . . . and what seemed to be a talking ball of glowing mucus? Iphigenia was still figuring that one out.

"Very well," she said. "But I'm not sharing a bed with any more monsters."

Thisby nodded, wondering when the best time would be to tell the Princess that she only had the one bedroll. By the shape of Iphigenia's scowl, she decided it would probably be best to wait.

And with that, they were off.

CHAPTER 10

Gregory had been walking for a day and a half and hadn't seen any stupid ladder. Maybe the girl with the backpack had tricked him. He knew it was equally likely that he'd just taken a wrong turn. He tended to take a lot of wrong turns. He was pretty sure he'd gone left at the fork but it was possible he'd gone right. Which one was left again? He held out both his thumbs and index fingers to see which one made a proper *L* and which one made a backward one, but couldn't remember if the trick was supposed to work with your palms facing in or your palms facing out.

He sat down on a reasonably flat rock and began to feel sorry for himself.

None of this would've happened if it weren't for Derrick, the blacksmith's son. Ever since Derrick started paying attention to Becca, Gregory had had to work twice as hard to win her favor. Derrick was broad shouldered and had hands like slabs of meat covered in sandpaper—which was a thing Gregory had learned that girls apparently liked for some reason. His own hands were soft, with oddly long fingers, but since being in the dungeon he had developed a blister from squeezing his sword so tightly. Maybe that was worth a peck on the cheek?

Gregory took out the bag of "wyvern beads" and examined them like he'd seen the appraisers do at the town market. He had no idea what he was looking for, but he screwed up his face like they did and nodded to himself, and eventually decided they were indeed genuine and quite valuable. When Becca saw these, she'd undoubtedly agree to marry him and forget all about Derrick and his viable career, natural good looks, and casual charm.

An awful guttural noise from nearby made Gregory jump. He hastily tucked his bag of treasure back into his belt and scurried ahead to see whatever it was that he should probably be running away from.

Gregory emerged from a twisty corridor to find himself standing on the edge of an enormous cavern shaped like a giant stone bowl. At the bottom of the bowl was a sort of odd drain. With a shrug of his gangly shoulders, Gregory proceeded to make his way toward the drain as if he were approaching the door of a tavern or a particularly friendly looking tree—that is to say, he simply walked toward it.

There was a horrible yowling from the dark.

Gregory hesitated and wondered if he should head back. If it were really dangerous, though, he figured somebody probably would've posted a sign, something like "Keep Out" or "Danger," that sort of thing. There was almost always a sign. He looked around. No sign.

He plodded onward.

It was hard work traveling down the slippery rocks, and by the time he reached the bottom, Gregory was ready for a break. He sat down on a boulder and stared out over the strange drain in the middle of the floor, pondering its existence. It seemed like this whole room could be a sort of bathtub for a giant, but he wasn't sure a giant could get very clean in here, on account of all the dirt. Also, where was the faucet?

As he pondered, a black cat the size of a small building staggered out of the dark. It appeared to be injured, or at least extremely tired, and it slumped down near the drain in exhaustion, breathing heavily. Gregory thought he saw blood matting its fur. It could have been tomato sauce, though. It was hard to tell. He wondered if he should say something. It seemed rude to just sit there.

Several small glowing doorways appeared on the floor near the cat, and from them emerged the most horrible creatures Gregory had ever seen. They looked accidental in their design, like children's drawings come to life. All their parts were jumbled together, arms growing out of heads, faces in stomachs, too many legs, wings and horns and tails all mixed up in a way that seemed to suggest they were created as some sort of cruel joke.

Strangely enough, a man appeared to be leading these monsters. He was squat and hairy and had a vicious grin across his smug face. Gregory thought that on his own, the man was ugly enough that if he were to fall asleep on a balcony he might be mistaken for a gargoyle, and yet, compared to the creatures he was leading, he seemed quite ordinary. He waved his arms, and the monsters charged forward.

Gregory hid. It was the first smart decision he'd made since walking into the dungeon two days ago.

The monsters pounced on the wounded cat. The cat fought back with the last of his strength but was inevitably overwhelmed. They tied him down with ropes and laughed at him as they did. In unison, several of the monsters each threw something small at the ground, aiming for the same spot, and a larger glowing doorway opened. At the hairy man's command, they dragged the monstrous cat into the doorway and then jumped in behind him. The doorway closed with a crackling *pop* of magical energy, which sparked and momentarily lit up the entire cavern with rainbow light.

Gregory stood up and scratched his head.

He wandered over to where the commotion had been just moments before and touched the ground lightly. There was no sign of where the glowing doors had just been.

On the ground next to him he noticed a bag that one of the creatures must've dropped. Inside there were several small black beads, which he added to his sack of wyvern beads. Hopefully these would be worth something, too, although honestly, they didn't look like much. Just boring old black beads. He looked around contemplatively.

Maybe the faucet is hidden, he thought.

CHAPTER 11

"We've been walking for hours," said Iphigenia, an hour and a half later.

"We can rest, if you'd like," said Thisby.

Iphigenia looked around and tried to imagine herself sitting down here to rest. To her right was a fountain that hadn't seen a drop of water in possibly hundreds of years. It was so covered in moss and lichens that it was hard to tell what the sculpture standing in the middle was supposed to be. To her left was an enormous set of heavy oak double doors banded with rusted iron. The doors were propped open just enough that she could squeeze through if she so desired, or more likely, something inside could squeeze out. In front of them were more hallways, tunnels, stairways, and passages. And behind them were yet more hallways, tunnels, stairways, and passages.

Everything Iphigenia had seen in the dungeon so far looked about as bleak as she felt. Hallway after hallway of boring gray stones that appeared as if they'd never been cleaned, random vines and gross moss, and rusted iron bars. Occasionally there'd be a natural cave path riddled with stalagmites, which was sort of pretty in its own way, but that was about it. There was also the smell, the constant, lingering smell, which never went away and which reminded Iphigenia of wet dirt mixed with boiled cabbage.

Iphigenia shook her head, and they continued on.

Thisby had a notebook open as they went and seemed to be spending more time looking at it than she did at the path ahead. It had quickly become a favorite game of Iphigenia's to watch the girl as she approached an obstacle with her nose buried in her books, and delight with anticipation at the impending collision. Yet somehow, every time, at the last second Thisby always managed to duck or dodge out of the way, narrowly averting disaster. It was very disappointing.

"What are you looking at?" asked Iphigenia.

Thisby raised her nose from her notebook. "Hm?"

She looked rather like a mouse, Iphigenia thought. Big, wet, curious eyes, a pointed nose; she even had fairly prominent front teeth.

"What. Are. You. Looking. At," she repeated.

"Maps," said Thisby casually, returning to her notes. "The tunnels got a little messed up around here after what the tarasque did. I'm trying to find a safe way back."

Iphigenia peered over Thisby's shoulder to get a look at her maps. She figured that it was likely that between the two of them, she was the only one who'd ever formally studied cartography—under one of the greatest mapmakers in all of Nth, no less—so she reasoned that she should probably be the one to read the maps. What Iphigenia saw, however, was a tangle of lines, all different colors and all coded with strange symbols that might as well have been an astrological projection as a physical place. It was nothing like the ornate, multicolored scrolls printed on vellum with which Iphigenia was familiar. The compass rose in the corner didn't even show the proper cardinal directions. Where most maps had *N, S, E,* and *W,* Thisby's had *U, O, D,* and *I.*

"What does this mean?" asked Iphigenia.

"Oh! That stands for Up, Out, Down, and In," said Thisby proudly. "It's my own system for navigating the mountain. Pretty handy, huh?"

"What about that way?" asked Iphigenia, pointing at what appeared to be a fairly direct route toward the castle. The slime dangling in a jar over Thisby's shoulder snorted, earning him a dirty look from the Princess.

"Well," said Thisby, clearly amused herself, "I mean, for one thing, that's going to take us right through the manticore's lair, and then there's the—"

"Is it faster?" Iphigenia demanded.

"I guess," said Thisby, "but not if we die."

"Is that supposed to be funny?"

Iphigenia had a look about her now that made Thisby realize it'd be best to tread lightly. Thisby tried to think of a better way to explain the situation to the Princess, but nothing was coming to mind. Something about the Princess and her backward logic made Thisby's brain go fuzzy. It was an effect that the Larkspurs often had on common people. It was as if their mere essence implied that they were always correct even when they clearly weren't.

"I guess we *could* go that way . . . ," Thisby muttered at last.

"Perfect!" said Iphigenia.

"*Thisby!*" scolded Mingus once the Princess was out of earshot. "What are you thinking? It's too dangerous!"

Thisby's face reddened.

"Yeah! But! Well . . . ," she trailed off. "Anyway, it *will* save time!"

"You don't have to listen to her just because she's the Princess! You're the expert down here, not her!"

"I know! I know! Don't worry! It'll be fine! If the manticore rips us in half, you could always use your mysterious slime healing powers to piece us back together!" teased Thisby.

"Thisby! This is serious!"

"Don't worry! I've got it under control," said Thisby, and then decided to add the only two words that immediately cause the listener to lose all confidence in the speaker: ". . . trust me."

Once they passed the second gate at the top of the long stone stairway, Thisby knew it was too late to turn back. If the manticore was around, they were in trouble. If it wasn't, they'd cut about half a day's travel time off their trip. On the way down to the lair, Thisby triple-checked her notes as if something definitive might surface, but the manticore was too mercurial to keep a regular schedule and too irritable to forgive them for trespassing. She knew it was a coin toss. Heads or tails if they'd make it out alive.

Thisby didn't like being so reckless, but the Larkspurs had a knack for getting their way. In fact, as the story goes, it's how the Larkspurs ascended to the throne in the first place. Most royal families throughout the bloody history of Nth had seized their kingdoms by brute force, but not the Larkspurs. Apparently, they'd simply asked the right people for the right favors at the right times, and those people had said yes.

In this way, Iphigenia wasn't much like her family at all.

For a Larkspur, Iphigenia had a tendency to rub people the wrong way. Not like her brother, Ingo. Ingo was a born charmer, the epitome of Larkspur heritage. Iphigenia was often too brutally honest for her own good. They say a dishonest man wants dishonest answers to dishonest questions, and nowhere was that more true than in the royal court of Nth.

Thisby had her doubts about their decision to take the

shortcut, but it was too late. She'd said yes. Upon entering the chamber and discovering that the entire floor was made of bones, Iphigenia was beginning to have her doubts as well.

"Don't worry," whispered Thisby, stepping carefully through the remains. "They're mostly not human."

Mingus suspected differently but figured he could correct her later, if they didn't end up somewhere in the piles themselves.

The girls clambered across the piles of bones, trying their best to be sneaky and failing miserably. Mandibles knocked into femurs, tibias bumped into rib cages, and metatarsals collided with patellas, creating a dry, rattling cacophony with every step. The piles peaked in little teepees of death scattered throughout the room, and the girls wove between them, guided by Mingus's light.

Thisby pulled ahead, leading the way as Iphigenia struggled to keep up. Her long dress was better suited for elegant brunches at the royal palace than it was for climbing across piles of skulls. Conversely, Thisby's outfit, though it wasn't much to look at, functioned quite well in this scenario.

"I don't think he's in here," whispered Thisby. "I guess, you made the right call, uh . . . Your Highness?" Thisby spun around.

But the Princess had stopped dead in her tracks. Out of the corner of her eye, amid the piles of bones, Iphigenia saw it. Her family sigil. Her brother's brooch.

Her heart raced as she bent down to pick it up. She

couldn't help but picture it being ripped from Ingo's cloak as he was devoured by the horrible beast that lurked down here in the dark.

She looked it over. It was a man's brooch, to be certain, and one that bore her family's sigil as clear as day, but it was hundreds of years old by even the most conservative estimate. Far too old to have belonged to her brother. Iphigenia let out the breath she hadn't realized she was holding. Apparently, some relative of hers had long ago tried his luck at the dungeon, and this was as far as he'd made it. She wondered what he could've been looking for down in this terrible place. The Larkspurs had always had wealth to spare, so mere treasure couldn't have been too much of a draw for one. Perhaps he'd just craved adventure.

Iphigenia sighed again. This time out of contempt rather than relief. People and their adventure. She never could figure it out. It was as if life somehow bored them, and yet so often the people who craved adventure the most had barely tried their hand at real life to begin with. She had no patience for it.

She tossed the brooch back atop the pile of bones where it belonged. But before Iphigenia could even wipe the knowing grin off her face, the entire pile collapsed, burying her underneath.

The percussive rumble of the tumbling bones echoed off the walls of the cavern and reverberated directly into the pit of

Thisby's stomach, where it rattled around as a sense of all-consuming dread.

"Mingus! Stop glowing!" she said as she scrambled to conceal herself behind an uncollapsed stack of bones. Mingus's light shrank in an instant until he was just a quivering mass of gray jelly, looking up at her, his mouth agape with shock.

"Thisby! What was that?" he asked.

"Shhh!" she scolded.

Thisby hid with her backpack pressed against the pile, waiting and listening. It was dark in the cavern without Mingus's light, but the last thing she wanted to do right now was draw more attention to herself. Thisby blinked hard, squeezing her eyes shut until she saw little purple spots and then repeated the process, desperate for her eyes to adjust to the darkness and somehow convinced this would help.

"Thisby! Thisby!" came a frantic voice.

Thisby could still barely see but she had an idea of the general direction.

"I'm trapped! Get me out of here—now!" yelled Iphigenia.

In the distance, beneath the collapsed pile, Thisby saw a pale white hand waving frantically in her direction. Iphigenia's hand appeared to be the only part of her that was free, and she was using it for all it was worth.

As her eyes adjusted more, Thisby made out Iphigenia's panicked face, peering out from beneath a ribcage.

"THIZBEEEE! THIZBEEEE!" she screamed.

"SHUT UP!" yelled Thisby.

For once the Princess listened. Or at least she fell quiet because she'd heard it, too. They weren't alone in the cave. Thisby heard a snuffling noise from somewhere off in the distance, and her heart sank to the very bottom of her boots.

CHAPTER 12

Thisby waited and listened. The manticore paced around the
cave, sniffing the air in big, heavy slurps like it was trying to
get every last drop of a milk shake through a narrow straw.

On her way to the cave she'd been brushing up on her
notes concerning manticores and had been reminded about
their keen sense of smell. It was probably only a matter of time
before it found them. Thisby, for the most part, smelled like
the dungeon and would be harder to detect, but Iphigenia's
flowery soaps would be a dead giveaway. Emphasis on the
word *dead*.

Thisby considered her options. There weren't as many
as she would've liked. She could hear the beast's footsteps

crunching over the carpet of bones. It was getting closer. Carefully, she peeked out to see exactly how close.

The manticore emerged from behind a tall pile. It stood at least eight feet high to the shoulder. Its face was almost human, but its body was entirely animal—like that of a lion, but with hideous leathery wings sprouting from its back. The wings seemed too small to lift the creature's bulky frame, and from what Thisby could recall from her notes, that much was true. Behind the beast trailed its most dangerous weapon: its tail. Long and scaly, the manticore's tail was capable of shooting poisonous arrowlike barbs. The poison in the barbs wasn't usually lethal—it was far more malicious than that: its intent wasn't to kill its prey immediately but to slow it down so that they were still alive, still fresh, when the manticore finally caught up.

Thisby watched until the manticore disappeared behind another stack of bones, and then she bent down to pick up a skull. With all her might, she heaved it as far away from her as possible, in the opposite direction of Iphigenia. The skull clattered noisily across a bed of its fallen compatriots.

Like clockwork, the manticore charged toward the noise, assuming his prey had slipped. Thisby used this momentary distraction to dash over to Iphigenia. She sprinted as fast as she could and grabbed Iphigenia by her one free hand, roughly yanking her out from beneath the pile of bones in one swift motion. The pile, of course, collapsed behind her.

Thisby knew they'd have only seconds now. The

Its face was almost human, but its body was entirely animal—like that of a lion, but with hideous, leathery wings sprouting from its back.

manticore reeled around at the sound of their escape and, realizing he'd been tricked, came charging back in their direction at full tilt. It was as much of a head start as the girls were going to get.

"Run! Straight to the tunnel!" shouted Thisby. "Go!"

Iphigenia was wild-eyed, and Thisby thought for a moment that she might be frozen with fear. She'd almost expected it. To her surprise, however, Iphigenia only paused to hike up her dress in order to make more room for her knees, before taking off fast as she could toward the tunnel. Iphigenia, it turned out, had the special thing that Thisby had so often observed to be badly lacking in the vast majority of outsiders who came into the dungeon. Iphigenia had survival instinct.

People who fancied themselves "adventurers" were often the worst offenders. Thisby figured there was something intrinsic in the idea of wanting to be an adventurer that meant you had to forgo your survival instinct, or else why would you willingly go where things were trying to kill you in the first place? Some people might mistakenly interpret this sort of behavior as bravery, but Thisby knew better.

Thisby definitely wasn't doing what she was about to do because she was brave. In fact, she prided herself on being prepared and, more often than not, considered bravery the antithesis of preparedness. After all, you don't have to rush headlong into battle if you've already won the war, now, do you? Rather, she was doing what she had to do to keep the

Princess alive, because if the Crown Princess were to die here, then a war on the dungeon was inevitable. This meant that not only would she likely be killed anyway, but so would the rest of the monsters who lived in the dungeon, whose care she'd been entrusted with. It was a simple decision, ultimately, but still not one she was thrilled with at the moment.

Thisby ran several steps behind the Princess, hobbling a bit as she went. Once she was certain that the manticore had seen her, she made her move, running off the path with her awkward gait to hide herself behind the nearest heap of bones. The gamble worked, and the manticore followed.

On their approach to the room, Thisby had come across an interesting note she'd written several years ago concerning manticores. *LAZY*, it said, in big capital letters. Thankfully, it turned out to be true. The manticore had chosen the path of least resistance and had gone after the slower-moving lunch—at least, the one Thisby had wanted it to think was slower moving.

As soon as Thisby was out of its eye line, concealed behind the remains, she took off, running as fast as she could toward the exit. The manticore was fast, but so was Thisby. She darted through the stacks nimbly, and as she did, she caught the break she needed. The manticore slipped on a loose skull and tumbled headfirst, rolling head over heels and sending skulls and femurs and tibias scattering as it went. By the time the manticore had righted itself, Thisby was only thirty-odd yards from the tunnel—a tunnel that, by her best estimate, was too narrow for the manticore to squeeze through.

Thisby was essentially home free! Her brief moment of triumph was interrupted, however, by a sharp pain in the back of her leg, and somewhere in the back of her mind, the word *essentially* repeated ad nauseum. Thisby looked down to see a needle about the size of a porcupine's quill sticking straight out of her right calf. Her heart raced—or rather, it would have, if the toxin rapidly spreading through her body hadn't already slowed her heart considerably.

It felt as if she were being slowly lowered into a warm bath. She pushed herself forward. In the distance, she thought she heard somebody calling her name, only whoever it was sounded as if she were underwater. Thisby tried to keep her focus, tried to continue to put one foot in front of the other, but it was becoming more difficult to stand, let alone walk. Her legs felt like wool socks stuffed with room-temperature yogurt, and it took all her energy just to keep her eyes open.

The tunnel was only a few yards away now, but she was slowing down even more. Her arms went limp—had her hands always been so heavy?—and as she tried to yell something, anything, she came to the horrible realization that her mouth wouldn't respond to her brain's instructions.

The footsteps of the manticore were getting closer. He was closing in.

Thisby made it as far as the threshold of the tunnel before her legs finally gave out. She collapsed. She had been so close.

Thisby looked up sleepily with a vague feeling that she'd wanted something a few moments ago. Wanted to be somewhere, perhaps. It was blurry. But it didn't matter. Everything felt fine now, anyway. She closed her eyes. It felt like she was floating in a pool of tepid water, caught in that perfect restful moment right before drifting off to sleep.

The manticore lunged.

Its teeth snapped shut inches from Thisby's foot, which had begun to somehow drift out of reach.

Thisby caught a glimpse of Iphigenia as the Princess dragged her by the backpack up into the tunnel. The manticore snapped its terrible jaws at them. Three rows of pointed, sharklike teeth biting and thrashing, desperate for one more inch to reach its dinner. Thankfully for Thisby, its shoulders were stuck solid in the tunnel, and there wasn't another inch to be had. Thisby gazed back at the manticore lazily, her eyes half closed.

"What a weird dog," she said dreamily.

Iphigenia dragged Thisby farther up into the tunnel, away from the manticore, and propped her up against a wall, where she smiled contentedly.

"Hey, buddy. Hey. Hey," said Thisby, adding a final, delayed, "Hey."

Iphigenia looked at her bewildered.

"I'm McGeepy." Thisby grinned.

"You're what?"

"I'm McGeepy."

"I have no idea what you're talking about."

"I'm McGeepy!" she demanded.

"I don't know what that means."

"I'M MCGEEPY!" screamed Thisby.

"Uh—"

Thisby laughed. "I'm Sleepy McGeepy!"

She proceeded to laugh so hard that she fell over.

"I think you need to get the barb out of her leg," said Mingus. "I think the poison is, uh, doing this to her." He pointed a nub at Thisby, who was attempting to see if she could stick out her tongue far enough to see it.[2]

Iphigenia wasn't exactly comfortable with the idea of performing surgery. In fact, she wasn't even sure she was completely comfortable with the idea of touching this strange girl who she had just met. The Larkspurs weren't exactly a touchy-feely kind of family. She thought she could recall her father giving her a pat on the shoulder once during a funeral, but it was possible he'd just lost his balance and used her for support.

"I can't . . . I don't know what I'm doing!"

"You just need to pull it out. I'd do it, but I don't have hands, and I don't think we're going to get too far like this," he said, motioning to Thisby, who'd moved on from trying to see her tongue to trying to lick her elbow.[3]

Thisby was the one who knew the way through the

2 Disclaimer: The author will not be held personally, legally accountable for any tongue strains or other tongue-related injuries that may happen to readers who just attempted to do this.
3 Ditto.

dungeon, there was no denying that. Iphigenia sighed and went over to look at Thisby's leg. There was a long quill sticking from the back of her right calf. Iphigenia resigned herself to the inevitable.

"Give me your leg," she insisted.

"No. I need them. I need both of them," replied Thisby, earnestly.

"Give me your LEG," she tried again.

"YOU GIVE ME YOUR ARMS! HOW ABOUT THAT?" shouted Thisby.

Iphigenia grabbed her leg, and Thisby began to thrash wildly. Thankfully for Iphigenia, Thisby's muscles were still weakened from the poison, and she was able to overpower the wild gamekeeper with a little effort. She grabbed the quill and yanked it from Thisby's leg in one swift pull.

The quill was about the length of a knitting needle with a hooked barb on the end. Iphigenia went to toss it away but stopped when Mingus yelled excitedly, "Sorry, Your Highness! I just know Thisby, and I know she'd want to keep it. To study. Would you mind?"

Iphigenia opened Thisby's backpack and was immediately overwhelmed by the sheer amount of stuff inside. It reminded her of a general store in southeast Nth that she'd been to once as a child on one of her rare trips away from the castle. Every inch of the store had been overflowing with wonderful items that triggered her imagination: boxes stamped with the insignias of their exotic places of origin, bottles full of strange elixirs with labels written in languages she couldn't comprehend, bizarre plants and gems and spell components, every sort of trinket one could ever need for a life out on the road. It was the first time she'd realized there was a whole other world out there beyond the castle walls, a world she was never meant to be a part of. Thisby's backpack was all that, only portable.

She picked a spot that looked suitable for the quill and stashed it away.

Hesitantly, she reached out and took Thisby's hand, much as Thisby had done for her when they fled from the tarasque, and helped her to her feet. Iphigenia felt like they were even now. Which was good. Now she wouldn't feel as if she had to speak up on the girl's behalf if Thisby was held accountable for what happened to the royal party while they were touring the dungeon.

It wasn't that she blamed Thisby for what had happened. So far, Thisby had merely shown up and offered to help her return to the castle. But Thisby was the gamekeeper, and technically that meant the tarasque was her responsibility. Iphigenia had been around politics long enough to know that blame always rolls downhill, and it was hard for her to imagine anybody lower down the hill than Thisby.

Still, that was an issue for later. For now, Iphigenia needed to get to the castle, and, whether she liked it or not, the girl who had moments ago been trying to lick her own elbow was still her best chance.

CHAPTER 13

Iphigenia sighed and looked at the map again. From where Mingus watched, he could see the frustration on the Princess's brow, but the last time he'd offered help, she'd snapped at him—something about not needing help from a talking booger—and hurt his feelings. Since then he'd kept his mouth shut.

Mingus's lantern swayed back and forth awkwardly as Thisby shuffled along, dragging her feet sideways like a zombie, barely able to keep herself upright beneath the weight of her enormous backpack. Normally, Thisby could bear the weight of the pack all day long without issue, but thanks to the manticore's poison, the poor girl could barely walk, let alone carry anything. Mingus thought it would've made much more sense for the Princess to wear the backpack, but he hadn't spoken up when the decision had been made, and he certainly wasn't about to say something now.

"Look at this stupid thing! Did you draw these maps with your feet? How could anyone make sense of this—this nonsense!" Iphigenia was fuming.

"Mmmmmmuuuuhh," groaned Thisby. Her senses were beginning to return, it seemed.

Iphigenia had her nose buried in the map. So much so that she wasn't looking where she was stepping, and by the time Mingus had mustered up the courage to yell, "LOOK OUT!" it was too late.

Squuuuuiiiiiiisssh!

The Princess recoiled in horror as cold, wet slime met the skin of her foot, squishing into her fancy shoes and wriggling between her toes.

"Ewwww!" she shrieked, pulling her foot back from a blue puddle of ooze.

Sliding across the path in front of her were several dozen semitranslucent blue slimes, each no bigger than a croquet ball and shaped like a spoonful of mashed potatoes dumped carelessly onto a plate. The slime on which she'd stepped spluttered helplessly on the ground in front of her as Iphigenia scraped the goo off her heel against a nearby rock.

"What are those disgusting things!" she demanded.

Thisby lurched to a halt, causing Mingus's lantern to swing to and fro.

"Slimes," he said.

There was an air of sadness in his voice, which Iphigenia decided to ignore.

"Is it going to hurt me?" asked the Princess. She was already wiping the residue off her ankle with a rag she'd borrowed from Thisby's backpack without asking.

"No," said Mingus. "But you killed it."

Iphigenia hesitated.

"In case you're wondering," he said, "I'm not a slime. They're mindless creatures. I'm different."

"Oh," said Iphigenia.

"But that doesn't mean they deserve to die due to carelessness," he added. "Please watch where you're stepping."

Iphigenia said nothing, and they walked on in silence for some time.

It was several hours later when Thisby fully returned to her senses, only to discover that they'd been wandering around hopelessly lost since the manticore cave. Apparently, Iphigenia's cartography instructor hadn't prepared her well. Neither, it seemed, had her manners coach.

"Finally, you're awake! Now help us get out of this mess!" Iphigenia demanded.

Thisby still felt a bit groggy from the manticore sting. She looked around, trying to place where they might be. It seemed likely that they'd backtracked and probably lost any of the time they'd saved by cutting through the manticore cave to begin with. It was a horrible feeling.

"Did you head Up or Out at the junction after the manticore cave?" muttered Thisby, rubbing her temples.

"How should I know!"

Thisby turned away from her and addressed Mingus.

"What do you think?" she asked quietly.

Mingus felt ashamed that he hadn't tried harder to get the maps away from Iphigenia even though he'd known that she was lost. He tried his best to recall what they'd done, but in the end, he could only guess.

"I think we went Up," he said, "but I'm not sure."

"Okay. Thanks, Mingus."

Thisby knew how bad Mingus was at stuff like this. It was Thisby's job to keep track of everything, to read the maps, to take the notes. Mingus was just there for company, and Thisby appreciated that. Thisby knew that loneliness was a poison in its own right. When you were down in the dungeon for days on end, loneliness could seep into your veins and ruin you as quickly as any manticore sting.

Unfortunately, now they were at a crossroads, both literally and metaphorically. Thisby would have to attempt to make an informed decision based on what little information she had. She looked around and compared the room they were in to her notes for the thousandth time. Nothing was jumping out at her.

"We should continue on the way we were going," said Iphigenia. "I had everything under control."

"I think I know which way we're going, but I just want to make sure. If we head down the wrong path, we could end up somewhere dangerous."

Iphigenia scowled. She wasn't used to being second-guessed.

"Like what?" she spat.

"Well," said Thisby, "from this junction, depending on the direction we're facing, we could be walking toward any number of things: giant beetles, wraiths, elementals, vampires—"

"Vampires?" interrupted Iphigenia. "Oh, let's go see the vampires! I've always wanted to meet a vampire!"

Thisby couldn't believe her ears. "Really? Why?"

"Oh, I don't know, they always just seemed so romantic in the stories. They're these eternal, haunted souls, wandering around their mansions, brooding over grand pianos."

Thisby laughed. "I've never seen a vampire play piano!"

"Don't laugh at me!" snapped Iphigenia.

Thisby held up her hands apologetically. She wasn't sure where Iphigenia was getting her stories about vampires, but she was happy to see the Princess at least taking an interest in something for the first time since setting foot inside the dungeon. Maybe they could go by the vampires. It probably wouldn't hurt anything.

"Okay, let's go see the vampires!" said Thisby brightly.

"Really?"

"Sure!"

Thisby checked her map a few more times before heading out, and off they went.

It took a few wrong turns, but finally the trio arrived at the vampire crypt. To enter the crypt, they had to walk down a spiraling stone staircase that was barely large enough for Thisby's backpack to fit through. Several times, Mingus's lantern banged off the wall, causing him to scream in alarm loud enough that Thisby to shush him.

Iphigenia's excitement was palpable. She tried her best to hide it, but her enthusiasm was infectious, and soon, even Thisby was getting excited by proxy. By the time they'd reached the bottom of the stairs, Thisby had a big smile on her face.

"Here we go!" she said pushing open the door to the crypt.

Iphigenia gazed into the room and immediately deflated.

The crypt was a long, thin room, maybe two hundred yards deep and twenty across, lined with decaying, moldy coffins propped up against the walls. The only decorations were a rotten old runner that went the distance of the crypt and a few iron sconces holding burnt-out candles. There were no pianos to be found.

Iphigenia waved the dust out of her face and squinted her eyes in the hopes it would make some difference, but the scene didn't change. Somewhere down the long corridor she could hear water dripping.

"What's this?" asked Iphigenia.

"Vampires, of course!" said Thisby. "Aren't they awesome?"

The girls gazed into the dusty crypt for several moments, Thisby grinning ear to ear and Iphigenia looking terribly disappointed.

"Come on!" said Thisby, waving Iphigenia forward. Hesitantly, she followed.

Once Thisby had closed the door behind them, Mingus was the only light, glowing a soft blue color. The room smelled like Grandma's house and mildew.

"Is—is this it?" asked Iphigenia.

The romantic vision of vampires she'd gleaned from stories was falling apart in front of her eyes. Where were the handsome young men in sharp formal wear hosting lavish parties? Where were the exotic women in masquerade costumes drinking from bejeweled goblets? Where were the pianos?

Thisby could sense Iphigenia's disappointment. She had no idea who was writing these stories about vampires, but she got the impression that the dungeon's vampires weren't the kind of vampires Iphigenia had in mind.

"Um, would you like to see one?" asked Thisby, against her better judgement.

Taking unnecessary risks wasn't something Thisby was known for, but seeing the Princess get so excited and then so disappointed had triggered something deep inside her. The Larkspurs just had that way with people. People bent over backward to make them happy.

Iphigenia nodded and followed her over to a coffin. Thisby grabbed the lip of it and pulled, drawing it slowly back. Iphigenia gasped when she saw what was inside.

The creature in the coffin was ghostly white and had a bulbous, bald head. Its eyes were enormous, almost insectlike, and its fangs stuck out over its lips, jagged and yellowed. Its two hands were folded over its heart, thin, gnarled fingers with long, curling nails. It looked far from human, let alone a handsome young man in formal wear. Iphigenia could barely stand to look at it. It was disgusting.

"Close it. Please," she said sadly.

Thisby, realizing she'd failed, closed the coffin dejectedly, and they made their way from the crypt.

They walked in silence for some time. Thisby had barely looked at the Princess since they'd left the crypt, so she was startled by her sudden outburst of laughter.

"Can you imagine trying to play the piano with those fingernails?" howled Iphigenia, clutching her stomach.

Thisby watched her for moment unsure of what to say.

Iphigenia mimicked a doofy-looking vampire playing the piano. "Donk! Dum! Dee! Donk!"

Before long, Thisby couldn't contain her laughter, either, and the two of them laughed until their sides hurt at the thought of it.

CHAPTER 14

The levity didn't last. By the time they'd reached the grotto of the acidic ooze, Iphigenia was at the end of her rope. It was their second day in the dungeon, and by now the Black Mountain was back in full swing, having recovered from the tarasque. Since their time with the vampires, Thisby and Iphigenia had been chased by death bears, hassled by banshees, hounded by bioluminescent wereplants, and of course, there was the incident with the spectral goat, which they'd both vowed never to speak of again.

Thisby sat in the corner of the room, next to a small, slow-moving waterfall, flipping idly through a notebook. Whatever she was looking for didn't seem to be in there, and after several minutes she tossed it back into her backpack and grabbed another.

Iphigenia, meanwhile, was stomping around impatiently.

"What are you looking for?" she demanded.

Thisby continued to scan her notes. "A map."

"More maps. Of course. Don't you know the way around here? Isn't that your job?"

Thisby paused but refused to look up.

"Do you know the roads in every city in your kingdom?" she asked as politely as she could manage.

Iphigenia looked like she wanted to say something rude, but Thisby continued before she had the chance.

"The Black Mountain is larger than your two biggest surface cities combined. Do you know how many passageways and tunnels and nooks and crannies and rooms and dens and pits and ladders and stairways and caverns and rivers there are in here? Not even a brainlodyte could remember all of it!"

"What's a brainlo— You know what, forget it. I don't care," said Iphigenia.

Thisby went back to her notes as if to imply that their conversation was over, but she had a sinking feeling this wasn't the case. She could feel Iphigenia's eyes burning into her.

"This place is terrible, you know," said Iphigenia at last. "Do you even realize that? Let me guess—this place is all you've ever known, right? So you probably think that it's okay. But it's not. It's not okay."

Iphigenia had moved on to phase two of her frustration,

in which she sought out ways to share her misery with somebody else. It was a trick she'd picked up from her father. Thisby kept her focus squarely on her notes, knowing she'd get too upset if she looked at Iphigenia's arrogant, pretty face.

"It's a *dungeon*. Full of terrible, filthy, disgusting, violent monsters that want to kill you! The only reason any rational humans ever come to visit is that they want to steal your gold! You're going to spend the rest of your life trapped here, and you're never going to get to do any of the things you really want to do—you know that, right?" Iphigenia concluded in a huff.

Thisby flipped another page. "How's that any different from your castle?" she asked.

Iphigenia's face turned bright red and she stalked away.

"Oh, boy. I think you've done it now," said Mingus.

Thisby continued to read her notes as if nothing had happened.

"You should go after her. She could get hurt."

"That's her own fault," said Thisby.

Thisby looked up from her notebook to see Mingus studying her with his fake button eyes. Somehow this didn't make her feel better like it usually did.

"She's just worried about her brother," said Mingus.

"I'm not so sure. I get the feeling she's always like this."

"Thisby!"

"Fine! Fine!" Thisby threw on her backpack and attached Mingus to his usual hook.

"But I'm only doing this for the sake of the dungeon. Not her," she said.

From the day she was old enough to carry her enormous backpack, Thisby had worked in the dungeon. It wasn't exactly cozy—Iphigenia was right about that—and it definitely was full of monsters that wanted to kill her—she was right about that as well—but the dungeon was the closest thing Thisby had to a home, and she worked hard to keep it running well.

But it was more than just a job. Thisby actually really liked it here. Possibly despite her better judgment, at times. And the monsters weren't all bad. Not all the time, at least. The monsters—just like all living things—had their idiosyncrasies. Thisby had just spent the time to learn them.

Even if she didn't like all the monsters in the dungeon, at the very least she respected them. Her bribery, if you could call it that, didn't hurt, either. It was nothing too extravagant, just some rosemary sprigs for the troll, sugar cubes for the nightmares, hambones for the gnolls, a child's blanket full of whispered secrets for the spectral goat, that sort of thing. It wasn't much, but Thisby knew if the Master ever found out, she'd be punished, which only made her all the more determined to find the just-right little bribes to give.

While Thisby liked to give the monsters treats, the Master believed in alternative methods of "encouragement." Starvation for the monsters who let the rare, wily adventurer sneak away with some of his precious treasure, beatings for the ones who saw it happen and did nothing. These punishments, as always, were dished out by his faithful servant Roquat, since the Master himself never seemed to make an appearance in the dungeon. Sometimes she suspected that Roquat was acting without the Master's authority since he was never there to give the orders himself, but of course, if Thisby or Grunda or anybody else ever brought this up to Roquat, he was quick to say that they'd just missed him, or laugh derisively and remind them that "The Master was always watching."

That part, at least, seemed to be true.

For a princess in a long dress, Iphigenia moved faster than Thisby had expected. Thisby had been following her trail for hours and was beginning to wonder if she'd somehow taken a wrong turn somewhere along the way. Her hopes of making it to the castle before nightfall were rapidly diminishing, while her concern was growing—not just about Iphigenia, but also about the situation in general.

Assuming that Iphigenia was correct—and Thisby had no good reason to doubt her—Roquat had kidnapped Prince Ingo, but why? Knowing him, it was possibly an ill-conceived attempt at ransom, but for all of Roquat's failings, he never seemed to care much for money. It would have to be something else then. Power?

And there was something else nagging at the back of Thisby's mind, something that she hadn't given a proper amount of time to consider since the events in the City of Night; namely, that something had passed through from the Deep Down. She'd been good to her word and kept Catface's secret, but now she wondered if she'd possibly made a mistake. Maybe Catface had known more than he'd let on. Maybe he was even in on it. Maybe after all those years of sitting in that stinking pit, staring at that impassible gate, escaping only for brief moments to hunt for food before returning to his post, maybe he'd given up on the Black Mountain. It seemed unlikely. But it was as fair a theory as any others she had right now—as absurd as it may have seemed.

The important thing was that somehow, something had passed through the Darkwell. Assuming Catface could be trusted, of course. But how? The gate was still closed. How does something pass through a gate with no hinges and not leave a mark?

The only way to pass through a solid wall in the dungeon was by blackdoor. But the Master controlled the blackdoor supply as tightly as anything in the Black Mountain. Besides, a blackdoor bead only worked one way, and they were made in the castle, not the Deep Down. Second, Grunda had told her once that not even magic could pass through the Darkwell, although that might've just been something Grunda said to keep Thisby from being too scared to venture down there as a child. Still, it had to be magic.

"Magic." Thisby sighed. Of course it was magic! That was why she hated the stuff.

Even the best magic was inherently flawed. Sure, you could ensorcell a stone to transfigure everything it touched into gold, but how did you pick it up? You want to summon some rain for your crops, well, hope you enjoy your flood! Maybe you just want something simple like a cape that makes you invulnerable to arrows, sure, just watch out for the troll who throws rocks. Magic broke the logic of the universe, and yet it always seemed to Thisby as if the universe managed to have the last laugh.

So she figured it was possible that something had somehow passed through the magic impassible gate, but even that theory gnawed at her guts. If it had been a blackdoor that had somehow overcome the magical protection of the Darkwell, there was still the question of how it'd gotten in there in the first place. Catface had smelled something that came *out* of the Deep Down, not gone into it. Somebody or something had to get that blackdoor down there to begin with. And the blackweave of the Darkwell was so tightly knit with metal bars that you couldn't even slip a blade of grass through it, let alone a blackdoor bead, as small as they were.

Thisby couldn't shake the feeling that there was a connection between the two things: something passed through the Darkwell and now the Prince has been kidnapped. It seemed like a big leap to get from one to the other, but it couldn't just be a coincidence. The idea made her nervous. She twisted her toes together in her particular way and tried not to think about it. She'd been thinking—and walking—

for hours, and so far all it'd gotten her were a sinking feeling in the pit of her stomach and sore feet.

Mingus swayed in his lantern. His glow had begun to shift from emerald green to aquamarine. It was getting late. Typically, when Mingus turned blue or purple, it meant it was night—or that he was feeling sad. Sometimes both. Before she'd had Mingus around, day and night were pretty arbitrary, since there weren't exactly windows in the sides of the Black Mountain, but since having him, she'd realized how helpful it was to be able to pretend there was a difference.

"Your Highness?" Thisby called out. It was a desperate move. Typically, the worst thing to do in the dungeon was announce your presence, but her patience was running thin.

"Maybe we should rest until morning," suggested Mingus.

Thisby didn't need to check her notebooks to know what a bad idea that was. Most of the creatures in the dungeon, especially the most dangerous ones, were nocturnal. She'd hoped they could make it back to the castle before midnight, but she'd known it was going to be close. Now it was essentially impossible.

They came to another fork in the tunnel. Thisby stopped. The two paths were identical. Same stone walls, same smell, no discernible noise, no footprints, no clues.

"Now what?" Mingus sighed.

Thisby thought for a moment and pulled out her most recent notebook. She thumbed through it a bit, and after a moment, she put the notebook away.

"This way," Thisby said, walking down the left-hand tunnel.

"How do you know?" asked Mingus.

"I don't," said Thisby. "But she's left-handed. Creatures tend to favor their dominant side when presented with two equal options. We might as well play the odds."

Mingus snorted.

"You wrote down she was left-handed?"

"I grabbed both her hands at some point as we ran from the tarasque. Her left felt stronger. I made a note of it. It's a guess, but . . . ," said Thisby.

"That's not much to go on," said Mingus.

"Is it ever?" said Thisby.

After a few hundred yards, the path began to slope down at a steep angle, and the air became thick and hot and stinky. Living in the dungeon, Thisby was quite used to thick and hot and stinky, but this air was something special. This air seemed to crunch when she moved through it, and it left a bad taste in her mouth, like week-old cave oyster soup. She clambered down the steep and slippery path slowly with one hand outstretched to brace against the wall for balance, while her other hand was busy pinching her nostrils shut. There was no need to check her map now. She knew exactly where they were heading, and she hoped beyond hope that Iphigenia had turned right at the fork after all.

The wyvern roost was one of the oldest structures still

intact in the Black Mountain, dating back to before the dungeon even existed. All along the walls of the roost were evenly spaced holes, giving the nest a distinct Swiss cheese look. In the corners of the vast room were four great stone towers, connected by narrow walkways that came to meet at a crossroads some one hundred feet above a towering, lichen-covered fountain. A sculpture of a wyvern with its wings outstretched and its mouth aglow with an otherworldly orange light perched in the dead center of the room. The sculpture was so lifelike that the first time Thisby had seen it, she nearly fell over backward.

"I don't see anything, do you?" whispered Thisby.

She watched the holes in the walls. Nothing moved.

Wyverns were nocturnal, but luckily for Thisby, it was still a bit early for them. Unluckily for Thisby, however, was that once she'd realized where she was heading, she'd checked her notes and noticed that it'd been three days since the wyverns were last fed. This was bad news indeed. Wyverns only ate every few days, but when they did, they'd gorge themselves on anything in sight. Since tomorrow was their feeding day, they would be ready to eat the first thing they saw when they woke up. Thisby hoped it wouldn't be her.

When she was younger, Thisby had once missed a feeding day. She'd gotten busy chasing a baby yeti through the ice caves, and by the time she was done, it had simply slipped her mind. The next morning, when she came down to the roost, she found all the nearby ogre dens empty. What she saw on the floor of the wyvern roost that morning was something she'd never forget. She never missed a feeding day again.

Thisby crept into the room, keeping an eye out for any signs of movement. Mingus dimmed his glow, which had been made unnecessary anyhow due to the supernatural orange light emanating from the mouth of the sculpture atop the old fountain. The light that shone from the wyvern statue's gaping jaws made it look as if the creature were breathing fire. This was a bit odd, because wyverns didn't actually breathe fire—at least, none of the ones Thisby had ever seen did. This was, of course, instead a reference to their supposed connection to dragons.

Thisby had never seen a dragon herself because, well, dragons weren't real. At least, not anymore.

When Thisby was only a few years old, Grunda had sat her down beside a crackling fire and told her the story of dragons and how the Black Mountain came to be. The legend went something like this . . .

Back when the world was still young, before people came to dot the landscape with their castles and kingdoms, before there were even trees and water, when the world was still raw and hot and angry with chaos, dragons ruled the world. They were great beasts the size of cities who fed on one another and drank fire from the mountains, who cracked the earth and darkened the sky.

Of all the dragons, by far the most horrible was the Black Dragon, the largest of all the beasts. The Black Dragon brought death with him wherever he went. He was the embodiment of hatred and fear, the ruler of chaos through sheer brute force and unrelenting terror. An unstoppable evil, the Black Dragon existed for millennia, seemingly eternal in his claim upon the earth, until one day, without warning, the world grew cold. And all the dragons, even the Black Dragon, perished.

Where the dragons' bodies fell, they became the earth. From their bodies grew trees and hills and valleys and mountains. Even animals, including man, sprung from their bodies, fully formed, ready to populate the world. But from where the Black Dragon died, only evil could grow. Over eons, a great mountain formed above his final resting place, a cruel, jagged dagger erupting through the skin of the earth, warning good creatures to stay as far away as possible: the Black Mountain.

But there are those who believe that the Black Dragon did not stay dead. That as the Black Mountain grew from its ashes, it in turn became his womb, feeding and nourishing his evil spirit back to life. And now, thousands of years later, the Black Dragon is ready to return, fully grown, to reclaim everything he has lost. They believe that deep below the Black Mountain, he lies in the darkness . . . waiting and watching: The Eyes in the Dark That Watch the World.

★★★

Of course, Thisby didn't sleep for days after hearing that story. Goblins weren't exactly sensitive to the fears of small children. As a matter of fact, they seemed to enjoy causing them—even the good ones like Grunda couldn't seem to help it.

That being said, the story was also very likely nonsense. Just a folktale to help explain things that people didn't understand. If you believed the wizards—which, again, Thisby never did—the world didn't grow from the bodies of dead dragons. They said it was created in some sort of cosmic blast. Humans, meanwhile, believed that the world was created by a gigantic, all-powerful human who lived in the clouds. Thisby had even read something once that claimed the world was held on the back of a giant turtle moving through space. She'd quite enjoyed that one. Yet despite the fact that these were all just stories, there was something about living in the Black Mountain that made the idea of the Eyes in the Dark hard to deny. It was hard not to feel as if there was something down there, deep, deep down. Waiting. Watching.

The Master quite enjoyed the idea of the Eyes in the Dark—of some vast, timeless evil living beneath the Black Mountain—because that was the kind of thing that drew the really good adventurers to the dungeon. But the truth of the matter was, even if there was something down there, it was well beyond the Darkwell and of no real concern to the day-to-day functioning of the dungeon. Whether it was an undead dragon, who could say? It was a striking image, at least, or as the Master would say, a "marketable" one.

Regardless, the wyverns fancied themselves direct descendants of dragons because they looked similar to how dragons were often depicted. Only instead of four legs like dragons, wyverns had two legs and arms that branched into wings—like a bat. They were also much, much smaller, if the legends about dragons were to be believed, although as far as Thisby was concerned, wyverns were quite large enough, thank you very much. Thisby was small for her age, but a fully grown wyvern stood at least three times her height— not including their tail—with a wingspan that made it hard for them to fit through most passages in the dungeon.

Thisby ran her hand along the cool stone at the base of the fountain as she crouched beside it, searching for traces of Iphigenia. The stagnant water that had pooled inside the fountain was so thick with algae that it was practically a solid, and it had the distinct aroma of a sea hag's bathwater.

"Look! Up there! The tower!" whispered Mingus.

Through an open, glassless window in the far tower, Thisby watched a pale figure in an emerald green dress climbing the stairs.

"YOUR HIGHNESS!" yelled Thisby, forgetting where she was for a moment.

Iphigenia turned and glared at Thisby before continuing off in huff.

"She's going to get herself killed!" said Thisby, turning to Mingus.

Thisby raced to the tower and up the long, winding stairs. By the time she reached the top, she could barely breathe and looked as if she'd just dunked her head in the fountain. It was possible that she smelled like she had as well, but that's a rude thing to say, so never mind.

"STOP!" Thisby wheezed.

Iphigenia, standing on a narrow walkway, turned around and crossed her arms defiantly. Thisby approached the Princess carefully, as if she were trying to walk toward a pigeon without frightening it away. The walkway was suspended between the towers, well over a hundred feet in the air, and the little guardrails tacked onto the sides looked a bit like an afterthought. It was possibly her imagination, but Thisby swore she could feel it swaying.

"What?" Iphigenia spat. Apparently all that walking hadn't settled her down one bit. If there was one thing the Larkspurs were good at, it was holding grudges.

"You're going to get yourself killed!"

"What do you care?" said Iphigenia, walking out to the crossroads directly between the four towers. She looked around, trying to decide where to go next. With a sigh, she placed her hands on her hips and turned back to Thisby.

"Which way goes to the castle?" she demanded.

"None of them!" Thisby exclaimed, exasperated. "This room's a dead end! And you would've known that if you'd stuck with me like I told you to!"

Iphigenia rolled her eyes. "After what you said to me?

How dare you speak to your future Queen like that!"

"You said the dungeon was horrible!"

"IT IS HORRIBLE! ISN'T THAT THE WHOLE POINT OF A DUNGEON? TO BE HORRIBLE? HOW COULD YOU HAVE A 'NICE' DUNGEON? WHAT WOULD EVEN BE THE POINT!"

"YOU DIDN'T HAVE TO BE SO MEAN ABOUT IT! I LIKE IT HERE! IT'S MY HOME, OKAY? AND I DON'T CARE IF YOU ARE THE FUTURE QUEEN, YOU'RE IN MY HOME, AND YOU SHOULD SHOW IT SOME RESPECT!"

The girls shouted until they were red in the face.

They shouted so loud, in fact, they didn't even hear the *whoosh*ing of wings bearing down on them.

*They shouted so loud, in fact, they didn't even hear
the whooshing of wings bearing down on them.*

CHAPTER 15

With a shriek that could curdle milk, a large gray wyvern dove for them. Just before the monster's ferocious talons could rip into Thisby, Mingus flashed a bright green, blinding the beast and causing it to miss. Its claws hit the walkway instead, gouging out chunks of stone from its surface.

The beast screeched angrily and circled back around. The beating of its leathery wings blasted gusts of wind that were strong enough to test Thisby's balance, and its horrible angry screams made her clasp her ears in pain.

"This way!" shouted Thisby, desperate to be heard over the noise.

Iphigenia and Thisby ran toward the tower directly across

from them, but before they could make it halfway across the narrow bridge, a second wyvern landed directly in front of them, blocking their path. It let out a cry of victory as the other wyvern circled around and landed behind them. Slowly, the two wyverns began inching forward, snapping their jaws.

They were trapped.

"Do something!" yelled Iphigenia.

Thisby had been in bad situations before. In the dungeon, finding yourself trapped between two hungry wyverns was pretty much par for the course, but this time there was a complication—and it was standing next to her, wearing an emerald green dress, desperately clutching her arm.

Thisby's mind raced. Clearly she had no time to get out her notebooks, so she was going to have to do this the hard way. Thisby scanned her memory for things she knew about wyverns. They're territorial, they hunt mostly at night, they only eat every three days, their favorite food is— Thisby froze. She knew exactly what to do.

"Open my backpack," she ordered Iphigenia. Iphigenia opened her mouth to protest at being spoken to like a servant but Thisby cut her off, "Just DO IT!"

Thisby crouched down as Iphigenia slid behind her and opened the backpack. The wyverns continued to walk toward them, snapping and screeching as they approached.

"There should be a canvas bag near the top. Get it out and hand it to me!" said Thisby.

Iphigenia looked into the overstuffed backpack and suddenly felt as if she were living one of those nightmares where she'd shown up at a grand ball being thrown in her honor and couldn't remember the names of any of the guests, and also, her farthingale was improperly tufted. Inside Thisby's backpack was an endless labyrinth of pouches, boxes, and bags, each one labeled in a manner so confusing that it might as well have been written in goblin, as far as Iphigenia was concerned. In fact, several of the care packages from Grunda actually were.

"Where is it? Everything's a mess in here!" she yelled.

The wyverns moved closer, calling out to each other excitedly.

"The bag's about the size of a watermelon. It has a blue snake and dagger emblem printed on the side. It should look like it's full of kidneys!"

Iphigenia held up a bag. "This one?"

Thisby looked at the bag and shook her head angrily.

"These are GALLBLADDERS! I said KIDNEYS!"

"You said it should *LOOK LIKE* kidneys!"

"Just keep looking!"

The wyverns moved closer. The beasts were only feet away now. The rancid stench of their breath combined with digging through bags of organs was making Iphigenia nauseous. The fear of being eaten alive wasn't helping much, either.

She tore through the backpack. There were several canvas bags marked with emblems, but none of them seemed like they were full of kidneys. There had to be a better system than this. She tossed several more bags aside until finally, after what felt like hours but was actually seconds, she found it.

"Here!" she shouted, tossing the bag up and over the backpack to Thisby.

Thisby caught it and pulled the drawstring. She reached her hand into the bag and pulled out a raw, dripping kidney. Holding it high over her head, she waved it back and forth.

The wyverns stopped in their tracks and bolted upright like dogs trying to peer over the edge of the dinner table. With every wave of Thisby's hand, they bent their necks in the same direction, following the kidney she clutched in her hand, fixated. They even let out a strange little cooing noise.

She tossed the kidney to the wyvern directly in front of her, and it snatched the organ from the air with terrifying speed.

"Come on!" she whispered to Iphigenia.

Thisby reached into the bag and grabbed another one. This one she threw off the edge of the railing between the two wyverns. They both dove for it simultaneously, the larger gray one getting there first. Thisby and Iphigenia hustled across the now-vacant walkway.

The whole way back down the stairs and out of the roost, Thisby tossed kidneys to the monsters until her bag was nearly empty, finally leaving them the remainder of the bag to finish off. The wyverns were still fighting over it when the girls disappeared out the doorway, back on their way toward the castle.

They walked in silence for a long time before Iphigenia finally decided to speak.

"That was clever."

"It wasn't," said Thisby. "It was just something I remembered."

Iphigenia sighed. "Can't you just take a compliment?"

"I can," said Thisby. "When it's the right compliment. Grunda used to say that cleverness is like magic: at the end of the day, it's all just smoke and mirrors, a parlor trick meant to impress gullible folks. I'm not clever. I don't want to be clever. I just take a lot of notes and pay attention."

Iphigenia smiled. It wasn't the toothy kind of smile like her brother, Ingo, might flash to impress the fat-faced dignitaries or cause the young barmaids swoon, but a tight-lipped, awkward smile that she made in spite of herself.

Thisby smiled back.

CHAPTER 16

By the time they were clear of the wyvern's roost, it was too late to press on any farther. Even when Thisby was by herself, she always tried to be back in her bedroom with the door barred tight before midnight, when the most dangerous monsters were out and about.

Unfortunately, there was no way to get back to the safety of her bedroom tonight, so Thisby decided to set up camp. In theory, if they camped tonight, they'd make it back to the castle tomorrow afternoon, and that seemed to be the safest bet. Iphigenia resisted at first, as spending another night in the dungeon wasn't exactly her idea of a good time, but she was so exhausted that she quickly acquiesced when faced with the alternative of hiking clear through until morning.

Thisby found a depression made of mud and stone in the side of a hill that overlooked Elphond's Escape and set up camp. This high up with their backs to the hill it would be nearly impossible for them to be snuck up on in the middle of the night, and the view didn't hurt either. It wasn't ideal to spend the night in the dungeon, but if you had to, the Escape was a nicer place than most.

Elphond's Escape was an entire level of the dungeon almost exactly two-thirds of the way to the top, and it was unlike any other area in the Black Mountain. Elphond the Evil had been the first Master of the Black Mountain and a wizard of the highest order. He'd built the Escape as a way to house certain creatures who couldn't thrive in the stony, dark conditions of the dungeon, and in doing so, made certain that his dungeon would contain the greatest menagerie of monsters anywhere in the known world.

The unwary adventurer who stumbled into the Escape might believe they'd somehow taken a wrong turn and ended up outside. There were plains and forest as far as the eye could see, bright blue skies—during the day, of course—and even a river that tumbled and burbled along until it terminated in a rather large waterfall, which cascaded down through several floors of the dungeon. Birds sang, wild beasts roamed the plains, and of course, fantastic monsters stalked through the woods and thundered through the fields. It was Thisby's favorite place in the entire dungeon, and it wasn't the first

Elphond's Escape

time she had camped there, although it was the first time she'd brought company, aside from Mingus.

Even Iphigenia was impressed.

"I suppose not all magic is stupid," she said.

Thisby quit digging through her backpack and looked up.

"No, I suppose not," she said. "This isn't like the kind of magic you probably saw from the current Master. This was Elphond's magic. Old magic. Cool stuff. You know, for a wizard. Do you have wizards back in Lyra Castelis?"

"Oh, sure," said Iphigenia with a sigh. "My father's Grand Vizier is a wizard. Little guy with a beard and awful breath. More into prophecies and giving my father warnings about dark, foreboding omens than he is about doing anything fun. No lightning bolts from his fingers or any of that."

"Now, that's magic I could get behind!" said Thisby. "Flying around, shooting fireballs, maybe even . . . *slime healing magic*?" Thisby looked over at Mingus but he didn't react. Maybe he was asleep.

"Like what?" said Iphigenia.

"Sorry, inside joke."

"Oh," said Iphigenia, staring up at the ceiling of the cave, which currently looked exactly like the night sky. She recognized a constellation known as the Hunter. A cool spring breeze even washed over them from the valley below and blew her hair around her face.

Below them, some centaurs galloped across the fields. The one who appeared to be their leader was carrying a lantern and shouting something in a strange language.

"We're safe up here," said Thisby before the Princess could ask.

After some time, she'd built a small fire, set a few basic bell alarms around their proximity, and removed from her backpack an odd, multicompartmented box that looked a bit like a tiny chest of drawers. Each drawer contained different snacks, some of which she offered to the Princess.

Iphigenia picked at them carefully.

"What's it like to be a princess?" Thisby asked finally, assuming that their awkward silence had gone on long enough.

Iphigenia paused. "I don't know," she said. "It's all I've ever been."

"Yeah, me, too," said Thisby.

Iphigenia looked at the filthy girl shoving some sort of jerky into her mouth.

Thisby realized the confusion. "Oh, I mean, I've always been me!" she said through a mouthful of food. "A gamekeeper, here in this dungeon!"

Thisby brushed her strawlike hair away from her face and suddenly felt the need to look dignified. It wasn't a natural look on her. Mostly she just stuck out her jaw for some reason and tried to chew with her mouth closed. It was better than nothing.

Finally, she swallowed her jerky and continued, "I mean, I like it. I just wish I could get out of the Black Mountain more often, maybe. I'm free to leave whenever I want, actually, but I can just never find the time. Even if I did, where would I go? Still, though, maybe I could travel a bit if I could find someone to take care of the dungeon while I'm gone. The monsters are all right, though, and Grunda's really nice—she's my friend, and a goblin. She took me into the dungeon when I was a baby and made sure the minotaur didn't eat me."

"I know the feeling. I can hardly ever get away from the castle. Believe it or not, this is the closest I've had to a vacation all year."

"And how's that going?"

Iphigenia smiled and lay down on her belly atop her bedroll. Since Thisby only had the one, she'd given it to the Princess and opted for some tufted grass for herself. It wasn't the softest thing she'd ever slept on, but it wasn't bad. They lay quietly for some time, side by side, staring straight ahead out over the valley. The centaurs had long since vanished into the dark forest in the distance.

"Nobody wants me to rule," said Iphigenia, breaking the peaceful silence. "Everybody wants it to be my brother, but I came out first so it has to be me."

Thisby kept her eyes fixed on the horizon ahead.

"Do you want to do it?" she asked bluntly.

"I don't have a choice," said Iphigenia.

"But if you did, would you want to do it?"

Iphigenia paused and considered this. She'd never really thought about it before.

"Yes. More than anything," she said.

"Then you'll probably be good at it," said Thisby. "There's all sorts of different people in this world, people who are naturally talented and people who struggle to tie their shoelaces, but the only ones who ever seem to do anything worth talking about are the ones who do the things they want to do just because they want to do them."

"And what about people who want to do nothing?" asked Mingus.

Up until this point, both Thisby and Iphigenia had assumed he was asleep.

Thisby laughed.

"I think most people want to do nothing. They just don't like to admit it," she said.

Something crossed Iphigenia's mind, and she suddenly rolled over onto her side to face Thisby.

"What was the deal with that candle the kobold gave you?"

"Huh?" said Thisby groggily. She sounded like she may have been ready to drift off to sleep.

"The candle! The nubby little one he gave you the morning after the tarasque attack!"

"Oh, right," said Thisby. "I'm not sure. Grunda told me something about kobolds and magic candles years ago, but it's hazy now. I think it was probably more of a gesture than anything, really."

Iphigenia paused.

"Do you get along with the monsters here?" she asked.

Thisby had forced open her heavy-lidded eyes and turned to face the Princess as well.

"Some of them. Some of them are my friends, some of them want to eat me, but at the end of the day, I just try to show them respect and hope they show me the same."

Iphigenia was reminded of something similar her father had once said about ruling a kingdom. She rolled onto her back and stared up at the stars. Thisby did the same.

The Princess and Thisby stayed up for a while, not talking, just lying silently beneath the magical stars of the Escape until they nodded off to sleep.

Iphigenia thought about her home and wondered if her parents were worried about her and her brother. Maybe they'd already sent out soldiers to find her. Perhaps, she thought, she'd wake in the morning to find a team of gallant knights standing above her, ready to escort her back to her soft, warm bed.

Thisby thought about all the chores that would be waiting for her when this whole adventure was over. She'd already lost two days of work roaming the dungeon, and it looked like tomorrow was going to be mostly a loss as well. She'd have to work overtime to try to get them all done by the end of the week, and she wasn't looking forward to that.

Mingus thought about—well, something. It was clearly something bad from the way that he was shaking, but that wasn't unusual. This time though, something was different. This time, he had good reason to be afraid.

CHAPTER 17

Mingus and Thisby had been inseparable since Thisby was seven years old, when she found him on her first ever trip to the Darkwell. She'd ended up there by accident, a strange turn of events that resulted in her being both hopelessly lost and lanternless in the lowest recesses of the dungeon. Stumbling around in the dark, she'd tripped over the lip of the Darkwell and found herself face to face with the nothingness that lay beyond.

She had spent what felt like an eternity there, crouched on her hands and knees, the cold blackweave gate pressing its strange patterns into her skin. All she could see was the darkness beyond. She was transfixed by it. That is, until a light caught her eye.

And that was where she found Mingus, sitting next to her on the Darkwell. A sad, glowing blob, halfway slipped between the bars of the blackweave. When she scooped him up, he shuddered in her hands, and to her surprise, he spoke.

"Don't let me fall," he said.

And so Thisby put him in an empty jar and took him home.

Since then, Mingus had never left his jar. On the rare occasion Thisby needed to clean it or change him over to a new one after it had gotten cracked or damaged beyond what a touch of ogre snot could fix, she'd simply slide him directly from his old jar into his new one, so he would only be exposed to fresh air for milliseconds before returning safely to his new home. Although, with the amount of complaining he did for a week before and after such an exchange, you might've thought she'd left him outside in a field overnight. When she was younger and more gullible, Mingus had convinced Thisby that he was desperately allergic to the fresh air and needed the enclosed space to survive, but over time she had come to realize that he got plenty of fresh air on a regular basis and this was just a ruse to convince her of the importance of him never, ever leaving his jar.

He was a quiet slime, for the most part. Unambitious and perfectly content to sit and do nothing for hours on end. Sometimes, Thisby would give him her notebooks, convinced that he must be bored out of his mind never leaving that jar, but he'd usually just stare at the drawings until he fell asleep. If there was one thing Mingus did enjoy, it was looking at her drawings, so much so that occasionally he'd ask her to tape a small one to the outside of his jar so that he could look at it more often.

They were close. In truth, they were more like siblings than friends. They'd occasionally fight, but always made up shortly thereafter. Thisby would make him a drawing as an apology or he'd put on a rainbow-colored light show for her, and the next thing they knew, they barely remembered what they'd been fighting about in the first place. But now Mingus wasn't so sure Thisby would forgive him so easily this time if she found out what he'd done. He couldn't bear the thought of it.

Iphigenia awoke groggily to the sound of birds singing. She rubbed her eyes and watched the sun as it climbed above the tree line, streaming ribbons of bright pink daylight through the leaves. Upon seeing Thisby and her talking slime, the realization that she was still stuck inside the dungeon took her disappointment to new, as of yet untapped extremes. It was like unwrapping a pony-shaped gift to discover that somebody had taped a bunch of wet old socks into the shape of a pony for no apparent reason. It was like drinking a frothy mug of hot chocolate somebody had made with pickle juice.

"Good morning!" said Thisby brightly.

Iphigenia rolled over to go back to sleep, but her pillow was gone.

She looked up to find Thisby stuffing it into her backpack.

"Only a few more hours and we should reach the castle!" she said. "Of course, we'll have to walk. We could cross through the mammoth grove to get there, but then we'd have to cross the cockatrice hollow. I suppose we could probably cut through the chimera pit . . ."

Iphigenia had already tuned her out.

She watched some strange-looking birds soaring above the forest down across the valley. They looked almost like lizards. She squinted her eyes and realized they were indeed lizards.

Iphigenia frowned at them as hard as she could manage. Her face was beginning to get sore from all the frowning she'd done in the past couple of days.

"I hope those pterodactyls don't give us any problems," Thisby said casually, sidling up to Iphigenia.

It took all Iphigenia's princessly powers not to sigh.

Elphond's Escape was muggy. So muggy, the expression went, that you could sweat through a shirt that you weren't even wearing. It had something to do with all the trees and water and being trapped inside a cave, which, as you may have figured, tended not to have the world's best ventilation. The fake sun also generated very real heat, which probably didn't help matters, either.

Nights in the Escape were quite lovely, but within only a few hours of sunrise, the humidity could make the journey from one end to the other unbearable. This was why Thisby had wanted to get an early start on the several-hour trek, but unfortunately for her, Iphigenia took a bit longer to get ready in the mornings than she did.

Growing up in the dungeon, Thisby had never witnessed anybody do anything that could even remotely constitute "primping," and as she watched Iphigenia wash her face in the stream and study her reflection, she wasn't quite sure what to think. Initially, at least, it had seemed like a profound waste of time. But then again, despite living in a cave, Thisby wasn't blind. She knew Iphigenia was radiant, and that she was, well, not so much. So perhaps there was something to it after all.

Thisby tried to play along and aped the Princess a bit, splashing water on her underarms and sighing at her reflection as she studied it in the water, but when Iphigenia asked for help with her hair braid, Thisby could only shrug helplessly. She'd briefly considered suggesting something like a sheepshank knot but figured that probably wasn't what the Princess had in mind. Honestly, Thisby only ever even combed or cleaned her own hair after it had gotten to be such a mess that it actually interfered with her field of vision or became so stiff that it poked her when she laid her head down on her pillow. In the end, Iphigenia settled on a more causal over-the-shoulder braid, which she could do herself, and Thisby watched her out of the corner of her eye as she did.

Ultimately, they had set out far later than Thisby had hoped to, but the notes she'd taken on Iphigenia's behavior seemed like they could be helpful at some point. It didn't feel like a complete loss.

Crossing the tree line at the edge of the forest turned out to be something of a mixed blessing. On one hand, shade was a welcome respite from the hot, magic sun beating down on them, but on the other, the jumble of trees, roots, and undergrowth made their walk much, much slower. Also, Thisby knew that out on the plains, they were in little danger of encountering any really dangerous creatures, but here in the thick gnarled woods of the Escape, they needed to be on guard at all times.

The forest was so heavily shielded by the canopy of trees that it took several minutes for Iphigenia's eyes to adjust to the dark. It seemed to her like Thisby didn't have that problem, being much more accustomed to the darkness within the Black Mountain than she was. There were strange noises in the woods—from those as innocuous as the rustle of leaves as something small and frightened scurried away, to the more exotic garbling of fantastic birds, the likes of which Iphigenia had never heard before. And as well-versed regarding the creatures of the dungeon as Thisby was, truthfully she'd never heard some of the strange calls before, either.

Thisby had spent some time in the Escape, occasionally as a well-deserved escape of her own, but much like the

City of Night, the Escape more or less regulated itself. Her interference as gamekeeper was largely unnecessary. Thisby's trips to the Escape were mostly for relaxing—in what little time she had for such indulgences—or for purely academic purposes. In truth, it was often both. There was nothing Thisby enjoyed more than coming down to the Escape to fill her notebooks with pages upon pages of scribblings and drawings about whatever exotic new creatures or plants she had discovered, but even as diligent as she was, there was still so much to the Escape that she'd yet to see. And it always seemed to be growing.

Actually, it was—albeit very, very slowly.

The Escape began as a room no bigger than a linen closet. It was there that Elphond planted a magical seed that eventually grew to become the Escape as Thisby knew it, only along the way, something unexpected happened—the Escape never stopped growing. Even when it reached the outer walls of the Black Mountain, the Escape continued to expand, and this was when things got really strange. By the time the current Master took over the Black Mountain, Elphond's Escape had grown beyond the edges of the mountain, but it didn't burst through it like an overfilled balloon; instead, it simply kept growing into space that didn't quite exist. At least, not in the way space is commonly understood. If you stood on the edges of the Escape, you both were and weren't inside the Mountain, depending on how you choose to understand the physics of it.

Magic was just kind of like that sometimes.

For the purposes of both cooling and mobility, Iphigenia had rolled up the bottom of her dress into a kind of makeshift skirt. Thisby suggested simply cutting it off, but apparently that wasn't a viable option. She said something about "silks from across the Nameless Sea," but Thisby had mostly tuned her out by then. Regardless of where the dress came from, it seemed like the Princess was struggling with the heavy fabric, and Thisby was grateful for once for her practical patchwork leggings, as ugly as they were. It was much cooler in here than out on the plains, but the humidity was far worse as the trees slurped up the thick wet mud of the forest floor and exhaled their sweet, warm breath back into the air.

"At least let me loan you a pair of boots," said Thisby, stopping to mop her brow with her sleeve. "It's no trouble, honestly. I have an extra pair in my backpack."

Iphigenia looked down at her shoes. They'd become so caked with mud that she could no longer even see the emeralds sparkling on her toes. And what good were bejeweled shoes if you couldn't even see the jewels? Iphigenia only sighed in response, but it wasn't a sigh of contempt; it was a sigh of capitulation. Thisby had become acutely aware of the distinction over the last two days. They stopped and rested by a small pond, sitting on toadstools large enough to support their weight.

"Oh! Thank you! Thank you!" exclaimed Iphigenia the moment her feet slid into Thisby's old leather boots.

Thisby had been mindlessly tossing pebbles into the pond, but now she froze and turned slowly toward the Iphigenia. It had just slipped out. They both knew it. When the Princess felt the difference between the pair of worn leather boots and her jewel-encrusted slippers, the feeling of relief had been so great that she'd just blurted out the words without even thinking.

"You're welcome, uh, Your Highness," muttered Thisby.

Iphigenia saw Thisby's face redden.

Despite her better judgment, Iphigenia felt the sudden urge to say something like, "Never mind the formalities! Just call me Iphigenia!" She could imagine herself and Thisby back at the castle, hanging out, laughing at all the other pompous royals. They'd dine together and ride horses and stay up late just talking. Maybe they could when everything was all said and done. Iphigenia had never had a best friend, maybe not even a real, proper friend, and the feeling made her uncomfortable. It was an embarrassing thought. So instead, she said nothing.

Iphigenia stood up and adjusted her dress, rolling it back up to an appropriate height. She puffed out her chest and mustered up the most dignified air she could manage given the circumstances.

"These will do quite well, I mean," she said, looking down at her feet.

"Great," said Thisby, whose mouth was still hanging a bit slack, as she searched for the right words to say.

She never found them.

Before she could, an arrow struck the tree beside her.

Mingus screamed as Thisby hefted her backpack onto her back just before two more arrows sank into it. One of them managed to pierce straight through the thick canvas near the bottom of the bag, where it punctured a bag of flour, causing Thisby to leave a snowy trail as she bolted through the heavy woods.

Iphigenia was thankful she'd managed to switch over to the boots in time for their sprint, but that was just about her only good fortune. Her dress was continually being caught and snagged by sharp roots and branches, once so badly that she actually had to stop and free herself from a thorny branch. As she bent down to untangle her dress, several arrows whizzed by her head, and she tore her dress badly as she ran away in a panic.

Thisby could hear the croaking chatter coming from the trees and recognized the voices as forest imps. Imps could be vicious hunters, but she'd never seen them attack outsiders like this. They were territorial but typically wary. Cautious, even. More prone to keep their distance than to risk an outright attack.

The imps of the Black Mountain were not what most people thought of when they heard the word *imps*. Due to poor translation of an ancient and quite popular folktale around Nth, imps were often confused with gnomes and depicted as diminutive, bearded folk with pointy red caps.

Actual imps, however, were froglike humanoids with bluish-green skin and soft leather shells on their backs. True to their name, forest imps lived in forests, always near a river, and had their own language and culture that couldn't be further away from that of the bearded, peaceful, hill-dwelling gnomes. They got the diminutive part right, however. Most imps only stood about three feet tall on their tiptoes.

There were several other species of imps throughout the Black Mountain, organized by color and habitat. Dark blue water imps had webbed hands and were amphibious, spending almost their entire lives underwater. They were typically the most aggressive of the imps and lived in the small lakes and ponds deeper in the dungeon than their cousins. Grayish rock imps lived near the top of the Black Mountain and had a tendency to develop a crusty buildup of soil on their shells caused by lying still for days on end, feeding off earthworms who happened to crawl into their open mouths. These imps were no trouble whatsoever, but they also weren't nearly as advanced as forest or water imps. In general, it was the forest imps, the ones who were shooting at them, who were considered the most reasonable of the three, but as their arrows whizzed overhead, Thisby quickly began to rethink her position.

Another arrow struck Thisby's backpack. This one hit something metal and ricocheted off, falling to the forest floor.

The sound of rushing water in the distance signaled to Thisby that they were headed toward the river. As another arrow flew wide of her shoulder by at least a foot, a bigger picture came into view. Something wasn't right. Forest imps were skilled hunters. They could hit a bat between the eyes at twenty yards, even on the run. Thisby knew that without even looking at her notes. Maybe the arrows weren't supposed to hit them. But why?

The sound of rushing water grew louder.

By the time Thisby had figured it out, it was too late. The river. They were being herded toward the river.

There was no time to turn around. Thisby and Iphigenia skidded to a full stop on the bank of the river. They were cornered, but the imps had stopped firing at them. What were they waiting for?

Iphigenia and Thisby watched as the small froggy imps stepped silently out from the woods, their arrows nocked and pointed straight at the girls. Behind Thisby, the river raged on through the forest, faster than she'd ever seen it move. Iphigenia squeezed Thisby's arm down by her wrist, silently imploring her to do something. There was a notebook in Thisby's backpack that held the notes she'd taken on the imp's language. It might offer some hope of communication, if only she could reach it, but she knew full well that reaching back for it now would likely end with an arrow sticking out of her throat. Thisby was going to have to improvise based on what she remembered. It wasn't much.

"*Krr-krooorrrr?*" said Thisby, adding as much of a verbal question mark as she could manage in a language made entirely of two consonants and one vowel.

The imps looked at one another, perplexed, keeping their bows trained on the girls.

"*Krroooo-koo-krrrrkrkrrr?*" added Thisby helpfully.

More blank looks. No good. She was going to have to get her notebook.

Thisby yanked her hand free of Iphigenia's iron grasp and held up both her hands submissively as a sign of good faith. Then she slowly began to slide her backpack off her shoulders as the nervous imps watched. When she went to reach for the top flap of her bag, one of the imps—the youngest of the hunting party—lost his nerve. The *twang!* of a bowstring was followed by the sharp *tink!* of steel hitting glass as the errant shot pinged off Mingus's jar, putting a nice crack in it.

Whether he'd intended to hit Thisby or simply fire a warning shot, it was now too late to try to find out, and with one confident motion, Thisby grabbed her backpack—and Iphigenia—and leapt into the raging river.

The cool blast of the river after their sweaty run through the forest would've felt pretty nice if it wasn't for all the drowning. Upon hitting the water, Thisby's backpack slipped free from her grip, and as luck would have it, one of the straps managed to become tangled around her ankle as the current swept them all downstream. The weight of her massive bag dragged her beneath the tumbling waves, pulling her down to where the water was coldest—which, again, actually would've felt pretty nice except for, you know, the drowning.

Iphigenia managed to get her head above the water just long enough to see that Thisby was nowhere to be found before the current washed over her again. The water was moving too fast to keep her head above for more than a second, so with each precious opportunity, she gulped as much air as her lungs could hold, not knowing how long it would be until she surfaced again.

Beneath the water, Thisby struggled to pull herself free of her backpack, but every time she came close, the current tugged in opposite directions and twisted her all around. Once she caught a glimpse of Mingus. His jar had completely filled with water—apparently coming in through the crack the arrow had put in its side. His fake button eyes had popped out and were floating lifelessly around the jar—as he himself was—so it was impossible to tell which way he was looking, but Thisby just knew it was at her. Mingus didn't need to breathe, so she knew he was still alive. It didn't take a best friend to know that whatever he was thinking wasn't good. Thisby held his gaze, or what she hoped was his gaze, for as long as she could, but in another moment she banged off a large boulder and was turned around yet again. Her ankle became more twisted in her bag, and to top it all off, it felt as if they were speeding up. Because they were.

It was Iphigenia who realized it first. On her next trip to the surface for air, she managed to catch a fleeting look down the river only to discover that there was only so much river left. She was pulled under again, and the next time she came up, there was even less river. Then even less. Then even less. The pattern continued for longer than she cared to admit before the realization sunk in.

Thisby, meanwhile, from her vantage point underwater, hadn't realized where they were headed at all until she was hurled, quite blue in the face and almost nearly unconscious, off a cliff and out into a large void, where she immediately began to plummet. The fresh air was actually quite a nice change of pace from drowning—you know, except for the plummeting.

It was hard for her to tell how long she fell. She felt her stomach drop, and there was enough time to realize that she was falling before it was over.

When she hit, the air went from her lungs, and she felt something slimy and cold and wet burst all around her. For a moment she lay completely still, too frightened to move, convinced that what she was feeling were her insides splattered all over the ground. Only it seemed a bit strange that she could feel them at all, seeing as how if her insides really were splattered all around, she assumed she would be dead. And she didn't feel dead.

Thisby coughed a bit and felt around, turning her head away from the water that she realized was still raining down on her from above. She grabbed something cold and wet beneath her and held it up in front of her face.

A fish gawped back at her, opening and closing its mouth. It looked almost as stunned as she was. Beside her, somebody groaned.

Thisby looked over to see Iphigenia. She was resting in a pile of fish. They both were, in fact, suspended in a sort of net that hung above a large hole, into which the river drained. Apparently, it was there to catch fish that otherwise would've been wasted when they fell to their splattered graves several floors below. Thisby couldn't help but lean over to look down into the void. There was no end in sight. Soon she was laughing despite herself, despite the dirty looks from a frazzled and sopping-wet Iphigenia, who didn't seem to get what was so funny.

She didn't stop laughing until the imps hauled them out. Fortunately, by then the chief had joined the hunters. Fortunately for Thisby, he was more skilled at languages than she was. It turned out the hunting party had been a group of young forest imps who weren't yet familiar with the ways of the dungeon, and the entire thing had really been just a big misunderstanding. The chief apologized profusely and even offered them some food and a chance to dry off, but Thisby thought it best to hurry on if they had any hopes of making it back to the top before nightfall. Iphigenia agreed.

As they walked away from the imps, cold feet squishing in their boots, absolutely reeking of fish, Iphigenia looked over at the mousy girl pulling notebooks from her backpack and fanning out the pages in a feeble attempt to dry them and realized something she hadn't considered before: she might be the first human Thisby had ever spoken more than a couple words to.

Thisby looked over to see Iphigenia. She was resting in a pile of fish.

Thisby dangled a wet notebook in front of her face, holding it delicately by the corner. Her brow was furrowed deeply. The pages hung limp and wet, the writing on them smudged.

"Oh, here! I think I figured it out," said Thisby. "'*Krroooo-krr-krrrrkrkrrr*' means 'We *are* your friends.' '*Krroooo-koo-krrrrkrkrrr*' means 'We *ate* your friends.'"

Now it was Iphigenia's turn to laugh.

Thisby glowered at her, but only for a moment before her resolve broke as well.

The only one who wasn't laughing was Mingus, who was distractedly prodding at the tape Thisby had used to seal the crack in his jar and wondering how long it would hold.

CHAPTER 17.5

By the time Iphigenia and Thisby finally reached the skystair at the center of the Escape, the pterodactyls had dispersed. During their trip the rest of the way through the forest, Iphigenia had to pull Thisby away several times when she stopped to take notes—mostly on her arms because her notebooks were still damp—about peculiar plants, but other than that, the remainder of their journey had gone smoothly.

The skystair, a spiral staircase, invisible from the outside, that rose up from the center of the woods, was the only way out of Elphond's Escape. From the inside, it looked like any other worked-stone stairwell in the dungeon: plain gray bricks, decaying from moss and age, lit by flickering torches. Iphigenia wondered if it was Thisby's job to keep all those torches lit. There were so many of them. She thought about Thisby, working alone, putting in long, thankless hours to keep the dungeon running, and for what? So some adventurers could come here and risk their lives for a little bit of treasure?

As far as Iphigenia was concerned, the whole dungeon should be shut down. She could always find Thisby a job in the castle, maybe in the stables. Her father would never allow it, though. He thought the dungeon gave commoners hope, that it distracted them from war and disease and—most important—poverty. He feared that without the hope of risking their lives to win fame and fortune in the dungeon, the commoners might rebel. And besides, he argued, who was it hurting?

Thisby walked ahead of Iphigenia with more bounce in her step than she'd had since they first met in the City of Night.

"It's great, isn't it?" Thisby called back to her.

Thisby sounded just like her brother. Always optimistic and jovial, perpetually fascinated by everything. Only somehow, she sounded more genuine than Ingo ever did. Ingo was great at fooling everyone, but his sister saw through him. She knew him better than anyone else.

Iphigenia looked out one of the skystair's windows and had to admit that it was a pretty nice view. Elphond's Escape was quite beautiful, when you weren't drowning or plummeting to your death, and from the skystair you could see pretty much all of it. Iphigenia had to struggle to maintain the bad mood she'd carried since the moment she set foot on the Black Mountain, and found herself slipping occasionally and accidentally enjoying herself. Soon enough, though, they were back in the bleak, stinky dungeon, and the spell of the Escape was quickly forgotten.

It took the better part of the day, but by late afternoon, the girls had made it almost all the way back to the castle. Despite her better judgment, upon seeing the end draw near, Iphigenia's optimism had returned. She'd begun to tell Thisby excitedly about all the food she was going to eat when she made it back home. She went through a long, mental list, reciting each delicacy one by one to Thisby, who nodded along even though she hadn't heard of over half the things Iphigenia mentioned.

"My father's probably waiting in the castle," said Iphigenia. "They probably already sent in a search party. I wouldn't worry about it. I'm sure my brother's fine and that horrible Roquat will get what he deserves, if he hasn't already."

Thisby nodded in agreement, but she wasn't so sure. She would've noticed if a party had come through the dungeon. There were always signs of intruders—even if it was often just their remains. Still, she didn't want to upset Iphigenia, who seemed much more pleasant than she'd been in the last two days, so she simply nodded along and smiled.

"Don't worry," said Iphigenia, sensing the consternation

on Thisby's face. "I've decided to pardon you. You won't be held accountable for what happened. I can't say the same for your Master, though. It's likely that blame will go much higher than that Roquat fellow."

Iphigenia had been thinking about this all day and decided now was the time to break her silence. Thisby wasn't to blame for what had happened, after all—Roquat was—and what's more, Iphigenia had begun to grow a bit fond of her. Sure, she was kind of gross and unmannered, and she seemed to sweat an awful lot, and more than once she'd outright insulted her, but despite all that she was good at her job, and she'd saved her life on multiple occasions. It simply wasn't fair to have her stand trial, to risk execution merely for being in the wrong place at the wrong time. To Iphigenia, this was the highest compliment she'd ever paid someone.

Thisby looked sideways at her.

"That's, uh, nice of you? Thanks," she said.

As they drew closer to the castle, the gray bricks and exposed caverns of the dungeon were slowly phased out in exchange for the shiny black stone walls of Castle Grimstone. Eventually, they turned into a tunnel that was entirely black stones, and they could clearly see the door to the castle up ahead. It was a large door, easily a dozen Thisbys high and adorned with a strange assortment of skulls, much like all the doors into the castle. In front of the gate were two guards, ghouls, from the looks of them.

That was a bad sign. Thisby knew that normally only one

lone goblin guarded this door. Since the Inspection, security had been heightened.

As the girls approached, the ghouls pointed their long barbed spears in their direction menacingly. The larger one spoke.

"Don't come no closer!" he barked.

The guards instead approached them, their weapons lowered and ready.

"What do you think you're doing!" snapped Iphigenia. "Don't you know who I am?"

"It doesn't matter who you are!" said the small one. His eyes were quick and jumpy. It made Thisby nervous. "Nobody gets into the castle! Master's orders!"

Iphigenia's face turned bright red. She wasn't used to being denied access anywhere, let alone by a pair of two-bit guards.

"NOW, SEE HERE—" she fumed, but Thisby cut her off.

"I'm the gamekeeper of the dungeon. I have urgent news for the Master," said Thisby. "Prince Ingo Larkspur has been taken captive. We need to speak to the Master right away."

The guards looked at each other.

"We'll pass it along," said the big one.

Iphigenia shoved her way past Thisby and stomped toward the guards.

"I am the Crown Princess of Nth, the rightful heir to the throne! My father, the King of Nth, YOUR KING, is up there right now looking for me! I DEMAND TO SPEAK WITH HIM . . . NOW!" Iphigenia said through gritted teeth. It looked as if her eyeballs might pop right out of her skull.

"There ain't no King here, girly," said the small one, grinning.

"And even if they was, we'd tell 'em to take a hike, same as you! Orders is orders!" said the big one. "And our orders is to turn away anybody an' everybody that tries to get through this door, ya got that?"

The guards stood upright, as tall as they could manage, making the Princess feel suddenly quite small. Even the small one was more than twice her size. Iphigenia deflated. She was at a complete loss for what to do next. Never in her life had anybody simply turned her down like that. Who would? With a snap of her fingers she could have them thrown in jail, or worse! But down here, she was beginning to realize that snapping her fingers might not have the same effect as it did back in the castle. For the first time in her life, she felt . . . vulnerable.

Iphigenia slunk back a few steps. The guards grinned broadened, sensing their victory.

Thisby stepped up.

"Look," she said calmly, "we're in a bit of a bind here. I know you have your orders, but I think this might be a special exception. This is the Princess of Nth. Her brother has been taken captive. If she doesn't get back to her family, we're all going to be in way more trouble than what the Master can dish out. Can you help us?"

The big one's face softened, ever so slightly. He leaned over toward Thisby and spoke directly to her, even though he spoke loudly enough for them both to hear.

"I know you, Thisby. I heard all 'bout you. But this is over your head, 'kay? Jus' turn around an' walk away. There ain't no King up there. Ain't no King comin'. An' no matter what you say or what you do right now, ain't no way you're gettin' through this door. Jus' turn around an' walk away."

His face hardened again. "That's the only warnin' you're gettin'. Walk away."

Thisby nodded to him and walked back to Iphigenia, who looked as if she'd been hollowed out.

"Come on," said Thisby taking her hand. For the first time since they'd met, Iphigenia didn't shrink away from her touch.

Together they walked back to Thisby's bedroom, climbed up the ladder, and passed over the gangways all without speaking a single word.

Despite her frustration with the guards, approaching her bedroom door made Thisby's heart sing. It had been three days since she'd seen the thick oak door, since she'd pulled it open and smelled the familiar fragrance of her room, the only room in the entire dungeon that belonged to her.

Suddenly, her heart raced for a different reason. She thought of how much her room meant to her and how surely meager it would seem to the Princess. She thought of Iphigenia mocking the few things she had, her tiny bookcase full of worn notebooks, her desk that she'd built herself from scraps of wood she'd found lying around the dungeon, and she felt as if her heart couldn't take it. It was all she had in the whole world, and if the Princess didn't like it, it would gnaw at her guts in a way she might never forget.

Thisby's hand hesitated on the iron ring before pulling it to open the door.

"It's not much," she said defensively.

It didn't seem like Iphigenia was listening.

At once Thisby was overcome with emotion. It was all there, just like she'd left it. Quickly, however, the panic set back in, and Thisby began to rush around, tidying up, much like Grunda had done the night Thisby found Roquat waiting in her room. The thought of Roquat being in her room now made her stomach feel all twisted up.

Iphigenia placidly sat down on Thisby's bed and stared at the wall. For some time, Thisby just watched her as she went about tidying up, not knowing what to say.

"Look, they don't know what—" Thisby began.

"My father isn't coming," said Iphigenia. "I never actually thought he would. I just . . . hoped."

Thisby stared at her.

"He knew the dangers of us coming here, and he wouldn't risk an open confrontation with the dungeon. It's too dangerous. The Kingdom comes first."

"But—"

"Whatever you're going to say, don't bother. He's making the right call. The right call for the Kingdom. For his people . . . ," she trailed off.

Thisby wiggled her pinky toe over her toe-which-comes-next-to-her-pinky-toe and stared at the floor, avoiding eye contact with Iphigenia at all costs. It would've been a nice time to see a bug or something. She looked around desperately for a spider to focus her attention on, but for once in her life, her room seemed painfully devoid of them. There's never a spider around when you need one.

"Thisby?" said Iphigenia.

Great, she thought, now she had to look up.

"Yes?" said Thisby, forcing herself to look at the Princess sitting on her bed like she was looking at a lamb carcass after the wyverns had feasted on it.

To her surprise, Iphigenia wasn't teary-eyed like she'd expected her to be. Instead, she sat upright on the edge of the bed with her hands folded neatly across her lap, looking as regal as Thisby had ever seen her.

"It's up to us to save my brother."

Thisby's heart sank.

"Also, I like your bedspread."

And then soared.

CHAPTER 18

It didn't take long to figure out that the Master had sealed off every possible entrance into the castle. Thisby went through the motions and checked them all anyway, but she was inevitably forced to give up and return to her room with the bad news. Apparently, the Master had gotten wind of what happened with the tarasque and the royals and had chosen the path of least resistance, barring himself up inside his castle and waiting out the storm. It was a cowardly move, but not an altogether surprising one.

The current Master of the Black Mountain took over the mantle when his predecessor, Hepsbeth the Horrible, slipped and fell while in her alchemy lab, landing on a knife. She landed on it several dozen times, to be precise. Coincidentally, the knife belonged to the man who would become the dungeon's current Master.

It wasn't an uncommon fate for a Master of the Black Mountain, as they quite often met similarly gruesome deaths after just several years—or if they were particularly unlucky, weeks—of service. Which was why, as a rule, the current Master didn't allow anyone to get too close to him. It was also why, as a rule, he refused to ever go into his own dungeon.

The current Master wasn't a great wizard, but he did have a knack for history. And one of the first things he realized during his ascension through the ranks of the dungeon— where he began as a lowly floor mopper—was that most of the former Masters met their ends while in the dungeon itself. The solution was simple, as far as he was concerned—avoid the dungeon and stay alive—and so far, it'd worked quite well.

The trick, of course, was figuring out how to manage an entire dungeon without ever setting foot inside it. The solution came quite accidentally when he found an old room, long untouched, that had once belonged to the original Master of the dungeon, Elphond the Evil. Thousands of years ago when Elphond created the dungeon, he'd begun work on a system that would allow him to travel anywhere in the Black Mountain instantaneously. He called it the blackdoor. Mysteriously, despite the machine being finished, it was never turned on—that is, until the current Master got his hands on it.

With the blackdoor beads at his disposal, the Master was able to send out his agents into the dungeon in his stead. He could even create temporary exits in the side of the mountain for his minions to slip out into town whenever he so wished. All he had to do was wait in the relative comfort of his castle for reports to come in. Most important, he would never have to go down into that vile dungeon and risk his life doing dangerous or menial tasks again. It was a perfect system. Almost.

Thisby walked back into her bedroom and set Mingus on the table. She shook her head solemnly at Iphigenia.

"What are our other options?" asked Iphigenia.

"Not many. My secret path under the castle is still open, but that leads out to a sheer cliff face. We could try to send Shabul for help. He's the guy who delivers my herbs and— you know what, never mind. Besides, he won't be here for weeks and—"

Iphigenia finished her sentence, "And by then it'll probably be too late."

Thisby sat at her desk and thumbed through her notebooks, trying to think of a plan. There had to be a way into the castle, somehow. The Master was diligent, she knew that. All the obvious ways would be blocked. There had to be some secret. Something she was missing.

It was early evening when there was a knock on Thisby's door. Before she had time to respond, the door swung open and a small old goblin trundled into the room.

"Grunda!" shouted Thisby, jumping from her desk and wiping the drool from the corner of her mouth—she'd fallen asleep on her books again. Most of her notebooks were severely drool stained for this very reason. The goblin looked at Thisby and then at the Princess.

"Oh, right!" said Thisby, "Sorry! Grunda, this is—"

"There'll be time for that later! Right now you girls need to come with me. There's somebody you need to meet."

Grunda waddled down the hallway ahead of them, lighting the way with a small glowstone that she'd tied to the end of a stick. She paused in front of a seemingly normal rock wall and tapped three times. The wall opened.

Thisby recognized it as goblin magic. The goblins had their own way of doing things, and as close as Thisby and Grunda were, Grunda still had her secrets. Thisby respected that. It was just the way it was with goblins.

Thisby and Iphigenia had to crouch to make their way down the small, crude tunnel, which seemed perfectly sized for goblins and little else. At the end of the hall was a tiny room with some sparse goblin-sized furniture, a table and several small chairs, one of which—surprisingly enough—was currently being occupied by a large, gangly human man.

"Hello again!" he said brightly, struggling to set down his tiny teacup on its tiny saucer.

He was all knees and elbows crouched in the goblin's chair

and made quite the spectacle of himself, stooping awkwardly so as not to bang his head on the ceiling.

"I thought I told you to *go home*," said Thisby. There was something undeniably motherly in her voice. Iphigenia smirked.

"I meant to, really I did!" said the man. "Only I got lost, see? It wasn't my fault! Really!"

"Iphigenia, this is Gregory. He's an, uhm . . ." She hesitated, "I suppose you'd call him an adventurer, who I met in the dungeon earlier. Gregory, this is . . ."

"Well, I know who you are!" exclaimed Gregory. He shot to his feet but made it less than halfway before his head collided hard with the low-hanging ceiling. There was a sickening crunch, which Thisby hoped was the ceiling. Amazingly, Gregory didn't seem to mind, and turned his doubling over in pain into an awkward little bow that he punctuated with a nervous "M'lady!"

"I—I mean, Your Highness!" he blurted.

For a moment, Thisby had forgotten Iphigenia was royalty. They'd been through so much together that she'd started to think of the Princess as just Iphigenia.

Grunda motioned for them to take a seat and offered up some tea, which Iphigenia accepted courteously. Thisby wondered if she should have done the same.

"There's no time to waste! Tell them about what you saw, Gregory," said Grunda once everyone was settled. "Tell them from the beginning."

"There's no time to waste! Tell them about what you saw, Gregory," said Grunda once everyone was settled. "Tell them from the beginning."

Gregory told the story about the Darkwell and the abduction of Catface. He told them about the squat, ugly man he saw leading the monsters and the magical doors they opened in the ground. Thisby couldn't believe her ears. She'd never liked Catface, but being attacked like that, especially by Roquat and whatever those things were, it made her feel sick to her stomach.

"You don't think . . . ," said Thisby.

Grunda nodded.

"Deep Dwellers? But how?"

"I don't know," said Grunda.

"It sounds to me like they used blackdoors."

They all turned and looked at Iphigenia, who'd been quietly sipping her tea up until this point. She dabbed delicately at her mouth with the corner of her napkin.

"Yeah, but . . . I mean, the Master controls the supply of blackdoors, right? There's no way!" blurted Thisby.

"Isn't it obvious?" she continued. "It was Roquat."

"But why? And how?" asked Thisby.

"I'm not sure why, but it has something to do with why he took my brother, I know it. As to how, I mean, he has access to the castle, right?"

"Yeah, but . . ." Thisby trailed off. She wasn't quite sure why, but something felt wrong.

Grunda walked around with the teapot and refilled Iphigenia's cup. The steam curled up in little wisps that Iphigenia gently blew away before taking another sip. Grunda eased herself back into her chair with a groan. Her knees weren't quite what they used to be.

"There's another problem with that theory," said Grunda, glancing at Mingus out of the corner of her eye. "I've been in this dungeon a long time, you see. I was here when the blackweave was first placed atop the well."

Thisby looked shocked.

"Really?" she asked.

"I know, I know! Ol' Grunda looks pretty good for her age!" She shot a playful wink at Iphigenia, who smiled back at her. "But I was there! Well before the new Master's time. Another age . . . ," she added wistfully.

"Up until that point, the Sentinel's job had been a lot harder. It was up to him to keep the Deep Dwellers out. There was a regular gate, of course, but then there was an uprisin', and next thing you know, suddenly a regular ol' gate and a big dumb cat didn't seem quite good enough anymore. That was when the Master commissioned the blackweave from the Dünkeldwarves. What was left of 'em at least.

"It was their gate, you see, but what sealed it off good and proper was goblin magic—as well as some other less important magic, I suppose—but goblin magic nonetheless! I was privy to its creation and I knew its secrets. It was more than just a gate. Not even magic could penetrate its surface. It created a barrier that permanently separated the Deep Down from the rest of the dungeon. Not even portals could pass from one side to the other, and that includes blackdoors!

Blackdoors are impressive magic, but at the end of the day, they're still just portal magic. In my day, portal magic was a dime a dozen. Most people didn't even walk across the room to use the pot! They'd just use a portal . . ."

Thisby gave her a sideways stare.

"Anyway, the point is that no simple blackdoor could've possibly gotten through the blackweave into the Deep Down—that is, unless . . ." She let it hang in the air a bit too long.

"Unless *what*?" asked Thisby impatiently.

"Unless something had already broken the Darkwell's magic spell," she finished, and took a long sip of tea.

"How would that happen?" asked Iphigenia.

"Something had to pass through the gate already."

The room fell silent. It was an impossible riddle.

You couldn't pass through to the other side of the gate, not physically nor by magic, unless you'd somehow already gotten through it. It was a paradox. An unsolvable problem. What can pass through an impassable gate? Well, nothing! Obviously! And yet something had indeed gotten through. But how? It made the mystery of how Roquat had stolen the blackdoors seem simple by comparison.

Thisby's head was starting to hurt. That was the whole problem with magic. It never worked like you wanted it to. It's not as simple as saying, "Abracadabra! Now this gate is sealed forever!" You need to bake in a logic puzzle. It needs to have a twist.

Thisby thought about what she did know. The gate was closed. It hadn't been opened. Something had gotten through it. But it didn't get through with magic . . .

On the edge of her mind a thought began to flicker. However, the moment she looked at it, it darted away, like the little floating dot in her eye that she would catch from time to time.

"With all due respect, how the magic was broken isn't my concern," said Iphigenia at last, getting to her feet. "I need to find my brother. If Roquat has him and Roquat is in the Deep Down, then that's where I'm going."

"ARE YOU CRAZY?" shouted Thisby.

Iphigenia pulled back as if she'd just been smacked in the face.

"Excuse me?" she said. "The plan all along was to find my brother, and up until right now, you've seemed perfectly okay with that!"

"I know that you've been in the dungeon for three whole days now and consider yourself an expert, but let me explain something to you . . . YOU DON'T GO INTO THE DEEP DOWN," Thisby said emphatically.

"Let me put this in a way you might understand. You know the horrible things we've seen in the last couple of days? The tarasque, the wyverns, the spectral goat? Those things are scared of what lives in the Deep Down. Terrified of it. We can't go down there. We'd die. We'd die in the most horrible, gruesome way possible. We'd—" Thisby stopped.

"My brother's down there," said Iphigenia.

The room fell silent.

"Look," said Thisby softly, "even if we wanted to go, we can't. There's no way in."

"Perhaps these would help!" said Gregory enthusiastically, dumping out the contents of the sack Thisby had given him onto the table.

Thisby gawped in disbelief as several portable blackdoors—along with the "wyvern beads"—tumbled out. It seemed impossible, but somehow, there they were. Maybe the Master wasn't as tight with his security as she'd thought.

Grunda stood up slowly and looked at Gregory, her black goblin eyes twinkling in the candlelight.

"I'm sorry," said Grunda calmly, "but would you mind getting your rock golem poop off my dining room table?"

CHAPTER 19

Roquat kicked a tiny, horned Deep Dweller that'd been gnawing on his leg underneath the table. It bounced off the wall, hissed angrily, and scurried away.

"I've fulfilled my end of the bargain," Roquat said gruffly, picking at his thumbnail with the tip of his dagger.

The creature sitting across from him blinked several times. It was about as much expression as it could manage. Its face was a pale, featureless white mask from which bulged two black, dead eyes, reminiscent of a shark's.

"I agree," hissed the arbiter.

"And what about your end of the bargain?"

The arbiter drew in a long breath that sounded like a

snake hissing backward.

"I do not have an end of this bargain, Mr. Roquat. I represent the interests of the King of Beneath the Mountain, the Eyes in the Dark."

Roquat stood up angrily and jammed his dagger into the table.

"And what about *his* end of the bargain?" he barked.

The arbiter did not flinch. It was hard to imagine he ever had.

"There are . . . complications. The Darkwell may have been stripped of its magic, but the gate itself is harder to remove than we imagined. And our supply of blackdoors, though we genuinely appreciate what you were able to procure for us initially, is practically drained. Still, with the guardian out of the way, it is only a matter of time before we open the gate. Our deal will soon be fulfilled."

"Soon!" snorted Roquat. "Hah!"

He walked over to a window and leaned outside. The tower he was in loomed above a decaying town that seemed to stretch on endlessly in every direction, a sea of rotting rooftops. In the few spaces where he could peek between them, he saw the wretched inhabitants of the Deep Down skulking in droves throughout the city. Their malformed bodies comprised mismatched parts shambling forward aimlessly in the perpetual night. The only light in the city came from the occasional torch, struggling helplessly against the darkness, casting eerie shadows and begging to be put out of its misery.

...he saw the wretched inhabitants of the Deep Down skulking in droves throughout the city. Their malformed bodies comprised mismatched parts shambling forward aimlessly in the perpetual night.

Everything in the Deep Down seemed to be put together incorrectly. A building with no doors might sit beside one made entirely of them. A stairwell might be turned upside down. A bridge might be placed over nothing, while meanwhile an adjacent lake of fire had only a diving board.

A ghoul or a werewolf seems awful . . . until you set foot in the Deep Down. Once a spider with an old lady's face unhinges her jaw to barf snakes at you, a guy who turns into a wolf doesn't seem so bad. But it wasn't fear that Roquat felt as he looked out over these loathsome creatures, only disappointment. The creatures of the Deep Down were quite disturbing, but they were far less impressive than the stories he'd been told as a young boy growing up in the dungeon.

"Do you want to know how I stole the blackdoors?" mumbled Roquat. He didn't wait for an answer. "I know the secret of magic. I whispered it into his stupid box, entered the chamber freely, and simply took them."

He watched as a four-legged creature stalked over the rooftops of the town, jumping from one roof to the next, landing silently as if it were hunting.

"People think I'm stupid. But I figured it out. I know the secret."

The four-legged creature found its prey and dropped down into an alley.

"I should be up there right now, taking my rightful place as the Master! I should be sitting in Castle Grimstone instead of this dump!"

The arbiter blinked.

"THE BLACK MOUNTAIN BELONGS TO ME!" Roquat bellowed.

The arbiter clapped twice sharply and the door to their chamber opened. A long-legged pink creature with a tray affixed to its back entered. Atop the tray were a jeweled decanter and two goblets. The arbiter casually poured himself a drink as he looked blankly toward the fuming Roquat.

"The Black Mountain belongs to me," Roquat repeated. "It's mine by birthright." His tone was suddenly much more somber. He plodded to the other side of the room and gazed out the window, hoping to see something better. It was more of the same. More horror, more dilapidated rooftops.

"The Dünkeldwarves lived in this mountain long before any of the so-called Masters laid claim to it. We were here before the dungeon. We're the rightful rulers of the mountain."

"And we," said the arbiter, "are the rightful rulers of the world." He took a long sip through the thin mouth-slit in the front of his mask. "And yet here we are," he concluded, setting the goblet down in front of him.

Roquat stomped over to the table and withdrew his dagger from the wood, leaving behind a deep scar where it'd been stuck.

"I don't care about Nth! I don't care about the world! You can have everything else! You can burn everything to the ground, for all I care! All I want is the mountain! I fulfilled my promise! I got you the blackdoors, I delivered the Prince safely to you, I got rid of the cat. If it wasn't for me, you'd have never even known that the magic on the Darkwell was broken in the first place! I figured it out! Me! I came here to strike up a deal with the Eyes in the Dark!"

"And who do you think willed you to come here?" asked the arbiter. "Do you really believe that you—*you*—are capable of orchestrating these grand machinations without his voice whispering in your ear? Do you think you are out of the reach of his influence there above the gate? You desire to be the King of the Black Mountain, but you are just a pawn. Worse yet, you are a pawn who is not even aware that the game is happening."

"I just want what was promised to me! I want what is owed to me!"

"Oh, believe me," said the arbiter. "You will get everything you are owed."

The arbiter clapped three times and the door swung open again. This time, four large cloaked figures carrying scimitars entered the room.

"I see," said Roquat.

The door closed behind them. From the hallway, a servant barred the door and waited. Inside, there was yelling and clanging and the sounds of things breaking. Then there was silence.

And with his final breath, Roquat finally got what he was owed.

Their preparations had been rushed. Thisby had run back to her room to gather a few items while Grunda and Gregory immediately set to work readying food, water, and any other necessities that they might need in the Deep Down. Iphigenia supervised.

When Thisby returned, she brought Grunda several bags that were practically overflowing with rags and horns and antlers and teeth; all the various scraps she'd collected from around the dungeon over the past few months. They were the parts she'd intended to trade to Shabul, only now she gave them to Grunda, along with some illustrations from an old book that Grunda whispered about excitedly. Some hours later, when Grunda returned from the back of her hovel, she handed Thisby several strange-looking packages in return.

Iphigenia meant to ask Thisby about the packages, but she was too anxious to think straight. There was no way to know when they might be back. Or if they even would be back. Even if they found Ingo, getting out could be as simple as throwing a blackdoor bead at the ground and stepping through a portal back into Thisby's bedroom, or as impossible as being stuck on the wrong side of the Darkwell with no way home. That was the risk they would have to run.

The problem was, there was no way of knowing where a blackdoor bead led for certain until you'd used it, and of course, once you did, you had only a short time—since it was impossible to know how long a blackdoor would hold.

Grunda checked all the blackdoor beads, sniffing them over and over with a look of great consternation, and she was ultimately convinced that at least one of them would lead them back home safely. Unfortunately, it was impossible for her to say which one. Like all goblins, Grunda had the ability to discern certain magical properties by smell. However, the blackdoor beads had rubbed together so much in Gregory's bag—not to mention the odor of the rock golem poop that they'd picked up—that it was difficult to tell one smell from the other. Of the three beads, Grunda was convinced that at least one of them smelled like the Black Mountain and the other two smelled like—something else.

Thisby was less than confident about Grunda's methods, but the first blackdoor bead that Grunda selected had indeed opened up a portal to the Deep Down, so she was one for one. At least, Thisby believed it was the Deep Down. She'd never been there, of course, but she knew that what she was looking at couldn't possibly be anywhere else within the Black Mountain. She knew the Black Mountain better than her own reflection, and the place she was looking at now was like nothing she'd ever seen.

Thisby, Mingus, Iphigenia, and Grunda stood before the blackdoor, which glowed brightly on the wall of Thisby's bedroom. Inside the portal, an old waterwheel slowly creaked along, powered by a river of dank green sludge that apparently passed for water in the Deep Down. Near the water wheel was a sort of mill grinding up who only knows. There didn't seem to be any sign of creatures moving about, but they'd been watching for several minutes, and Thisby was still working up the courage to step through to the other side.

"I'm not sure how long the blackdoor will hold, dear," said Grunda.

Mingus had been beside himself since they'd decided to go to the Deep Down to bring back Prince Ingo. He'd simply refused to come at first, but Thisby had managed to convince him that if she could do it, there was no reason why he couldn't. In the end, he'd relented, but now that Thisby was faced with the prospect of actually stepping through that portal herself, suddenly the assumption that "she could do it" didn't seem so certain.

Thisby stared at the blackdoor like an executioner's stand. Her heart thumped against her rib cage, and it felt as if she'd forgotten how to move her feet. But then something strange happened. She felt a pulling in the pit of her stomach, and her feet began to move, almost on their own.

She stepped forward.

Slowly.

One foot after the other.

Everybody in the room watched as she edged closer to the doorway. Her face was vacant but determined.

Thisby could smell the rank stench of the river, feel the hot air on her skin. She stood mere inches from the blackdoor, close enough to where it was all that she could see.

The pulling grew stronger.

And she jumped in.

Thisby landed awkwardly on the other side, wobbling under the weight of her backpack, and clutching a terrified Mingus in her hand. He swayed in his jar. He'd changed to a purplish color so dark it was almost black and had pressed himself up against the wall of his jar as tightly as he could manage.

"Thisby, oh, Thisby . . . ," was all he could say.

"Shhhhhhh," she said. "It's okay."

Moments later, Iphigenia joined them on the other side.

Thisby turned back to see Grunda smiling at them from her bedroom. Thisby went to say good-bye, but before she could speak, the door blinked out of existence and the last trace of home vanished before her eyes.

She knew that tens of thousands of feet above them, her room still existed, that her notebooks and her desk and her bed were in the exact same place as they'd been a moment ago, but the thought wasn't any comfort now. The only thing that made her feel any better was reaching down her hand to feel the two other blackdoor beads nestled safely in her pocket. Those were her only way back home, her only lifeline in this terrible place. But for now, they were trapped. Trapped in the most horrible place on earth. Trapped in the Deep Down.

CHAPTER 20

Only one map of the Deep Down existed and unfortunately for Thisby, it was hundreds of miles away on the absolute opposite end of the kingdom, tucked away in one of the many libraries of Lyra Castelis. Strangely enough, its resting place was also only about a ten-minute walk from Iphigenia's bedchamber, not that she, nor anybody, for that matter, even knew it existed. The map had ended up there in much the same manner as the other valuable, rare, and extraordinary things that ended up in the royal castle did, simply because there was no other place that made sense for it to be.

The closest thing that Thisby had on hand to guide them were some drawings that had fallen loose from an old book.

They were more like illustrations from a child's storybook than proper maps. Assuming the drawings could be trusted at all, Thisby knew that the Deep Down was shaped like a funnel, or perhaps an upside-down mountain, and the farther you went down, the smaller it became. It also appeared as if at the center of the funnel, stretching all the way down to the bottom, was a city, built layer upon layer like a wide spiral staircase.

They wandered through the outskirts of the city—or at least what Thisby hoped were the outskirts of the city. For all Thisby knew, they could be on the opposite end of the Deep Down, miles away from where Ingo was being kept. This was, of course, assuming he'd be kept in the city at all. Which, in turn, was assuming the supposed city even existed. Still, it was the only lead they had.

Thisby was completely out of her element. There were no notebooks she could check for advice, no maps she could reference. It reminded her of her first few years in the dungeon. For those first few years, she'd struggled every day not to be eaten by a troll or mauled by gnolls. She'd mostly just fumbled around in the dark trying not to die a horrible death. She'd done it then. Somehow. Now she wasn't so sure she could do it again.

The Deep Down was different from anything she'd ever encountered in the Black Mountain. It was darker than she'd expected and there was chaos everywhere. Once, when hiding from a wandering group of monsters, she'd accidentally almost led Iphigenia into the mouth of a wall-sized creature she'd mistaken for a cave. And that was just in the first few minutes. By now, it'd been hours.

To say they were lost might imply they had a plan to begin with. Thisby thought that her familiarity with the Black Mountain would be more help than was the case. In the Deep Down, tunnels led to nowhere, and the logic of how everything was arranged seemed designed to intentionally confuse travelers. Perhaps it was. Overwhelmed and frustrated, she'd already considered trying to use one of the blackdoors to return to the dungeon several times. If it hadn't been for Iphigenia, she probably would have.

Iphigenia wasn't doing much better at not being scared, but her determination to rescue her brother seemed to blot out the hopelessness of their situation.

"I think we're getting closer," said Iphigenia, apropos of nothing.

This was a markedly different girl than the one Thisby had met only three days prior, and one who she liked quite a bit better, honestly, only given the current situation, Iphigenia's newfound optimism was beginning to rub her the wrong way.

Thisby grunted dismissively.

"It feels like it, at least," said Iphigenia.

"I guess you're the expert," said Thisby pointedly.

Mingus stirred nervously in his jar. He'd barely said a word since they first entered the Deep Down, opting instead to curl up in his jar, barely glowing, shriveled and terrified.

"We should just go back," Thisby muttered under her breath.

Iphigenia looked wounded.

"It's been hours! It's not like we're doing any good down here!" said Thisby. "Do you want to just wander around here forever? How does that help anyone? We could go back and regroup. Try to come up with a better plan."

"We tried to come up with a better plan and we failed. Besides, we don't have time! For all we know, Ingo . . ."

"I'm sorry, okay?" blurted Thisby. "I'm sorry! We tried and it didn't work! What do you want me to say? We're not any good to your brother dead."

"But . . . ," said Iphigenia.

"Maybe we should, um, try that way," interjected a small voice.

The girls stopped and looked at Mingus. He shifted anxiously in his jar.

"Maybe we could just try it," he said quietly.

"We've already been that way," scoffed Thisby.

"I don't think so," he said. "Can—can, uh, we just try it, please?"

Mingus had a strange tremble in his voice that made Thisby feel uneasy.

"We can try it," said Iphigenia reassuringly.

They walked in silence for nearly an hour down a small winding path, until at last the path let out onto a thin ledge overlooking a sea of rooftops that stretched on as far as the eye could see. Strange machinery clanged and acrid smoke billowed from between the buildings. In the distance, a crooked tower stretched from the top of the cavern to the bottom, supported by thin bridges that connected it to other, smaller structures, jutting off the sides of it like the spokes of a wheel.

"The city! How'd you know it was this way?" asked Thisby.

If Mingus had shoulders, he would've shrugged.

"Lucky guess," he muttered.

Thisby had read exactly one book about Deep Dwellers. Truth be told, it was more of a picture book intended to frighten children away from playing near the Darkwell than a textbook, but it was better than nothing. She'd found it on her first trip to the City of Night years ago and had kept it safe since then, despite the fact that the illustrations in the book had caused her more than a few sleepless nights—the book's intended effect had worked like a charm. She was embarrassed to admit that she still kept the book on the very bottom of a very tall stack of very heavy tomes, on the off chance that the creatures from the illustrations sprang to life and came for her in her sleep. It was unlikely, sure, but why take the chance?

The scant text in the book was written in Dünkeldwarvish, and the little bit she'd managed to translate wasn't particularly helpful in their current situation. But among the tattered and browned pages it was only the frightening illustrations she'd really needed anyway. Before they left for the Deep Down, she'd given the book to Grunda, and with the help of her nimble goblin fingers—as well as Thisby's ample supply of spare monster parts—Grunda had managed to cobble together two rather horrifying costumes, intended to allow Thisby and Iphigenia to pass undetected when and if they reached the city.

Thisby's costume was a tattered black shroud that covered her entire backpack and body beneath the same patchwork blanket, allowing only her head and arms to stick out. On her head she wore a grotesque mask with pointed ears and antlers. The seams of the mask were concealed by the hood of her cloak, which pulled double duty by providing even more shadowy spots to hide the flaws of her disguise. Overall, the effect was quite good. The costume made her look like an old hunchbacked monster, the likes of which she'd seen in one of her book's illustrations. She didn't have a dozen legs, of course, but she did her best to hide that with a floor-length cloak.

Iphigenia was much harder to disguise, being one of those unfortunate people who can still somehow manage to look good even when dressed in a grotesque monster costume. After several failed attempts, Grunda had decided the best approach was to wrap her from head to toe like a mummy with yellowed gauze bandages. She'd then stuck on some various items like horns and whatnot to accent the fact that she was indeed a monster and definitely not a princess. The illusion had almost worked. But still, through the small gaps in the bandages that Grunda had been forced to leave open so Iphigenia could move and breathe, it was easy enough to catch a glimpse of her sparkling green eyes, or notice a lock of her thick, raven-colored hair sprouting through her wraps like a beautiful flower blooming through the cracked floor of a gulag, and the whole effect was ruined.

The costumes were far from perfect. Thankfully, it was very dark in the Deep Down.

The city was walled off, forcing them to enter through a tall stone-and-iron gate. Leading up to the gate was a long line of creatures of every imaginable shape and size, shuffling forward miserably in the darkness, one step at a time.

The air here was hot and thick as they approached, and Thisby began to sweat profusely beneath her mask. Beads of sweat streamed down her forehead and stung her eyes, while her own breath was cruelly reflected back at her face, warm and damp. Through the constantly shifting eyeholes of her mask, she scanned the crowd as she walked.

Each Deep Dweller was different. The thing that stood in front of her was black and oily, large globs of itself sloughing off as it craned its long neck around. It had no visible eyes, but Thisby felt as if it was watching her. Studying her. Maybe it could see through her costume. She could feel her heart thump in her ears.

Beside her, Iphigenia clung tightly to her cloak like a child might hold on to her mother's dress as they walked through a crowded market. There was something charming about it. In fact, there was more to like about the Princess than Thisby had expected. They had their differences, but somehow, the more time they spent together, the less important those differences seemed. She wondered if Iphigenia felt the same.

Her train of thought was interrupted when a furry brown creature, round and fat, pushed past them in a hurry. Its stench caused Thisby to gag.

They shuffled along, trying to stay inconspicuous as they approached the gate. The crowd up ahead came to a point as the Deep Dwellers forced their way into several tight tunnels leading into the city, the creatures' horrible bodies mashing together as they attempted to squeeze through the narrow passages. Thisby felt Iphigenia tug on her cloak and looked over. Through her bandages, Iphigenia's eyes were wide and frightened. Thisby tried to look comforting, but her nerves were frayed as well, and with a final glance that she hoped would communicate some sign of reassurance, the girls pushed into the tunnels.

It was a waking nightmare. A churning sea of bodies mashed together, creating a teeming mass of hair and sweat and slime and warts and hooves crushing down on them from every direction. Iphigenia could barely breathe. She felt Thisby's cloak pull from her grasp and suddenly, horribly, she was alone. Desperate and not thinking clearly, she called Thisby's name but it was lost amid the cacophony of snorts and hisses and growls bouncing off the tight stone walls. In every direction she looked, in the faintest light by which she could still see, she would catch flashes of the monsters who surrounded her on all sides. Beaks snapped open and shut mere inches from her face. A clawed foot stepped on her heel. Something sharp jabbed into her side. And worst of all, she was alone.

When the crowd finally broke through to the other side of the tunnel, Iphigenia wanted to cry. She ran from the stream of monsters and pressed her back against a cold brick wall. When a hand touched her shoulder, she jumped.

"Are you okay?" asked Thisby.

Iphigenia waited for her pulse to return to normal before answering.

"I'm fine."

Thisby waited for a real answer.

Iphigenia tugged her bandages away from her mouth just as something hot and vile exploded out. She managed to turn her head away from Thisby just in time. Thisby waited as the Princess finished retching and wiped her mouth on her bandages.

"Okay. Now I'm fine," she said.

As they walked the streets, Thisby was struck by how much the Deep Down felt like the City of Night as seen through a funhouse mirror. Stairways and roads led to nowhere, creatures lurked just outside the periphery of their vision, and unnatural voices gibbered at them from darkened alleys. It was eerily reminiscent of walking through a nightmare, so much so that at times Thisby felt certain that if she were to attempt to run, she very well might find her legs had turned to jelly.

Aside from the bizarre arrangement of everything, the most striking difference between this place and the City of Night was that while the ruins of the City of Night had been abandoned long ago, these ruins were very much inhabited. Deep Dwellers scurried in and out of houses and alleys going about their business. Carts pulled by abominable warty toads the size of horses clattered along the road up ahead on their way to the market. This city wasn't dead. It was very much alive.

Yet squalor was everywhere. The monsters who lived in the Black Mountain had room to breathe; some even had chambers entirely to themselves. They had room to run and explore. Here the Deep Dwellers seemed to be hiding in every nook and cranny they could find. Rat-tailed lizards dashed from the sewers only to be grabbed at by several angry, hungry hands that followed it. Dozens of creatures piled into tiny standing-room-only sheds, huddled close together. Thisby watched, curious, through the holes in her mask as they moved down farther into the black heart of the city. She'd heard so many stories about the Deep Down growing up that she'd always known it would be awful, but she was beginning to suspect it may be that way for reasons she hadn't quite expected.

Mingus flickered dimly from time to time, but his fear had rendered him largely unable to glow, leaving Thisby and Iphigenia to stumble around in the dark as they made their way. With every corner they turned, it seemed as if they uncovered a new sight they would never be able to unsee.

Down one alley, they passed by some robed creatures opening two large wooden barn doors to reveal the gigantic, thrashing head of some sort of bird, the structure barely able to contain its size as the creature angrily snapped its sharp beak. A small group of robed lizards ushered several other bewildered creatures forward at spearpoint, and Thisby, as accustomed as she was to the brutality of nature, still had to look away when the bird began to devour the offerings. She'd caught her own reflection in the inky black mirrors of the bird's bulbous eyes as it ate, and it was more than she could take. There was something different here. Something in the way the Deep Dwellers seemed to prey on one another unnerved her.

Thisby felt torn between the urge to record these strange new sights in her notebooks and the urge to erase them from her memory completely. She finally settled on writing it down if and when she returned home, although Thisby had never felt more uncertain she would make it out of somewhere alive, so the compromise felt like a bit of a cop out.

They moved as stealthily as they could manage. Even with the costumes, their best bet was to stick to the shadows, avoiding any ambient light. Thisby took point, carrying Mingus and trying to move carefully enough to keep anything in her backpack from rattling or jingling, with Iphigenia following closely behind. She jumped when she heard a rattle behind her and turned to see an eight-foot-tall giant carrying its own head in a small birdcage. The head was crying bloodred tears.

The creature brushed by the girls, clipping Thisby in the shoulder and partly uncovering her beneath her shroud, but it continued on without so much as a second glance. Thisby straightened her costume and looked around. All around them, Deep Dwellers hurried this way and that, seemingly paying no attention to the girls and Mingus. They might as well have been invisible.

"I guess the costumes are doing their trick," Thisby intoned as a group of kids with the heads of various animals—a lion, a tiger, a ram, and a snake—ran by. Thisby watched them run on ahead, laughing hysterically. It took her some time to realize they were all part of the same creature, physically joined at the hip. Behind them, they were dragging something in a crude rope sack. Thisby felt sickened when she realized what it was. It was another kid, one who for all intents and purposes looked just like them, only he had just one head, the head of a rabbit. The rabbit locked eyes with her for only a moment, and Thisby could feel his panic. And then, just like he came, he was gone, dragged behind the kids, their shouts and laughter trailing off into the city streets.

Apparently, the creatures of the Deep Down had their own pecking order. At first glance it was easy to dismiss a place like this as chaos, but Thisby knew too well there was no such thing. The strong always ate the weak. That's the way of nature, out in the wild and in the dungeon. The difference down here was that there was no keeper. There was no Thisby. There was nobody to make sure certain types of creatures never crossed paths, nobody to make sure everybody was well fed and taken care of. There was a sharp pang of guilt in Thisby's stomach that was hard to ignore.

After hours of wandering through the winding streets, they reached the foot of a large, important-looking building formed from uneven green bricks. The base of the building was slanted on each side, like a pyramid, and from the top of that base rose a single green stone block that comprised the bulk of the structure, windowless and brutal in its design. The building looked thousands of years old. The irregular green bricks from which it was made looked almost softened by time, moldy.

Two sentries stood watch at the main entrance atop a wide set of steps. They were immense creatures, at least a dozen feet tall, with apelike bodies covered in black fur that swallowed every bit of light that dared to touch it. Atop their shoulders were long, thin necks and vulturelike heads that scanned the vicinity. In their hands were tall pikes topped with barbed spears. Thisby and Iphigenia ducked back behind a steeply inclined wall to avoid being spotted in the light emanating from braziers nearby.

"What do you think that building is?" asked Iphigenia.

"The prison," said Mingus automatically.

He stared out toward the building, deep in thought. So deep, in fact, that he was more than a little bit startled to look up and see Thisby and Iphigenia staring at him, brows furrowed quizzically.

"I mean, I think so. It looks like a prison to me," said Mingus.

Thisby wanted to know more about how Mingus knew so quickly what the building was, but Iphigenia had already moved on.

"Ingo could be in there," she said hopefully. "Come on, we have to check it out!"

They took several laps around the building, sticking to the perimeter of the surrounding buildings before coming to the unfortunate conclusion that the only way in was through the front door. The really unfortunate part, of course, being the two giants guarding the entrance.

"What do we do?" asked Iphigenia. The bandages had slipped even farther off her face, making her costume less convincing than ever.

"I guess we could try just walking up there and seeing what happens . . . ," said Thisby, although the tone of her voice betrayed her conviction that this was a good idea.

Mingus quivered. "No, no, absolutely not!"

"Do you have a better plan?" asked Thisby.

Mingus hesitated.

"That's what I thought," said Thisby, and with that, she adjusted her mask and began to walk toward the guards. She took one fleeting glance behind her to look at Iphigenia. The Princess walked delicately, her head held high. Even the bandages had now draped around her face in what might be considered a rather flattering framing. The feeble costume was simply no match for her inherent grace.

Thisby sighed. She wondered if this was where they would die. If they did, she thought about how different her and Iphigenia's funeral services were likely to be. Thisby would most likely be tossed into one of the Black Mountain's oubliettes until she became a skeleton. Grunda would maybe say a few words to the couple other goblins who showed up—and that would be that. Iphigenia's death, on the other hand, would likely result in a period of mourning across the entire kingdom. She would be laid in a glass coffin—which she would undoubtedly make beautiful just by her mere presence—surrounded by wildflowers. She would probably be lowered into the ground beneath a statute as tall as the Black Mountain itself.

Thisby didn't begrudge her any of this, though. Iphigenia was the closest thing Thisby had ever had to a human friend. Maybe they could still hang out when they were both dead. As ghosts or something.

Up close, the guardians looked much bigger than they had

from the street below. They stood nearly as high as Catface and were more than twice as wide. Even though their necks were thin, Thisby had to imagine they could easily swallow her whole without much risk of choking. As they approached, the guardians craned their heads in the girls' direction and studied them without saying a word.

Iphigenia held on to Thisby's arm.

"Uh, can we go in?" asked Thisby politely.

It was a bit of a long shot, but it never hurt to try the direct approach.

The guardians looked at her impassively, their black eyes unblinking.

Mingus, who had turned a rainbow of pale greens, whispered to Thisby, "Offer them something!"

"Like what?"

"I don't know, anything!"

"But I can't get into my backpack without taking my costume off!"

"I'll get it!" said Iphigenia who hurried behind Thisby while Thisby smiled at the guards.

Iphigenia lifted up the back of the cloak and began to dig around in Thisby's backpack. Navigating her way around the boxes and pouches in the light was a difficult enough task, but attempting to do so in the dark was next to impossible.

"What am I looking for?" asked Iphigenia.

"Anything! Just—anything!" said Thisby through clenched teeth.

Iphigenia rooted around until her fingers found something interesting. She quickly snapped the backpack shut and made her way forward to present the object with all the reverence appropriate for a royal court, which seemed a bit out of place considering the circumstances. With an elegant curtsey and a wide sweeping of her arms, Iphigenia proudly placed the stump of a mostly burnt-out candle on the ground before the two towering guards.

There was a long pause as Thisby, Iphigenia, Mingus, and the two guards stared at the candle, not sure what to make of it. The pause was broken when the barbed tip of a spear as wide around as a ship's mast whizzed past Thisby, missing her but managing to rip the shroud clean off her. An exposed Thisby scrambled between a guard's legs in a break for the door, but the right foot of guard number two came crashing down just in time to block her entrance.

Iphigenia ran and took cover behind a flickering brazier just in time for it to block the point of a spear headed her way. The brazier was flung aside and sent hot ashes flying, scattering them over the landing. Iphigenia stood exposed as the guard drew back his spear for another strike. There was nowhere for her to hide.

As if on cue, the candle burst to life with a brilliant blue flame. The flame spewed three sparks and each hit the ground between Iphigenia and the guard, expanding and growing into a fully formed kobold. Ralk stood in the middle. He turned toward the stunned Iphigenia and took a short bow.

Interestingly enough, the kobolds didn't seem to be thrown by the fact that they were in the Deep Down. Rather, Ralk seemed only interested in the task Iphigenia had in mind for him, looking at her quizzically with his head cocked to the side. She raised her hand and pointed over his shoulder toward the guards. Ralk turned and studied the flummoxed guard for a moment, and then he and his brothers were off like a shot, leaping nimbly toward the two giants easily a dozen times their size.

The guards began their attack immediately, swinging their massive spears and smashing everything in sight, but the kobolds proved too nimble for their clumsy blows. Iphigenia ran between the legs of the giants to Thisby, and the two of them hid in the doorway, close together, pressed up against the wall to avoid the fervor of the battle.

Ralk clambered up one of the giants' backs as easily as if he were running up a staircase. The other giant spotted Ralk and lunged forward with his spear, but he was too slow. Ralk had already deftly jumped out of the way by the time the attack landed, and the spear instead found only the back of the first guard. With a sickening *SPLUTCH!* the spear went right through the first guard. And then there was one, standing defenseless and wondering what in the world had just happened.

The kobolds set upon him next, and in moments, the second guard was lumbering around trying to get the monsters off his back. He staggered, managing to successfully knock one of them off before ultimately losing his footing and tumbling down the stairs. By the time he hit the bottom, the kobolds had jumped free and made their way back over to girls.

The girls looked at the small kobolds, stunned.

"*Mara'wak kombeh*," said Thisby at last, bowing awkwardly, parroting the words Ralk had said to her in the City of Night two days ago.

At this, Ralk grinned. He made a little whistling sound by putting his fingers into his snout, and the candle, which was still burning on the landing, blew out. In a flash of blue flame, the three kobolds were gone, leaving behind only a wisp of smoke where they'd just been standing. The only sign that they had ever been there at all were the two vanquished giants dead near the stairs.

"What does '*mara'wak kombeh*' mean, anyway?" asked Thisby, turning to Mingus in his jar. He stopped shaking and looked at her.

"It's kobold for 'Master of the Black Mountain.'"

"Oh," said Thisby. She wasn't sure what to make of that. It seemed like an odd sentiment, but at least she'd understood why the kobold had grinned at her when she'd said it to him.

They entered the building. Thisby had never seen anything like it. Inside it was full of pipes that gave the impression of a tangled ball of wires, green metal tubes darting in and out of the walls at irregular angles. There appeared to be no logic to their placement, and trying to figure out what they might do or where they might lead made Thisby's head spin.

Iphigenia wandered over to the wall, catching something strange out of the corner of her eye. But when she reached out her hand to lean against the wall, Iphigenia yelled out, causing Thisby to turn around. Iphigenia recoiled from the wall, holding her hand.

"Ow! Something bit me!" she yelled. "I'm bleeding!"

"It's a good thing you're covered in bandages," said Thisby mindlessly as she got closer to the uneven green bricks that comprised the wall. There was something strange about them. Something she'd been unable to see when they were farther away—it almost seemed as if the bricks were moving. It was ever so slight, but sure enough, they were. At first she thought it was an illusion caused by flickering light, but from up close, there was no denying it. She leaned in closer to study the bricks. Their shine wasn't from glaze, but rather that they were wet. She leaned in until her nose was practically pressed against one of the bricks. With a hiss, the brick parted in half, revealing a row of sharp yellow teeth! Thisby jumped back. Disgusted, she looked around. The building itself suddenly seemed to be breathing.

"It's alive," whispered Mingus.

They hurried on through the building, out of the main room, trying to ignore the hissing of the walls. At last they found a stairwell leading down into the basement of the structure and were relieved to find that down here, at least, the walls were made of seemingly normal bricks. Thisby breathed a sigh of relief. In the Deep Down, sometimes you had to celebrate the minor victories.

Mingus was right about it being a prison. They entered a large, dimly lit room filled with cages stacked floor to ceiling, at least a hundred feet high. The cages were aligned in narrow rows, stuffed into little metal cubbyholes like drawers on an apothecary table. Some of the spots where the cages might go were empty, as if that cage had been temporarily removed, but most of them were full—and occupied. There, hidden inside those darkened cages, were creatures that even the Deep Dwellers would rather forget.

Thisby studied an empty cage, and she finally had an answer to where all those tubes from the entry led, although she was beginning to wish it had been left a mystery. From the back wall behind the cage, a tube that seemed to be made out of the same stuff as the living bricks hung limply. Thisby leaned up against the cage bars and watched as a glop of green goo spurted out from the tube and landed in an overflowing food bowl on the floor of the cage directly below it. This was how they were feeding the prisoners.

They walked down an aisle, which was narrow enough for Thisby to stretch out her arms and touch the bars on either side. Not that she did, of course. She wasn't stupid. In fact, Thisby scrunched up as tightly as humanly possible, terrified of what might be lurking inside those cages. The cages were pitch black inside, and Thisby tried her best not to look at them. The last thing she needed was to imagine what horrors were locked inside. The noises and the smells of this place made her skin crawl, and Iphigenia was squeezing her hand so tightly that she knew it would be sore and bruised when they finally got out of there—if they got out of there. She almost missed the walls of living bricks.

The prison seemed to stretch on and on, and eventually, they found themselves completely engulfed in a sea of cages. No matter where they looked, the only thing they could see were more cages. It was as if the end of each hallway had ended in a mirror, creating a reflection of a reflection of a reflection, and so on. An inescapable infinity of cages.

As they walked, Thisby tried her best to draw a mental map so they could find their way back out of the prison in a hurry, but it wasn't her strong suit. They'd taken too many turns, and her memory wasn't very good, especially not under this kind of pressure. It was the reason she took such detailed notes. One of the reasons, anyway.

"INGO!" Iphigenia screamed at last.

Thisby whirled around. "What are you doing?"

"Trying to find my brother!"

"Not like that!" scolded Thisby. She looked around, half expecting to see cage doors suddenly flying open as the prisoners, newly alerted to their presence, came rushing out. Of course, rationally, Thisby knew that prison doors weren't typically left open, as it kind of defeated the point of the whole thing.

Iphigenia looked sullen. "Then how? It's not like you

know what you're doing!" she said.

It was Thisby's turn to feel hurt. She was trying her best. For days she'd been way out of her depth, but she'd been trying as hard as she could to make things work. The fact that Iphigenia didn't appreciate all that she'd done for her stung.

"I–Iphigenia?" called a weak voice from several rows over.

It was Ingo.

CHAPTER 21

Iphigenia had taken off running before Thisby had a chance to stop her. She ran through the rows of cages toward the voice as fast as she could, dizzy with excitement.

"Ingo!" she called out. "Ingo, I'm here!"

A weak voice responded from several rows over, and Iphigenia turned down another aisle. Thisby trailed behind her.

"Iphigenia, wait!" yelled Thisby.

Iphigenia wasn't listening now. She turned down a row that was wider than the rest and heard Ingo's voice calling to her from a cell at the end.

"Iphigenia? Is it really you?" said Ingo.

She walked forward as if in a dream. The voice was pulling

her forward. For a moment, it felt like she was underwater, and her body was swaying helplessly with the current.

"Ingo, it's me!" she said.

The cage was dark as she approached it. There was something moving in the darkness, but it was hard to make out. She got closer and leaned in toward the bars.

"Ingo?" she said.

Thisby turned the corner and saw Iphigenia bending close to the cage. Behind her, inside the cage, Thisby saw something move in the dark. Only it wasn't Ingo. It was something much, much bigger than Ingo.

"IPHIGENIA! GET BACK!" shouted Thisby, but it was too late.

Tentacles shot from the cage and wrapped around Iphigenia, pulling her in toward the bars as she struggled and thrashed against them. Thisby sprinted toward her. She grabbed Iphigenia's hand to free her, but the tentacles were too strong. In the cage, Thisby saw a beak full of razor-sharp teeth snap hungrily.

"OVER HERE!" bellowed a familiar voice.

Thisby glanced over her shoulder as she pulled helplessly on Iphigenia's arm. There across the aisle, in several crudely welded-together cages, was a face she wasn't sure if she should be happy to see or not . . . the Sentinel of the Darkwell.

"Catface?" yelled Thisby.

"FREE ME!" he boomed.

Catface had seen better days, but he was still an intimidating sight. Even cramped in that cage, filthy and beaten, he still somehow managed to look proud and dignified.

Thisby's mind raced. She thought of all the times Catface had messed with her, bullied her, made her feel frightened and weak. She wished for all the world she could leave him in his stupid cage. Make him suffer for all the times he'd been mean to her. For what a jerk he'd been. But now wasn't the time for petty revenge. There were bigger things at stake.

"HOW?" she yelled back, suddenly realizing it might not be as easy as he'd made it sound.

"There's a lever that opens the cages! It's an emergency release! Over there!"

"WAIT! IT OPENS *ALL* OF THEM?" Thisby exclaimed.

"Yes! There's no time! I'll get you out of here! Your friend is going to die!"

Thisby looked him in the eyes, trying to see if she could see through them. She had to trust that he was as good as his word. That he would get them out of here. If not, once those cages were open, she was as good as dead. Still, if she did nothing, Iphigenia was dead regardless.

Thisby threw the switch.

With a lurching metallic noise, all the gates swung open, and for a moment everything was hauntingly, mind-numbingly silent. This particular type of silence is sometimes called the calm before the storm. It's the moment when everything seems to freeze and the world has one last fleeting moment of peace before everything gets turned upside down. This was that moment. It was actually pretty nice.

And then it was over.

With a horrendous din of banging bars, trampling footsteps, and otherworldly screams, all the worst creatures in the Deep Down burst forth from their cages and started destroying everything in sight—the building, one another, themselves. It was a prison riot, yes, but it made a normal prison riot look like a couple of kittens tussling over a ball of yarn. It was as if the entire world had exploded into violence and screaming and mayhem.

Thisby turned to see Iphigenia being dragged into the beast's cage. She looked around, but there was no sign of the Sentinel. Catface had broken his word. This is it, she thought. This is how I die.

Thisby couldn't think, so she acted instead, rushing headlong into the beast's cage. She pushed her way through a mass of tentacles, which were whipping all over the cage like stays on a ship that had burst free in a storm, until she found Iphigenia. She was braced against the creature's beak, fighting with all her strength to avoid being pulled inside its angry jaws.

Doing the first thing that came to mind, Thisby charged forward and jammed her hand into the beast's one enormous eye as hard as she could. To her surprise—and the beast's—it went in quite easily, and moments later, she found herself elbow deep in monster eyeball. The creature let out a horrific shriek and began to thrash harder than ever. One of its tentacles caught Thisby in the side of the head and sent her sprawling to the floor of the cage.

Her head swam. The next thing she knew, she was being dragged out of the cage by her ankle and tossed up onto a big furry back. She felt Iphigenia's arms wrap tightly around her waist, and it was all Thisby could think to do to grab two handfuls of fur and hold on tight.

Catface was off like a rocket, bounding through the prison, knocking over monsters as he went and finally spilling out onto the streets outside. Armed guards rushed toward them, trying to contain the situation, but the chaos was too much.

Catface sprang from the ground, and Thisby felt the wind rush through her hair. She felt the freedom of weightlessness followed by the sinking jolt in her stomach as they landed on the rooftops above. Iphigenia squeezed tighter. Mingus swayed in his jar, screaming in some language Thisby couldn't understand. He was probably cursing something awful.

"My brother! We have to go back for my brother!" Iphigenia shouted.

"Your brother's not in there, Princess," said Catface. "We need to get out of here."

Catface bounded over the rooftops, knocking tiles loose as he ran, occasionally shattering them entirely. Once his large paw even smashed entirely through a weakened patchwork roof. As he regained his balance and withdrew

Catface was off like a rocket, bounding through the prison, knocking over monsters as he went and finally spilling out onto the streets outside.

his foot, Thisby looked down to see some rather frightened-looking Deep Dwellers shouting up angrily at them through the brand-new hole in their ceiling.

The girls held on tightly as Catface ran, leaping from building to building. Occasional arrows flew past and alarms sounded, but they weren't the only prisoners who'd escaped that night, and in the chaos, even a cat the size of a house running across the rooftops of the city could become easily lost in the commotion.

"You didn't use the blackdoors," said Iphigenia, her hair blowing in her face.

"What?" said Thisby, but even as she said the word her mind was already being overwhelmed by her own stupidity. In the chaos she'd forgotten about them entirely. They were right there in her pocket the whole time. But for some reason she'd run into the cage anyway. She'd thought she was going to die, but she ran in anyway. How stupid could she be?

"I guess I forgot."

"That's pretty stupid," said Iphigenia, squeezing Thisby tighter than she had been previously. It was as close as either Thisby or Iphigenia had ever come to giving or receiving a hug. Neither one of them was really sure it was actually happening.

"Yeah, I guess it was," said Thisby.

Catface slowed when they reached the outskirts of the city.

"I need to rest," he said at last, admitting defeat against

his wounds once the adrenaline of their escape had worn off.

He found a small cave that appeared to be unoccupied and bent down, letting the girls slide off his back. It turned out Catface could be considerate when he wanted to be. Thisby and Iphigenia slumped down onto the cave floor, not realizing how exhausted they were until they took a moment to let their guards down.

Thisby set her bag beside her. Mingus sat still in his jar, saying nothing. He hadn't spoken since they'd left the prison.

"Mingus . . . light?" Thisby asked weakly.

Mingus didn't respond. Or glow. He just sat there. Catatonic.

It was uncomfortable when Mingus didn't respond. Since he didn't need to breathe or blink or do any of the other basic functions that almost all living things do, when he didn't respond it seemed for all intents and purposes as if he was dead. One time he'd slept for two days in a row, and Thisby had almost considered burying him.

Catface began to clean his wounds just like any cat would, and the girls watched him from the other side of the cavern. He paused momentarily when he noticed them staring, but then continued unabashed.

"Where's my brother?" asked Iphigenia after watching him for some time.

He paused his licking and looked at the Princess.

"Direct. I like it," he said.

"This is not a game, cat," she said.

Catface turned to Thisby. "Hah! You two are cut from the same cloth, aren't you? Although I'd have to say that her end of the cloth is much nicer looking. Yours is a bit frayed and stained in comparison. A bit worse for the wear, wouldn't you say?"

"Please just answer," said Thisby pleadingly.

"Oh, very well," said Catface. "I've just been desperate for interaction, that's all."

He looked back at Iphigenia, who was now scowling at him.

"I don't know where your brother is, but he wasn't in that prison. The last thing I overheard was that he was being taken to the meet with the Eyes in the Dark."

"I thought the Eyes in the Dark was just a story. Something to frighten children into behaving," said Thisby.

"It's hard to say for sure. It's possible that it's just a title they give to their King. Sort of an honorary thing. But either way, the Deep Dwellers were taking their orders from somewhere. Once the Darkwell opens, we won't just be dealing with some monsters flooding the dungeon—it'll be an army."

Thisby stood up. "So how do we stop them from opening the Darkwell?"

For the first time, Catface looked gravely serious. He settled into a sphinx pose and studied Thisby's face. It made her nervous.

"I'm afraid it's too late. They may not have opened the Darkwell yet, but the magic is broken, and they're heading for the surface. It's only a matter of time."

"So, what, we should just sit back while they take over the dungeon? That's my home! It's our home!" said Thisby, standing up. She was wobblier than she'd realized. Apparently, she was still a bit woozy from that hit to the head.

Catface furrowed his brow.

"Perhaps you shouldn't have broken the magic seal in the first place!" he snapped.

Thisby looked confused, "Me! What did I do?"

"Not you!" snarled Catface. "Him!"

Mingus turned around in his lantern.

"Thisby," he muttered. "I'm so sorry."

Thisby couldn't believe her ears.

"What's he talking about, Mingus? You didn't do anything . . . right?"

Mingus glowed a faint white, so faint it was almost not visible at all.

"I was born in the Deep Down. I never told you because I was afraid you'd send me back, or at least, someone would. One day, I just came through. Into the dungeon. I had to get out, Thisby! I had to! That was the day you found me. I didn't realize until later that passing through the Darkwell could undo its magical protection."

"What do you mean?" asked Iphigenia.

"Ah! Just as I suspected!" said Catface, turning to Iphigenia. "Years ago, when the Darkwell was created, a magical seal was placed on the gate that could only be opened by a sort of paradox. The spell stated that the only way the gate would ever open, regardless of force, was if something had already physically passed through it. The spell served two purposes: one, you couldn't simply smash the gate open, and two, you couldn't use a blackdoor to reach the other side because you'd never physically traveled through the opening. Brilliant, isn't it? The gate will only open if something has already opened it. Only they forgot one thing: What if you didn't need to open it to physically pass through it? What if you could simply slip between the blackweave and come out the other side? Well, then the spell would be broken. And our boneless friend here managed to do exactly that!"

"But how did Roquat figure it out?" asked Iphigenia.

Mingus was silent for a moment before finding the courage to speak.

"Two weeks ago, when you were out feeding the salamanders, I woke up to find Roquat in your room. He must've been coming and going with blackdoors to get past your locks. He was reading your journals. He told me he'd figured out where I was really from and that he'd send me back there if I said anything to you! He'd been reading your journals for months, and somehow he'd put it all together! I'm so sorry, Thisby! I should've said something, but I was so scared!"

Mingus didn't have real eyes and was incapable of crying, but Thisby heard tears in his voice. But how had he not told her? How could he have kept this from her for so long?

"Why didn't you tell me you were born in the Deep Down?" she asked.

"I was scared. Scared you'd send me back. I couldn't stand the thought of coming back here, Thisby. I can't."

"You should've told me about Roquat, at least! You knew he was up to something! Maybe we could've fixed this before it was too late!" Thisby was getting angrier the more she thought about it. If Mingus hadn't been such a coward, they might've been able to avoid this whole thing.

"He just took your notebooks and he left! He must've realized that because the spell was broken, he could use the blackdoors to pass through the gate. What was I supposed to do? It's not my fault, Thisby! I was scared!"

"Enough!" shouted Thisby. "I can't believe you didn't tell me!"

She got up and walked over to Mingus, peering angrily into his jar.

"You know what? You're a coward. That's all there is to it. You live in your little jar and you try to keep yourself safe, but you don't care what happens to anybody else, not really. Now the whole dungeon is in danger because of you. Because you were too much of a coward to speak up. I wish you'd stayed in the Deep Down."

With that, Thisby stormed out of the cave. Iphigenia tried to follow her, but Catface put up his big paw to stop her.

"She'll be fine. Just give her a minute," he said calmly.

★ ★ ★

Thisby stomped off into the darkness. She'd known Mingus for so long, and this whole time he'd been keeping a secret from her that put the whole dungeon at risk. How could he have been so selfish?

She thought of the day she'd met him, hanging through the grate of the blackweave gate. She'd thought he was falling through it, but in retrospect he may have been coming out. It hurt her to think of their whole friendship being built on a lie. From the moment they met, he'd never said a word about it. Never said a word about the Deep Down or his life before her. Maybe she hadn't asked the right questions. Maybe if she'd been a better friend or made him feel more secure, he would've told her. Maybe it was her fault after all.

Roquat had figured it out somehow. Mingus was right—he must've stolen her notebooks. He'd figured it out. He was cleverer than she'd thought, and if she hadn't kept those notebooks . . . Maybe it was her fault after all.

Thisby looked around and suddenly realized she was a long way from the cave.

It had taken her longer than she cared to admit to remember she was still in the Deep Down, and almost instantly her anger was transposed with fear. She had no backpack, no lantern, no Iphigenia, no Mingus, no Catface, and was wandering aimlessly around in the place that haunts the dreams of the things that haunt people's dreams. Her heart sank.

She turned to go back and found herself face to face with several Deep Dwellers, clicking and hissing as they closed in around her. They'd snuck up on her. She had been so lost in thought that she hadn't even been paying attention.

Thisby looked around, but there was nowhere to run. She was cornered, backed up against a wall. She tried desperately to think of a plan, but her mind was racing too fast for her to keep up. The Deep Dwellers moved forward, slowly, methodically, until all at once, as if a switch had flipped, the monsters stopped, frozen in place.

The crowd parted and a person walked through. He was clad in golden armor and a long red cape, but his pretty face was unmistakable.

"There you are!" said Ingo. "I've been looking all over for you!"

He snapped his fingers and the Deep Dwellers pounced on Thisby, knocking her to the ground. She fell poorly, facefirst, and ended up with a mouthful of dirt and a bloody nose. Thisby struggled underneath the weight of her attackers, but it was no use. She was completely overpowered.

It took all her strength just to get her head up, and when she did, she found herself face to face with Ingo, who was leaning in to get a better look at her, bringing them within mere inches of each other. For somebody who'd just spent several days in captivity, he seemed shockingly well put together.

"I heard that you saved my sister," he said with a soft smile.

"Y-yes," Thisby muttered.

"Pity," he said.

And with that, a hood was pulled over Thisby's head, and everything went dark.

CHAPTER 22

After what felt like an eternity, the hood was pulled off Thisby's head and the world flooded with light. She struggled for breath; the air was almost as hot and sour as it'd been inside the hood. Before her eyes could even adjust to the light, some gruff voice yelled, "Drink," and a cup full of warm water was thrust in her face. Very little of it made it into her mouth.

As her eyes adjusted, she saw Ingo standing on the other side of a campfire, looking out of place in the horrible company he kept. He patted some Deep Dweller—an unfortunate-looking creature covered in ratty brown fur whose face was in its stomach—on the shoulder before walking over to

Thisby and kneeling down.

"This place is terrible, isn't it?" He chuckled.

Thisby was silent. Her mouth was still caked with dirt and blood from where she'd face-planted after his guards had tackled her.

"Here," he said. He reached around and cut her hands free. She rubbed her wrists, fighting the temptation to punch him in the mouth.

Ingo handed her a damp towel, and she began to clean off her face.

"I'm sorry for what happened earlier. It was honestly a bit of a misunderstanding. Let's start again, okay?"

Thisby was silent.

"You have the look of somebody who has been traveling with my sister for days." He laughed. "I probably don't need to tell you this, but she can be a bit of a handful. You see, that's the problem. She was chosen by birth to rule the kingdom, our kingdom. But she's not fit to rule. At least, that's what the Eyes in the Dark thinks, and I'd have to say I agree. I'm a much more natural leader. So I did what I had to do . . . or at least, I tried to."

Ingo sat down on a rock nearby. He leaned so casually and smiled so nonchalantly that he could have just as easily been talking about the weather as he was talking about trying to murder his sister.

"I see that look. I know what you're thinking. 'What a monster!' But I want you to know that I never wanted things to play out this way. I'd always thought I'd do my power grab like a proper gentleman, through politicking and the law, usurping her from the throne through more . . . legitimate means. I'm not a violent man! Murder? How crass!"

Thisby almost could have believed him, the way he said it. She found it hard to believe that somebody so beautiful, so delicate, could be such a monster.

"This isn't my style! But the Eyes in the Dark can be very . . . persuasive. And once we had a deal, there was no backing out. I follow his plan; I take my rightful place as the ruler of this kingdom. Simple as that.

"Or it should have been, until you showed up! I have to give you credit, Thisby! You know this dungeon better than I ever thought possible!"

He reached out to take the towel from Thisby, sensing she was done with it. He was right, but Thisby held on to it anyway. It made her feel better to deny him something. Ingo shrugged.

"Which brings me to my next point. I'd actually like to talk to you about a promotion. Things are changing in the Black Mountain, Thisby. Heck, things are changing in the world! And I think there's a place for you. Here. In the Black Mountain. Do you get what I'm saying?"

Thisby squeezed her towel and imagined she was wringing his neck.

"Of course you don't. I'm being too obtuse. Lemme just come right out and say it: I want you, Thisby Thestoop, to be the new Master of the Black Mountain."

Thisby hated that her heart raced at those words. She knew it was a trick. Every bone in her body was telling her it was, and yet, she couldn't deny feeling a strange sense of elation at the idea. Worse yet, somehow Ingo had sensed it.

"Great! Perfect! You know the dungeon better than anyone! You'll be perfect for the job! There's just one little change we need to make, part of upholding a deal on my end—you know how these things go—we need you to keep the Darkwell open. So from now on, the Deep Dwellers can come and go in the dungeon as they please. It's something the Eyes in the Dark has been very insistent on and, well, a deal's a deal. Before you say anything, I know, I know, it's not ideal, but this is how things get done in the world. You understand that, don't you, Thisby?"

Thisby hesitated. Ingo grinned.

"Or we can do this the hard way. Now, before you answer, let me tell you about the hard way. The hard way is where I take my army of angry Deep Dwellers, smash through the weakened Darkwell, march through your precious dungeon, and kill every single monster in sight. That doesn't seem like a good compromise, though, does it?"

"What about Roquat? You're working with him, right?" Thisby asked, keeping her tone as flat as possible. She was beginning to realize Ingo was quite good at reading inflection.

Ingo beamed at her.

"Ah! Very clever! Very clever! So you figured it out,

huh? I was working with, uh, Roquat did you say? Right. Roquat. And he was indeed promised the position of Master in exchange for his, uh, assistance in opening the Darkwell, but it seems he'll no longer be able to fill the position. His contract was . . . terminated early. I'm afraid he's passed on."

Thisby had been furious at Roquat for days since he'd loosed the tarasque and started this whole mess, but something about Ingo grinning over his death rubbed her the wrong way. She felt sick in the pit of her stomach. She and Roquat had never gotten along, but he didn't deserve to die as a casualty of Ingo's insane quest for power.

"Roquat does your dirty work, tries to kill your sister, gets rid of the Sentinel for you, and you, what, stab him in the back? That must've been it, right? From the looks of it, I doubt you could take him in a fair fight."

"And you're worried that we'd do the same to you, right?"

For once, Ingo was way off the mark.

"Don't worry," he said. "Roquat was a means to an end. He never would've been able to maintain a lasting peace between the Deep Dwellers and the rest of the dungeon, but I believe you can. I believe you can control these monsters. I've seen it."

Thisby spit out some blood and wiped her mouth with the towel. She almost felt like laughing at his sheer arrogance.

"Nobody controls these monsters. Especially the Deep Dwellers. Was that your plan for lasting peace? To just open the gate and hope nothing bad happens? That was your bargain: you get the throne and just leave the Black Mountain in chaos? What do you really think will happen then? Once that gate is open, the Deep Dwellers and whatever it is down there that's driving them, it isn't going to stop at the mountain. They're going to show up in your villages, in your towns, at your gate. You're playing right into their hands. They promised you the Kingdom, just as they promised Roquat the Black Mountain. Don't you see? This is a game where everybody loses. You, Roquat, the Deep Dwellers, the monsters. After spending time with Iphigenia, I'd started to think that maybe you royals weren't so stupid after all, but apparently it's just her," said Thisby.

Ingo stood up, enraged. His face was red and several locks of his black hair slid across his forehead.

"How dare—" he started.

"No, no, no," said Thisby, standing up. "I'm not done yet."

Several of the Deep Dwellers who'd been escorting the Prince rushed over with their weapons drawn, but he held up his hand to stop them. Ingo Larkspur was far too proud to have his guards protect him against some scrawny unarmed little girl.

"You tried to kill your own sister, your own sister who's spent the last three days worrying about you, searching for you, so that you could enact what has to be the worst thought-out plan in history! This is why you weren't meant to be King! You'd be terrible at it!"

Ingo drew his sword. Thisby took a step back and glared at him.

"Now I've gotta go try to undo your stupidity before it's too late! And one more thing!" Thisby added. "Next time you take somebody captive, check their pockets first!"

And with that, Thisby threw a blackdoor at the ground and jumped through.

Ingo scrambled to his feet but hesitated just long enough at the edge of the portal for it to snap shut with a definitive crackle. Unlike Thisby, he had the good sense to look before he leapt. And where Thisby was headed, Ingo had no interest to follow.

CHAPTER 22.5

Shabul peered through bundles of drying herbs through the leaded glass window of his cobblestone cottage as ranks of soldiers trudged past up the Black Mountain. He'd been watching for the better part of an hour as the rows upon rows of soldiers carrying purple flags emblazoned with the crest of King Larkspur—a silver lyre entwined with flowers—bumbled past, and still the army had yet to thin out. Wherever they were going, whatever they were doing, they were bringing an army.

A few days ago, a convoy carrying the Prince and Princess up the Black Mountain for the Royal Inspection had passed by Shabul's shop, but unfortunately for the potion maker, he wasn't able to entice them to stop. He'd even gone so far as to tailor the signs in front of his shop to things he believed would steal the royal twins' attention:

POTION OF FUTURE TELLING: WILL YOU BE ASSASSINATED? FIND OUT!

HEAVY IS THE HEAD . . . THAT DOESN'T HAVE SHABUL'S SPECIAL ELIXIR!

ROYAL BOIL? TRY MY SPECIAL NO-SPOIL BOIL OIL!

The last one he'd thought was particularly brilliant, but it was all to no avail. The royal carriage had passed by without even so much as slowing down. Now he found himself with an opportunity to upsell an entire army, and he'd been caught completely unprepared. Fortunately for Shabul, this was a large army, which meant he had time to rush prepare some Luck Potion—a perpetual favorite for those brave soldiers about to rush headlong into a fray of people wielding extraordinarily pointy things. He'd wait for the back of the army. At the back of the army were the generals, and they were the ones with the money anyway.

After some time, Shabul finally caught sight of a woman riding a beautiful white horse wearing the most resplendent armor that he had ever seen. The woman's armor was not so shabby, either. Shabul grabbed up his Famous Luck Potion, straightened his turban, and ran outside, eager to make a sale.

The woman on the white horse gave him a side-eye as he walked briskly up to her, waving happily and holding his finest basket full of potions.

"Hello, hello!" called Shabul.

The woman did not answer him, but also did not take her eyes off him. Shabul saw this as a good sign.

The woman's white-gold hair was cropped short and pushed back away from her face. She was tall and thick, with broad shoulders, and she looked as if she'd seen her fair share of battles. Shabul did not know it, but she was General Elspet Castor, the Hero of the Battle of the Nameless Sea. Even if he had known, he probably would not have behaved any differently.

He bowed awkwardly as one might to a lady.

She gazed at him stonily but stopped her horse anyway.

"My name is Shabul, and I have just the thing for you!" he said, rifling through his potion basket. He knew full well that he was going to try to sell her his Famous Luck Potion— but that would be the final act of the play. Opening with that would spoil the whole thing.

Shabul rifled around for a bit more before he withdrew a green flask and proudly held it up.

"This one will make you very, very rich!" He beamed. "It is made with real cockatrice feathers, known the world over for their fortune-enhancing properties!"

General Elspet had begun to ride again, following her army at a slow trot. Shabul walked alongside her, pretending he hadn't noticed the discourtesy.

"Never mind! Never mind! I should've known you were too discerning for that!"

Shabul went back into his basket and began to root around again. He made a great show of clinking the bottles together. General Elspet kept her eyes on the path ahead.

"This," he said, producing a small bag of crushed leaves, "produces a tea that will heal any infirmity of the mind or body. It is made from . . ."

"I do not want your snake oil, peddler."

Shabul deftly turned around his bottle of Genuine Snake Oil so its label was no longer visible.

"My elixirs and potions are the best in all of Nth! I assure you!"

Elspet sped up enough so that it was hard for Shabul to keep pace.

"I'll have you know I get my ingredients from the Black Mountain itself! They are harvested in the dungeon by hand!"

Suddenly, Elspet stopped riding. For the first time since he'd approached, the General turned to face him, and Shabul found himself retreating a bit beneath her cold glare.

"What did you say?" she demanded.

Shabul, ever the professional, continued on. "I said, my elixirs and potions are made from finest ingredients, which come from the dungeon of the Black Mountain itself."

Elspet rode over to the peddler, her eyes trained on him.

"When was the last time you were there, in the dungeon?" she asked.

"Hm. Maybe three or four days ago." Shabul paused. "What is it you're doing there, anyway? Is something wrong?"

Elspet considered him for a moment and decided there was no harm in telling him the truth. He was of such little importance that it was as harmless as talking to a tree.

"A royal caravan passed through here several days ago. Inside that caravan were the Prince and Princess of Nth. They were expected to return days ago and have yet to. We're here to find out why."

"And start a war, from the looks of it," said Shabul, despite his better judgement.

The general didn't smile. In fact, she didn't even blink. It gave Shabul goose bumps. Here was somebody who knew war, who understood it. And who was definitely willing to make it again if need be.

"Have you seen anything strange around here lately?" asked Elspet.

Shabul combed through his recent memory. The other day, a raven the size of a small carriage had carried off a baby from Three Fingers. He'd watched it fly over his cottage on its way back to the mountain. He'd also caught a goblin stealing carrots from his garden. And there'd been that horrible disembodied voice that had begun talking to him over the last few days as he tried to fall asleep, but all things considered, there was nothing he'd call "strange."

He shook his head.

Elspet turned to ride away.

"Be careful, Mister Shabul. There are bad things coming to the Black Mountain."

"I've lived here all my life. I'm used to it."

Elspet paused.

"Then you know this is different."

Shabul felt a chill go up his spine at her words. He knew she was right, but hated to admit it to himself. Something had been different lately, although he couldn't quite put his finger on it.

"Good luck, General."

"Thank you," she said sincerely. "I need it."

She rode away, leaving Shabul standing dumbstruck, staring after her. It took him several minutes until his brain kicked back in, and he realized he'd just missed a sale.

CHAPTER 23

To her surprise, Thisby didn't find herself back in the dungeon. At least, she didn't think she was in the dungeon. In all her years there, she'd yet to come across any place this horrible.

Everything was dark and extremely hot—so dark that she couldn't see her hands in front of her face, and so hot that it immediately felt as if all the air had been sucked out of her body.

She inhaled sharply, trying to catch her breath, but the sudden blast of heat inside her lungs made her feel as if her chest were on fire. Thisby collapsed. She braced herself against the fall, but the hot stone burned against the skin of her palms, making her cry out in pain. She rolled over onto her back, trying to remove her exposed skin from contact with the ground, but the heat quickly radiated through the back of her thick shirt and made her feel as if she had lain down on a frying pan. Thisby rolled onto her knees where her leggings were thicker and stood up, coughing and wheezing.

She pulled the neck of her shirt up over her mouth and breathed through it, desperate to take some of the edge off the unrelenting heat. She sipped the air in short little breaths, trying her best not to breathe it deep into her lungs again.

Everything was pitch black.

Back on her feet, she reached into her pocket for the second blackdoor, but it was gone. Her mind went blank with panic. She'd dropped it.

She knelt down and felt the ground. It burned her skin, but she had to keep looking. It had to be there somewhere. She groped the ground desperately but came up with nothing. After several minutes she accepted the inevitable. She was going to have to find another way out.

Hands outstretched in front of her, Thisby stumbled through the dark, hoping beyond hope to bump into something. Anything. If she could find a wall, maybe she could follow it to an exit, but her fingers touched only terrible, endless darkness in every direction.

She staggered forward. Something shifted in the darkness, just beyond where she was standing, and an awful feeling began to creep up from the base of her spine. She wasn't alone.

"I know you're in here!" yelled Thisby.

Nothing responded. Not even an echo.

A hot gust of air grazed the back of her neck, causing her to shiver despite the overwhelming heat. She stopped dead in her tracks and listened. The only noise she could hear was her own labored breathing.

Perhaps she was already dead. Maybe she'd dropped through the blackdoor straight into a volcano and this was some sort of torturous limbo. After all, there was no way to know where a blackdoor let out unless you'd made it yourself. When she'd thrown it, she'd thought anywhere would be better than being stuck in the Deep Down with Ingo. Apparently, she was wrong.

"You have a dream," said a raspy voice. It came from everywhere at once, as if the cave itself were speaking. "You wake up. You get out of bed. You walk to the ladder. You look down. And then . . ." The voice trailed off.

Thisby felt the darkness drawing in more tightly with every word. It was heavy, weighing her down from every direction and keeping her stuck to her spot. Thisby forced herself to respond despite her every instinct telling her to stay still and quiet.

"Then I jump," she said.

There was hideous laughter all around her.

"Then you jump," it parroted. "How nice."

Thisby felt the words wrapping around her neck like a noose. She felt the urge to scream and run away but couldn't find the strength to do either.

"Where would you go if you ran?" he mocked. "Would you run forever? Just run and run and run and run? You belong here, Little Mouse."

Thisby thought for a second she saw Catface stalking around in the darkness, but shook the image from her head. It was just her imagination. This was something far worse. It knew her. It knew what she was thinking. She shook her head. For all she knew, it could also just be her mind playing tricks on her.

"Maybe it is, and maybe it isn't," said the voice. "What is it you want, Thisby Thestoop, the sweet, lonely girl who was left at my doorstep? Tell me, and I would be happy to oblige."

He paused. Thisby could feel thin, invisible fingers digging around inside her head. She struggled to keep her mind clear.

"Strange . . . for an orphan, you seem to have no desire for your parents. Good. Most parents are idiots, yours especially. Neither do you want power. How rare for someone so pitiful as yourself to not to want to be powerful! You truly are a kind, gentle girl, aren't you? Are you sure you wouldn't like to be Master? To have the whole dungeon serve you?"

The fingers poked deeper into her brain and she winced, trying to keep focused.

"Now, Ingo Larkspur, there was a simple boy. He wanted power, he wanted to be King. So I brought him here and we made a deal. Easy. Done."

"You made him do it?" Thisby choked.

The hideous laughter almost swallowed her.

"Made him? I barely had to ask. He would've done it anyway. Displaced her the moment he had the opportunity. But he was a coward and I was impatient. So I gave him a nudge. The deal was perfect: he gets the kingdom and I get my freedom. Best of all, one day he can sleep easy on his ill-gotten throne. Who could blame him, after all? It was me, the great manipulator. The Eyes in the Dark. The corrupter of 'innocent' men. You see now, Thisby, don't you? He could have done it any time. He had all the opportunity in the world. Why jump through all the hoops? Ingo isn't stupid. Why free me? Why? Why risk everything?"

Thisby felt the answer welling up inside her like she'd eaten something rotten.

"Because once I gave him the nudge, it was no longer his fault."

Thisby felt sick.

"That was what he wanted. It's what everybody wants, my darling! Freedom from the responsibility of their awful, selfish decisions! I can provide that. And there's nothing more valuable in the entire world."

There was something about being here in this place. Something that made her angry, hateful, and, more than anything, scared. It made her feel as if giving in to those horrible feelings, giving in to the darkest parts of herself, would somehow make it all go away. But that wasn't quite it. It was more like, the fear and the hatred would still be there, only she'd be able to view it all from the outside, from a place where she'd be safe from the worst of it.

She thought about the Deep Dwellers. About how living so close to something that made her feel like she did right now might twist you over time. After all the stories she'd heard from Grunda when she was a child, had the Deep Dwellers really seemed so evil? Or were they just scared? If she'd had to live with this feeling, the one she had right now that was eating up her insides, did she really think she'd be any different?

"You make them afraid," she said.

The Eyes in the Dark choked on a laugh. It was the most terrible noise Thisby had ever heard.

"Humans are afraid of everything! Even your Master is afraid of his own monsters! Meanwhile, the monsters are afraid of the Deep Dwellers and, yes, the Deep Dwellers are afraid of me—that is true. But I don't need to *make* anyone afraid, my darling. They were born afraid. Everyone is born afraid. Just like you.

"Without fear, there would be no dungeon. So you can bury your head in the sand if you'd like, or you can grow up, my sweet girl. You can grow up and I can help you. I can help you have your heart's desire, and nobody will blame you. You won't even blame yourself. Doesn't that sound nice?"

Something stirred inside Thisby. It was an awful, wretched

little black spot near her heart, and it did want something.

"Tell me, Thisby. Tell me, my sweet girl . . . ," said the Eyes in the Dark. "Everybody wants something. You don't even need to say it out loud. I know what's in your heart. Just tell me. Just tell yourself. What is it that you want?"

Thisby tried her best to clear her mind, to not allow him into her head, but she couldn't resist. It turned out there was something she wanted. Something she wanted more than anything in the entire world. She felt embarrassed by how obvious it was. It was something she hadn't realized she'd wanted herself until recently, but now it was the only thing that she could ever remember wanting . . .

"YOU WANT ME TO CRAWL UP MY OWN *WHAT* AND DIE?!?" the voice boomed.

Thisby had already turned and was running full steam back in the direction she'd come. At least, to the best of her knowledge she was. It was impossible to tell in the dark. The heat swelled behind her, and she could feel a horrible anger burning inside her head. Screaming at her. She'd gotten its attention at least.

She dove to the ground, ignoring the burning, and began to frantically search for the blackdoor. No more games. She was going to find that stupid bead or die down here looking for it, but she wasn't going to spend another minute talking to some creepy disembodied voice in the darkness, poking around inside her brain.

The room felt as if it were growing smaller. Either that,

or something was closing in around her. The darkness began to swirl, and faint patterns began to emerge. Thisby tried to convince herself it was all in her head, but it was easier said than done.

Her hands groped around on the floor, burning against the hot stone. Finally, her fingers touched something small and round. She grabbed it and smashed it against the ground.

The cavern lit up in a flash of magical light, piercing the darkness, and for a moment, in the sparkling glow of the blackdoor, she saw it. She wasn't standing on solid ground at all. As the scales moved beneath her feet, she realized what she was actually standing on was the back of a dragon as big as the mountain itself. The Black Dragon. Its voice boomed from beneath her feet, its curses echoing off the cavern walls. The moment before she plunged through the blackdoor, she saw something far off in the distance. It was something she would remember for a very long time. The horrible yellow eye of the dragon, as big as the moon, staring right at her.

It was something she would remember for a very long time.

CHAPTER 24

The Master of the Black Mountain lay back in his bubble bath trying hard to soak off the stress of the last few days. He'd been in there for hours, however, and he was beginning to have the sneaking suspicion that all the Epsom salts and rose hips in Nth weren't going to bring him any peace of mind tonight. He reached around blindly, refusing to open his eyes lest he risk knocking off the precariously placed cucumber slices, until his pruny fingers found a little silver bell that had been placed on a nearby table. He rang it gingerly.

A large creature, stitched together from several of the Master's previous servants who had since expired, galumphed into the room, letting some of the steam escape through the crack in the door. It was wearing an apron because it had been baking. Not for the Master. Just for fun. Monsters have hobbies, too.

THOOOOM!

The entire room shook violently, knocking several bottles of neatly arranged toiletries to the bathroom floor. The Master sighed heavily.

"Harold, is there any news?"

Harold nodded glumly.

"Honestly, I can't believe they're still at it! Don't they know when to quit?"

The Master took the cucumber slices off his eyes and climbed out of the bath. Harold handed him a towel and tried his best not to look at the wrinkled old man drying off in front of him.

He sighed again as he pulled on his bathrobe. "Well, I suppose I better check in and see how it's going."

The banging had been happening every few minutes for the last twenty-four hours. It was a horrible racket. So far, it had ruined two baths, quiet reading time, naptime, snack time, and his violin practice.

THOOOOM!

The halls shook as the Master waddled through the castle, still in his bathrobe, leaving wet footprints as he went. He made his way down to the chamber and whispered the secret of magic into the door. Then in he went, over to his machine, flipping everything on as if by rote and plopping down in the seat.

The machine whirred and ground to life, grabbing the proper crystal ball and setting it down into the slot. On a nearby screen, it projected the image contained inside the scrying sphere, large enough for him see.

He sighed yet again. He'd been doing that a lot lately.

He watched the Deep Dwellers on the other side of the gate ready their machine and throw the switch. The Master grabbed on to the arms of his seat, knowing what was coming.

THOOOOM!

The whole room shook as the Deep Dwellers' machine smashed into the blackweave gate above the Darkwell yet again. The crystal balls in his chamber clinked together like wineglasses after a toast. He squinted and tried to study the screen.

The gate was badly damaged. It wouldn't be long now. Soon they'd smash it down and be inside the dungeon. His dungeon. It was only a matter of time before they made it all the way to his castle.

He wondered how long his guards would stick around. They weren't very loyal. He'd given them very little reason to be. They weren't paid well, and he wasn't particularly kind to them. In fact, he thought sometimes it was a miracle they hadn't revolted already. How long they'd risk their lives in a full-blown Deep Dweller raid was anyone's guess.

THOOOOM!

He pulled some levers on the blackdoor machine, and one of the arms swung around in a broad, sweeping arc, coming to rest over a different crystal ball. It was promptly loaded into the slot, and a new image graced the screen. It was Roquat. Or at least, it used to be Roquat.

The Master sighed. He'd never particularly cared for the Dünkeldwarf, but Roquat had served him well over the past few decades. Well, until he'd struck up a deal with the Deep Dwellers to become the new Master of the Black Mountain, thus betraying him. Still, this brand of treachery was nothing new to the mountain, and at least Roquat usually showed up to work on time.

The Master had been watching the entire drama in his dungeon unfold from the safety of his machine for the past several days. It'd been quite the exhausting emotional roller coaster, and he had a sneaking suspicion it wasn't over yet. His suspicion was confirmed when he looked down to see somebody crawling through a blackdoor on the floor near the machine in which he sat.

"Hello?" he called.

THOOOOM!

A filthy girl with a pointy nose crawled up through the portal and nearly collapsed on his floor. The Master studied her from his seat in the machine. She looked familiar.

"Can I help you?" he asked.

Thisby picked herself up.

"You work in the dungeon, right? You're the gamekeeper?"

He'd seen her involvement in the last few days but he'd forgotten her name. He must've heard it a dozen times. It was right there, on the tip of his tongue.

"Thistle, right?"

Thisby staggered over toward him. The Master stayed in his seat, elevated high above her. He was getting a bit nervous by her lack of response and starting to wonder if he should yell for his guards.

"We need to stop them," she said at last.

The Master thought for a moment. She had a point. The Deep Dwellers were definitely going to kill him, and yet, from his current position, he didn't really see all that much he could do. He also didn't particularly care for the familiarity of her tone when she addressed him.

"It's too late. They'll be through the gate any minute now, I'm afraid," he said. "I suppose you're welcome to stay here, although it's only a matter of time before they get in here as well."

Thisby looked up and saw Roquat's body on the screen. He was lying on the ground facedown in the dirt, somewhere in the Deep Down. It almost looked like he was sleeping.

"Can this show me anybody in the dungeon?" Thisby asked, pointing at the screen.

The Master's face lit up. Finally, something he was interested in!

"Why, yes! It does! You jus—"

"Show me Iphigenia," interrupted Thisby.

The Master made a face like a child who'd just dropped his ice cream, but obediently followed her instructions anyway. He pulled the levers, and a new orb was slotted into place. Iphigenia and Catface appeared on the screen. They were still in the Deep Down, making their way toward the surface.

Thisby smiled. Iphigenia was wearing Thisby's backpack, and for the first time she was able to see what it looked like on someone else. It was enormous. It looked like Iphigenia might be crushed beneath it. Mingus swayed from his usual hook. He was glowing again. That was a good sign. Poor Mingus. He hadn't meant to do anything wrong; he was just terrified of ever going back to the Deep Down, and yet he'd gone anyway. He'd gone back to the place that he feared the most simply because Thisby had asked him to. He was a good friend.

"Good," said Thisby. "They're still alive. Can we get them out?"

The Master shook his head.

"Even though the magic of the Darkwell is broken, blackdoors to the Deep Down aren't like normal ones. They take time to make. Sometimes days. It's a real hassle. You have to plan for that sort of thing way in advance."

"Like Roquat did? He must've made a dozen of them without you even noticing," said Thisby.

The Master frowned at her. She wasn't being very nice.

"You know, I'm still in charge here," he muttered weakly.

Thisby ignored him.

"Iphigenia will be safe with Catface for now. Start

working on bringing them out. In the meantime, there's something else I have to do," said Thisby, dusting herself off. "Tell me . . . how long do we have until the Darkwell breaks and how fast can you make blackdoors?"

CHAPTER 25

Iphigenia's legs had sunk so deep into Catface's inky black fur that from a distance she looked like a floating torso—a torso wearing an enormous backpack, of course. Mingus swayed in his jar as they trotted along. Iphigenia watched him staring off into the distance, glowing faintly.

After Thisby had stormed off, they'd gone looking for her, but by the time they got to where she'd been, all that was left was the disturbed earth where she'd fallen and a trace of blood in the dirt. Iphigenia had wanted to stay, wanted to keep looking, but before long more Deep Dwellers arrived, and they had had no choice but to leave. She'd told herself that once they reached the Master's chamber and found

Ingo, she'd be able to look for her, that once they found her, she'd use her father's army to bring Thisby back from the Deep Down if she must—but it only helped so much.

Since they'd parted ways, Iphigenia had begun to find herself wishing Thisby was still around. She missed talking to her, being around her. She'd even caught herself thinking it might be nice if Thisby came out to the castle to visit her sometime. Maybe they could go down to the shops together, or take in a play. It was all very confusing, and Iphigenia didn't know what to make of it.

Iphigenia had never had a friend before. Being her friend required certain levels of patience, and the sort of people who tolerated her hardheadedness usually had ulterior motives—such as getting closer to her brother or father—and they could hardly be considered real, genuine friends. Honestly, she'd never minded the solitude before. She was too stubborn to be lonely and too proud to lower her standards, and yet now, after having a glimpse of what it felt like to have an actual friend . . . the thought of losing that feeling made her miserable. It was like living in the cold your whole life. It was fine, so long as you never got to spend a day on the beach. After that, the cold could feel almost unbearable.

Mingus wasn't taking it well, either. Iphigenia couldn't read people as well as her brother could, but since Thisby had gone missing, Mingus had barely said a word. It wasn't hard to realize that he blamed himself.

"She'll be all right," she said, both for Mingus's and her own benefit.

The absurdity of her desire to comfort a slime monster didn't sink in until the words had fully left her mouth. She knitted her brow and stared straight ahead, straightening her posture a little under the weight of Thisby's backpack.

"I should've said something sooner," Mingus said somberly, forgetting to move his mouth when he spoke.

Iphigenia almost said something else, but instead her mouth just opened and shut several times as the words got stuck somewhere between her brain and tongue. Finally, she just sighed, surrendering to an awkward silence.

They lurched to a stop and Catface's ears stood on end. Iphigenia could feel the fur on his neck bristle around her.

"Quiet!" he said.

He crouched down low to the ground and crept forward, moving with the shadows. He darted out from the tunnel into a much larger chamber and then jumped back and forth, climbing like a mountain goat to the top of a rock wall. Moving silently, he passed through a stone archway and peeked out to the other side.

Iphigenia's jaw dropped. Hundreds upon hundreds of Deep Dwellers of every shape and size imaginable—from lumbering giants to creatures no larger than a common goblin—flooded the chamber below. There were more here than Iphigenia had seen in her entire time so far in the Deep Down, and worse yet, they were organized.

Hundreds upon hundreds of Deep Dwellers of every shape and size imaginable—from lumbering giants to creatures no larger than a common goblin—flooded the chamber below.

In the center of the room, below the Darkwell, stood a device the size of a tall ship that was shaped like a child's swing set. Several ropes hung off the sides of what looked like a large steel drill, which hung from the crossbars like a pendulum. Creatures that must have been as big as Catface grabbed hold of the ropes, and to the beat of a drum they drew them back, back, back . . . and then . . . released.

THOOOOM!

The entire cavern shook as the drill swung forward and smashed into the blackweave gate. They'd heard the noise on their approach to the Darkwell and prepared for the worst, but Iphigenia still felt unnerved by what she saw. These weren't mindless monsters smashing at the gates with their fists. Catface was right: this was an army.

They crept around the outside of the cavern, keeping low to avoid the gaze of cautious or bored monsters who might be looking around. They were high enough above to move with little risk of being spotted, but all it would take was one stray eye to catch sight of them, and suddenly they'd be at the mercy of an entire army. Catface crouched low, his belly flat against the rock as they watched.

"It's not going to hold much longer," he whispered.

Iphigenia nodded. He was right. The gate was barely hanging on at this point, and it seemed likely that one more hit would be all it would take. They were too late to save the gate, but it was a mixed blessing. What was left of the blackweave gate was the only thing holding back the army of

Deep Dwellers, but without the blackdoor beads that Thisby had taken with her, it was also their only way out of the Deep Down.

A horn sounded.

The sea of monsters that filled the room began to part as a small group of Deep Dwellers made their way through the crowd. Something was off about them, though. A figure that seemed far too normal, too human, was walking out in front of the group. Iphigenia strained her eyes to get a better look, but Catface saw it first.

"Isn't that—"

"Ingo!" exclaimed Iphigenia.

Ingo led a small company of Deep Dwellers up to the front of the machine, which stopped swinging for the first time since they'd entered the chamber. In fact, all activity seemed to suddenly cease. Iphigenia watched her brother ascend a small flight of stairs onto a makeshift stage. He turned to face the crowd, beaming with delight. The crowd looked on in silence.

"We need to get closer!" whispered Iphigenia.

Catface began to slink closer to the stage as the audience watched her brother with rapt attention.

"Today!" said Ingo triumphantly, pausing for effect as he liked to do. "Today you cast off the bonds of subjugation, the bonds of oppression! Today you take your rightful place back in the mountain—the mountain that by all right belongs to YOU!"

The crowd roared its approval.

"What the heck is he doing?" whispered Iphigenia.

"I don't know," replied Catface.

"The mountain belongs to you! Yes, YOU! RIGHT THERE!" he said, pointing to a random Deep Dweller in the crowd. "Of course it does! It belongs to you, and you, and you, and you! Not to any Dünkeldwarf!"

The crowd hissed angrily at the mention of that name.

"I know! I KNOW! The Dünkeldwarves built your prison! They built the blackweave gate that held you, and then what did they do? They left you to rot in it! And who helped them build it? The goblins! Your jailors! All of them! But you know who's even worse than them? The monsters who have lived above you for centuries, lording their freedom over you!"

The crowd booed and hissed even louder. He was whipping them into a frenzy.

"This is your mountain! It certainly doesn't belong to any . . ." He paused. He was relishing this moment. ". . . MASTER!" He spat the word with disdain.

The crowd was frothing mad. Some of the Deep Dwellers had begun to throw things indiscriminately at the mention of the Master's name.

"The Black Mountain belongs to YOU! IT BELONGS TO ALL OF YOU!" said Ingo.

The crowd exploded into cheers. Ingo paused and soaked it in. He had a way with speeches. He always had.

"And now, with one final swing of the Hammer of Righteousness, we will smash open the gates of our prison once and for all! On my mark! ONE . . . TWO . . ."

Ingo raised his arm and the crowd roared in anticipation. They roared so loudly, in fact, that if you had unnaturally sharp hearing, you could have heard them in the next town over.

This was not an exaggeration. It was however, the reason why all the dogs in Three Fingers had begun to spontaneously howl in unison, much to the confusion of the local citizenry. Over the next few weeks, the incident became so publicized that a special inquisition was formed to investigate the bizarre occurrence, but despite putting their brightest minds on the case, nobody in Three Fingers ever managed to come up with a feasible explanation for the phenomenon. They did manage to execute several people on suspicion of witchcraft, however, so it wasn't a total loss.

"WAAAAAAAAAAAAAAAIT!" screeched a familiar voice over the din.

Ingo froze, his arm suspended in midair, and looked up to see his sister racing down the side of a cliff with an anxious-looking giant cat in hot pursuit. At least, he thought it was his sister. She was much filthier than he'd remembered his sister ever being, and she was carrying a backpack that had to be at least three times her size.

The crowd parted, partially out of sheer shock, and the raven-haired girl, stumbling under the weight of her oversize backpack, found her way onto the stage. She approached

Ingo, out of breath, and he waved away the guards who tried to intervene.

"Iphigenia?" he said. "Is that really you?"

"Ingo!" she yelled and threw her arms around him.

Catface wasn't granted the same warm welcome, and instead was met with a wall of Deep Dwellers pointing spears in his direction, yelling angrily. Several of the giants stomped over, ready for a fight. Catface backed up and hissed, arching his back.

"WAIT!" Ingo commanded. The Deep Dwellers obeyed, but kept their spears fixed on the enormous cat, who had started pacing nervously back and forth.

"Ingo, we've been looking for you for days! What are you doing here?" Iphigenia asked.

"What does it look like I'm doing? I'm freeing an oppressed people!" Ingo laughed with a casual air that undercut the fact that just moments ago he'd been firing up an army to go to war. It was possible his nonchalance was phony, a ploy to make himself seem unflappable, but it was just as likely that leading an army to war affected Ingo Larkspur about as much as discussing the weather.

Iphigenia pulled back and looked at her brother, half expecting him to shoot her some sort of sly wink. Something to let her know this was all a trick and they were on the same side. It never came.

"These 'people' kidnapped you! They're going to destroy the dungeon!"

Ingo scoffed. "The *dungeon*? The dungeon! Seriously, Iphi! Who cares? They've been keeping these poor creatures locked away in their basement like prisoners! Yet they committed no crime! And besides, the dungeon is terrible! You know that! If it were up to you, you'd have this whole place shut down! I know it!"

Ingo smiled at her and squeezed her shoulders. He was capable of saying things in such a way that you felt foolish for ever disagreeing with him. Iphigenia felt turned around.

"But these things are dangerous . . ."

"Not with the right leader." He was grinning ear to ear now. He was about to play the ace up his sleeve. "I ran into your new friend. The filthy dungeon girl. I know, I know! For some reason you two are all buddy-buddy now! I don't want to question it—look, you're friends, I get it!"

Iphigenia turned bright red. First with embarrassment, and then with shame for being embarrassed by her only friend.

"Anyway, there was a little misunderstanding, but the short story is that I asked her to be the new Master. Here in the mountain. She can stay here and watch over everyone! I'm not saying I want to be her best friend like you do, but she's good at her job, I'll give her that!"

"Stop doing that!" snapped Iphigenia.

Ingo stepped back, nonplussed.

"You think you can make me feel bad because I have

a friend? Well, I don't feel bad! I like her, okay? She's my friend!"

"Just calm down—"

"No, I won't calm down! And by the way, you can't do this! You can't destroy the dungeon. Maybe you're right. Maybe the Deep Dwellers don't deserve to be locked away but—but this is not the way to handle things! War isn't the answer! It would risk destroying the entire dungeon and everything that lives in it. The monsters up there are living things. Besides, it's Thisby's home and you can't do it."

"And what are you going to do to stop me?" Ingo scoffed. "I have an army, Iphi. I will kill everything in here if I want. Even your friend. If I feel like it."

Iphigenia's mind raced. Her brother's horrible, cruel smirk cut into her, driving out all rational thought. Standing there, laughing coldly as he discussed the fate of the dungeon, the fate of her best friend, in front of an army of abominations, she could see him clearly for the first time.

She dug her hand into a side pocket of Thisby's backpack and withdrew something that looked very much like a knitting needle, barbed on one end. She pointed it threateningly at her brother.

"I won't let you!" she yelled, frightened at the honesty and desperation in her own voice.

Ingo had heard it, too. For the first time, he looked visibly shaken. It didn't last long.

He laughed cruelly. "What is that supposed to be? Are

you going to darn me to death?"

"I won't let you hurt Thisby or the residents of this dungeon!"

"Residents? RESIDENTS? They're monsters, Iphi! MONSTERS! Since when do you care about monsters?"

"I don't! Not really! But Thisby does, and more important, I trust her. Turn this army around right now and march them back to where they came from."

Iphigenia stood unblinking, the manticore needle pointed at her brother. Ingo glowered at her, rage welling up inside him. She was trying to take another thing away from him. He smirked. Then laughed. The anger that had built up inside him had melted away and revealed something far crueler at its core.

"Why would I do that? I have an entire army at my command. Why would I listen to you?" he asked, brushing the hair from his face.

"Because I'm your Queen and you're—nobody."

"Nobody? Nobody! And you, a Queen?" he said.

Ingo drew his dagger and rushed toward her so quickly she didn't have time to ready herself. The impact toppled her over onto Thisby's backpack, and she landed hard, feeling the wind go out of her. By the time Iphigenia realized what had happened, her brother was already climbing back to his feet, and the blood was pooling thick and black on the front of her dress. The wound from his dagger ran several inches deep into her stomach.

Ingo stared down at his sister and felt disgusted. Not with himself, of course, but with her. With what she had made him do. There was a strange feeling just beneath his ribs. He looked down and began to curse very loudly.

From where Iphigenia collapsed, she could see her brother yelling, clutching his side where she'd managed to stick him with the manticore barb, but she couldn't make out his words. Sound and light blurred together in a warm, hazy fog that made her feel like she was swimming underwater on a midsummer day. Iphigenia was lying on her back. The backpack beneath her made her feel like a turtle who'd tipped over onto its shell, helpless. Up above she saw the Hammer of Righteousness—what a stupid, stupid name, she thought—glinting in the torchlight.

Ingo yelled something, but the sound was muffled, like she was trying to listen underwater.

The Hammer pulled back, back, back . . . and then swung forward in a large shining arc, leaving trails of brilliant light in its wake.

THOOOOM!

Everything shook.

Dust billowed from the ceiling.

And the Darkwell burst open.

CHAPTER 26

Catface leapt over the guard's pointed spears and dashed toward the stage. Stray arrows flew by him like a swarm of gnats buzzing past. With one quick movement, he snatched up the Princess, grabbing Thisby's backpack into his jaws, and jumped away, sailing over the crowd.

Where he landed, the crowd scattered. He turned to see the giants closing in on him, rushing him with their swords and axes flashing above their heads. He looked around the room until he found his path and then exploded into action, jumping from platform to platform, higher and higher, until there was only one last big jump to make.

He coiled down, sinking back against his hips, and

waited. Angry screaming came from below, mixed with the confusion and excitement of the gate being opened. He tuned it out.

The Hammer of Righteousness swung closer, carried by the residual momentum from smashing the gate. As it reached the back of its parabolic arch, Catface jumped. He flew through the air, the Princess dangling like a ragdoll from the backpack he held in his mouth. His feet hit the cold steel of the Hammer and scrambled to find something, anything to hold on to. He slipped.

Catface fell splayed over the Hammer as it continued along its path, swinging back toward where the gate had been just moments ago. He tried to find his footing but couldn't, and before he knew it, the Hammer had reached its apex and begun to move backward yet again. Arrows flew overhead as the Hammer returned to the back of its arch. With each swing of the Hammer—and no one left to power its flight—the momentum had begun to slow dramatically. Each swing took Catface farther and farther away from the leap he would inevitably have to make. He knew he was running out of time.

The Hammer swung forward again. This time Catface managed to find his footing. Digging into the steel with his claws, he crouched in wait until the last possible moment, and when the Hammer swung toward the Darkwell, he jumped.

His claws searched frantically for an edge to catch on and thankfully found a piece of the loosed blackweave gate. It was enough.

Catface pulled himself up through the Darkwell, while down below, the Deep Dwellers had already begun to move their siege ladders into position. It would only be moments now before they began to climb through the gate themselves and start their assault. Catface crawled out through the Darkwell into the basin that surrounded it. He was finally back in the dungeon. Back in his home. It was so familiar, so quiet and peaceful compared to where they'd just been. Up through the Darkwell rose the clamor of war, but it sounded surprisingly distant for something so close, so inevitable.

He walked over to his bed calmly and set the Princess down as gently as possible. It wasn't much of a bed, more like a well-worn groove where he'd often slept, but it was warm here and dark and out of the way, and at least the ground was soft. It was the least he could do for her. Iphigenia was shaking and bleeding through her dress. She didn't have long now. He'd seen enough injuries in his time to know that. He tried his best to make her comfortable and then walked back over to the Darkwell.

From here, he'd have a tactical advantage. He knew he'd be able to take out a lot of them as they came up through the well, but eventually he'd be overrun. It was inevitable. The well was big, and no matter how many of them he eliminated, eventually, some would get through. It was only a matter of time before he got tired, and then that would be the end of it.

He peeked down into the well.

Their ladder system was quite clever. It circled the outside of the well so he couldn't simply knock it over. The Deep Dwellers were much smarter than he'd given them credit for.

He sat upright and licked his paws idly. There was nothing left to do now but wait, so he might as well be well groomed for the fight.

"Iphigenia?" said a small voice.

Iphigenia rolled over and looked at the backpack placed beside her. There was a faint pink glow in the jar that hung from it.

"Mingus?" she said.

Speaking made everything hurt. It felt like her stomach was on fire.

"Iphigenia, you need to open my jar. Can you do that?"

Iphigenia nodded. She was so lightheaded that even this small movement made the room spin. She stuck her hand out to reach the jar but it felt so far away. She forced herself onto her side. Everything in her stomach flared painfully.

She grunted.

"Come on, Iphigenia. You've got it," Mingus said soothingly.

Iphigenia dragged herself over to the jar and pulled it off its hook. With every turn of the lid she felt her guts burn like someone was jabbing her insides with a red-hot poker. Finally, the jar opened. She collapsed onto her back, taking labored breaths and trying not to move her stomach as she did.

Mingus slid to the edge of his jar.

When he'd first escaped from the Deep Down, the only thing Mingus had known for certain was that, more than anything in the world, he wanted to feel safe. He'd lived his whole life up to that point feeling frightened and for once, he just wanted to know what it would feel like to not be afraid anymore. For years he'd thought that if he could only make it over to the other side of the Darkwell, there everything would be perfect, and yet, when he got there . . . life was still dangerous, still unpredictable.

It turned out that there was nowhere in the whole world where he felt safe. Until Thisby had given him his jar. He'd never left it by choice before. Thisby had forced him out a few times to clean it, but she had always been there with him, and somehow that had made it not so bad. But here, in the Darkwell, in the place he hated more than any other . . . he quivered.

If Mingus had a heart, it would have been pounding in his ears (if he had ears). All that he had to keep him safe was his jar. It was the only thing he had in the entire world. He couldn't just leave it.

He paused.

Iphigenia looked at him—the sad little slime, too scared to leave his jar.

"I'm sorry," she said, closing her eyes.

Mingus watched her for a moment, and then slid out of his jar.

He slid over to her and climbed onto her stomach, just above the wound. Her dress was soaked through with blood. She winced in pain as Mingus settled down on top of her and then, slowly, he began to glow.

The Deep Dwellers made their way up through the well in a fury of flying spears and arrows intended to drive Catface away from the edge, where he stood batting down the overly ambitious creatures who tried to cross the threshold too soon.

Every time he managed to knock down one Deep Dweller, two more took its place, and soon, they were beginning to breach the gate. Catface took a swing at a giant who'd been climbing the ladder and missed wide, snagging his claw on remnants of the blackweave gate. It was the opening the Deep Dwellers had been waiting for. Before he could free himself, twenty or thirty Deep Dwellers scrambled up through the Darkwell, and Catface had no choice but to abandon his post at the top of the gate and chase after them.

With nobody left to guard the Darkwell, it was the beginning of the end.

Hundreds of Deep Dwellers, creatures of all shapes and sizes, flooded into the dungeon, their terrible bloodlust fueled by millennia of pain and torment at the hands of the Eyes in the Dark. They were horrific, unstoppable beasts, out for—there was a flash of light—out for, um—there was another flash of light—horrific, unstoppable beasts out for—there was yet another flash of light.

...slowly, he began to glow.

Blackdoors had begun to open all around the Darkwell. The Deep Dwellers stopped in their tracks and looked around. All around the edge of the basin, blackdoors were flashing open, bursting with magical energy.

From one of the blackdoors on the center of the hill stepped a small, filthy girl with a pointy nose, clutching a notebook to her chest. She raised her right hand above her head and held it there. The Deep Dwellers looked at her and then at one another. The room was eerily silent. If a snail had sneezed somebody probably would have said "gesundheit."

With a tremendous battle cry, she thrust her fist forward, and monsters burst through the blackdoors, charging down the hill.

The battle of the Darkwell had begun.

CHAPTER 27

Werewolves, ice wraiths, gargoyles, kobolds, vampires, ghouls, rock golems, wereplants, hydras, griffins, death bears, dire rats, centaurs, man-snare plants, acidic oozes, gnolls, nightmares, mummies, ogres, trolls, wyverns, and more had all shown up to fight. They spilled from the blackdoors and charged down the hill, a mess of claws and teeth and vines and ooze, rumbling like a runaway train toward the Deep Dwellers below.

Some of them had come willingly, some begrudgingly, some Thisby had even had to trick, but she'd gotten them all here, and that was what mattered. It'd taken every bit of knowledge she'd painstakingly gathered over the years to convince them all, and when this was all said and done, she'd have a lot of promises to fulfill—so many, in fact, that she had to start another notebook just to record them all—but thanks to her, they'd gathered an army, and thanks to the blackdoors, they'd arrived just in time.

Thisby whirled around to see Grunda, accompanied by several other goblins who she didn't recognize as well as Ralk the kobold, approach her from behind.

"Are you sure you can do this?" asked Thisby, yelling over the din of battle.

"It's goblin magic. We can do it," she said.

"We'll clear the way; you just have to seal the gate. We just need enough magic to hold it for now. We can figure out the rest later," said Thisby.

"Don't worry about us, dear! Go! Find the Princess! As long as Ingo is out there, she isn't safe!"

Thisby nodded and took off down the hill in the wake of the chaos. She ducked through the maelstrom of clashing monsters and weaved her way through toward the Darkwell. Iphigenia had to be down there somewhere.

She passed by a wyvern fighting off two Deep Dwellers at once. It grabbed one of them in its massive claws and took to the sky as the other fled. Just a few days ago that could've been her or Iphigenia, she thought with a smirk.

WHOMP!

A massive war hammer barely clipped Thisby's shoulder, but it was enough to send her flying, tumbling end over end

They spilled from the blackdoors and charged down the hill, a mess of claws and teeth and vines and ooze, rumbling like a runaway train toward the Deep Dwellers below.

until she spilled into the dirt. She'd let her mind wander for just a second, but that was all it took. Her shoulder ached. It felt like she'd just run full steam into a brick wall. The giant thundered toward her, drawing back his massive hammer, but before he could bring it down, an enormous paw swiped sideways and knocked the giant aside as if he were a ball of yarn.

Catface pounced on him, and the giant was finished before he even knew what hit him.

"Iphigenia's hurt," he said, running back over to her. "You need to get her out of here."

"Where is she?" yelled Thisby.

"Get on, I'll take you," said Catface.

Ingo Larkspur climbed out of the Darkwell behind his army, expecting to see a triumphant victory. He was mildly disappointed. He'd had a speech ready and everything. A whole night's worth of speech writing and practicing his "power poses" in front of a mirror, all down the drain. He sighed. What a waste.

There was a stinging pain radiating from where his sister had poked him with that needle. His guards had attempted to remove it, but the barb held fast below his skin, so it had been broken off for the time being, leaving a little black rod jutting out of his side. He'd brushed it with his elbow several times while he was climbing and had quite nearly fainted from the pain. He'd have to have it removed when he got back to the castle. Back home. Back to the safety of his own bed. A bed that was sounding better and better by the moment. He felt unnaturally tired for some reason. Sleepy. Sleepy *McGeepy*, even. What a strange phrase, thought Ingo, to have just popped in there.

All around him, Deep Dwellers scattered and fled under the onslaught of the dungeon's monsters, who'd apparently caught them with their proverbial pants down. It turned out the Deep Dwellers weren't exactly the well-trained soldiers Ingo had hoped they were. They were more like monkeys with sharpened sticks. Sure, they were big, horrifying monkeys, and their sticks were quite sharp, but at the end of the day that wasn't enough to win any wars. A simple surprise attack was enough to derail their entire "strategy"— what little of it there was to begin with.

Ingo wondered how the Eyes in the Dark ever thought this was a war the Deep Dwellers could win. Another thought immediately pinged into his brain with an answer he felt as if he'd known all along. The Eyes in the Dark didn't think they could win. Maybe he didn't care. Then why? Why go through all this trouble?

Even in the haze that had begun to form around his mind, Ingo knew the answer. Ingo was bad at many things, but reading people wasn't one of them. Strange then, how he'd never managed to see it all clearly until now. The Eyes in the Dark didn't care about the liberation of the Deep Dwellers. Of course he didn't. He only wanted the gate opened for himself. He didn't care who died in the process. Not the Deep Dwellers, not the monsters, not Roquat, not Iphigenia, not Ingo.

It was ambition Ingo understood. Admired, even.

His guards circled around him, forming a defensive perimeter around their fearless leader as he surveyed the scene. Ingo yawned. They were fighting a losing battle. The good guys—or were they the bad guys? Ingo wasn't sure and honestly didn't care—either way, he was pretty sure they'd lost.

Ingo shrugged. At least, he thought he did. In truth, he didn't have the energy to properly raise his shoulders, and merely imagined himself shrugging. Close enough.

Nearby, he saw some goblins attempting to seal the Darkwell with magic. Spell books were lying open at their feet. It was pretty obvious what they were doing, but none of the Deep Dwellers seemed to be paying much attention. They really, really weren't any good at war.

Ingo wondered if he should stop the goblins, but his sister was probably right. It didn't really make any sense to let Deep Dwellers run around free in his kingdom. He'd gotten what he wanted out of the deal anyway. Iphigenia was dead and he'd soon inherit the throne. It was kind of a win-win. And furthermore, so what if he broke his deal? Once he was back home, he'd be safe from the Eyes in the Dark.

Anyway, there was no shame in backing out now. Get out while the getting was good, he figured. It was exhausting work and he deserved a break.

Ingo turned to his guards. His eyes were half closed and his head had begun to droop.

"Okay, well, see you later, I guess," he said dreamily.

And with that, Ingo simply turned and walked away, dragging his feet clumsily and leaving behind a rather confused-looking group of guards who were moments ago ready to protect their leader with their lives, if it came to that. If there'd been a proper order to the Deep Dwellers' military, somebody—perhaps a general or other high-ranking officer—would've surely stopped their leader from loping off by himself in the middle of the battle, but as it were, nobody said a thing or even followed after him. They simply watched him go for a few moments before they turned back to the fighting.

Ingo walked for almost an hour before the thought even crossed his mind that he might be lost. In truth, not much was crossing his mind at this point, aside from a strong desire to sleep and a lingering curiosity as to why it felt like he was walking through a warm bath. Days ago, before Roquat's untimely demise at Ingo's order, the Dünkeldwarf had explained to him how to find his way to the castle from the Darkwell, but he hadn't written anything down, and if Ingo was being perfectly honest—which he almost never was—he hadn't even really paid attention. At the time, it'd seemed fairly straightforward. Now, though, it felt as if something were clouding his mind. He looked disapprovingly at an oblong rock for a minute or two before surrendering and sitting down on it to think. It was as uncomfortable as he'd expected, and yet somehow still seemed as if it would be a nice enough place to fall asleep.

He sat there for some time, mindlessly rubbing his side where the barb was buried beneath his skin and fighting off the urge to sleep, before the sound of approaching footsteps got his attention.

"Hello?" said Ingo. "I think— I think— I'm lost. Can you . . . um . . . help?"

A gangly young man, at least a handful of years older than Ingo, rounded the corner. He looked fairly lost himself and studied Ingo with some fascination.

"I need to find the way out of here. I need to go home," said Ingo.

Gregory studied him. The boy he was looking at was dressed nicely, perhaps too nicely for the dungeon. He was handsome, but tired. And there was something familiar about his face that Gregory couldn't quite place. The recollection was likely due to the fact that in Gregory's pockets, he had several copper coins with the Prince's face printed on them, but who looks that closely at coins anyhow?

After considering him for what felt like an appropriate amount of time, Gregory chimed in, "I'm actually trying to find a battle, myself. I was supposed to meet some people there. Ultimate stand against evil and whatnot. But I'm 'fraid I took a wrong turn somewhere."

Ingo shut his eyes for a moment and had to shake himself back awake.

"Yes, yes. Well, do you think you could point me toward the way out of here?" asked Ingo.

Gregory scratched his head. It didn't itch, but he really wanted to indicate that he was seriously pondering Ingo's question, and this seemed like the best way. He momentarily considered doing that thing where you rest your chin between your thumb and forefinger, but it felt like it might be overkill.

"I think you want to head straight from here. When you get to a little pond up ahead, turn left. Then, uh, another left at the fork. That should just about get you there."

Ingo nodded again and almost fell asleep. His head tipped forward and then rocked back. He woke with a start and got to his feet. Gregory watched him and considered offering help, but realized it was probably best if he hurried on to the battle. There was a chance it would determine the fate of the world, and he'd be pretty embarrassed if he missed that. So he watched the boy who he didn't know was a Prince shuffle off alone, and then hurried on himself in the opposite direction.

Ingo pulled himself along for some time, dragging his feet and bracing himself against the wall when he needed to, until finally, near the fork, he had to stop and rest. Another left at the fork, the gangly man had said. He was so close. He had almost drifted off again when he heard a noise that sounded like wet sandpaper on stone. It startled him awake.

"Hello? W-who's there?" Ingo mumbled weakly.

There was a faint glow coming from just around the bend, as if somebody was holding a lantern.

There was no answer.

Ingo mustered all his strength and stood up. Since the invasion had begun, his nerves had been a little frayed. Before the invasion, the monsters in the dungeon wanted to kill him for food. Now, he suspected, correctly, most of the monsters in the dungeon wanted to kill him for vengeance . . . well, and for food still, probably. Although with every passing minute his concern diminished. If Ingo had had his wits about him, he likely would've headed in the opposite direction of any noise down in the dungeon. As it were, he peeked around the corner.

He stared blankly at what he saw. It was no vicious monster out for revenge—or even food, for that matter. Just a faintly glowing goat, levitating several inches off the ground and contentedly licking the moss off some rocks with its eyes closed. Ingo laughed.

"Jus' a sssstupid goat," he slurred.

Ingo slumped to the ground on all fours. The stone beneath him felt like soft, warm bread as the remaining manticore poison in the barb finally won out. His limbs felt as if they were full of wet sand, and sleep crept in through the cracks in his resolve to stay awake.

The licking stopped. There was a momentary silence

followed by the rhythmic clack of goat hooves on stone growing louder and louder from where Ingo lay, fighting to keep his eyes open. The hooves stopped. He could smell the hot, pungent breath of the animal. With all his remaining strength, Ingo picked his head up from the ground and craned his neck to look at the goat standing over him. They were practically face-to-face.

"Stupid goat," Ingo whispered.

The goat looked down at him and slowly began to unhinge its jaw, revealing several sets of long, serrated fangs. Its eyes became glowing bloodred pools with several pupils each, and its body doubled in size, legs extending from it like a spider as it grew.

It was the most horrible thing Ingo had ever seen, and he watched it all with unblinking eyes, unable to move, unable to scream, as the goat—or whatever it truly was—descended upon him.

In his final moments, Ingo didn't feel regret for what he'd done, only sleepy. So sleepy that he didn't even feel frightened as the spectral goat began to devour him whole, and all things considered, it was probably a better ending than he deserved.

Catface bounded across the battlefield to where he'd left Iphigenia. Thisby slid from his shoulders.

"Thank you . . . Catface," she said.

"You're welcome . . . Little Mouse."

He bowed quickly and charged back into the fray.

Thisby ran over to Iphigenia. She was lying on her back and barely conscious. She was so far from the Iphigenia Thisby had met when she'd first entered the dungeon. Her beautiful dress was torn and dirty, her hair had fallen out of its neat braids, and her eyes were puffy and red.

Thisby touched her shoulder and tried to gently rouse her.

"Thisby?" Iphigenia said wearily.

"Iphigenia! What happened?"

Thisby saw the blood on her dress, but there was no wound, only a rip in the fabric and a bright pink scar. There was also a mild glowing where the wound had been.

"What—what happened?" muttered Thisby.

"Mingus . . . he . . ."

Thisby looked over to see Mingus's empty jar, and tears began to stream down her cheeks. She wiped at them with dirty fingers, leaving smudges across her face. She had no idea what had happened, but between Iphigenia's tone and the empty jar . . . it couldn't be good. She'd never even had a chance to tell him that it was okay, a chance to forgive him.

Iphigenia's eyes began to well with tears. Then her nose began to well with snot. Even her mouth began to well with something . . .

Iphigenia rolled over and began retching. A ball of glowing slime oozed out of her nose and mouth and fell with a wet *splat* onto the floor beside her. Thisby stared at the blob of quivering goo, unsure what she'd just seen. Iphigenia hacked something up and spit, wiping her mouth with the sleeve of her dress.

"Mingus?" said Thisby, staring at the slime.

Mingus gurgled something weakly in response. "Can I please go back in my jar now?" he asked.

"He saved my life," said Iphigenia.

Thisby's eyes grew to the size of dinner plates as it all began to click together. The scar, the blood on the dress, Mingus being sneezed out of her friend's face . . .

"SLIME HEALING MAGIC IS REAL?" screamed Thisby.

CHAPTER 28

Thisby watched anxiously from a distance as the monsters dispersed back home to their own special corners of the dungeon, leaving the Darkwell behind. It was the part of her plan that had made her the most nervous; even if they were successful, would the temporary truce last long enough for the monsters to make it back to their lairs, or would the basilisk get into a staring contest with the cockatrice, or the fire bats melt the ice wraiths?

In the end, it'd worked out about as well as she could have hoped. The monsters, so exhausted from their confrontation with the Deep Dwellers, had for the most part loped back to their respective homes calmly and in an orderly fashion. It was a temporary unity. Thisby knew that better than anyone. Yet still, there was something hopeful about looking out over the edge of the Darkwell and seeing that whole menagerie of monsters working together toward a common goal. It was only a shame that it had to be drenched in so much violence.

Leaderless and disorganized, it hadn't taken long for most of the Deep Dwellers to be driven back down through the Darkwell. Some even went willingly. Following the battle, Catface had quickly begun hunting down any remaining Deep Dwellers who'd fled or hid out during the fighting, but there was no way to find all of them—not even with Catface's amazing sense of smell. Too many had escaped out into the dungeon, or perhaps even out of the Black Mountain itself, where they'd found the freedom they'd so desperately craved. Thisby couldn't blame them.

As Grunda and the other goblins placed their temporary magic seal over the Darkwell, Thisby even found herself wondering if they were doing the right thing. Not all the Deep Dwellers were bad. They were just angry and scared. She figured she would be, too, if she'd spent her whole life trapped on the wrong side of that gate, so close to the Eyes in the Dark. But that was the whole problem. If she opened it, he might get out as well.

Yet during the battle, there'd been no sign of the Eyes in the Dark. Perhaps it had simply all ended too quickly—the whole thing had only lasted mere minutes after Thisby and the monsters arrived—but she suspected there was more to it than that. She'd met him down there in the darkness below the mountain, wherever they had been, and she knew he was far too large to fit through the gate himself, which she'd assumed had been his plan. Maybe it had been the magic that had held him in place, but then again, Roquat had figured out some time ago that the magic on the Darkwell had been broken, and surely he'd informed the Eyes in the Dark about it. So what, then, had kept the Eyes in the Dark at bay? Was the gate even necessary, or was it just a prison holding the Deep Dwellers in? And if so . . . why? Maybe—the thought crept into her mind uninvited—just maybe, the Eyes in the Dark had actually done the right thing in trying to destroy it, even if he'd gone about it the absolute wrong way.

No, for now they were better safe than sorry. It made more sense to keep the Darkwell in place, and that meant the Deep Dwellers had to stay right where they were. She'd have plenty of time later to figure out a better solution. The dungeon was safe now—well, at least as safe as a dungeon full of monsters could be.

When things seemed as if they were under control, Thisby brought a blackdoor bead over to Iphigenia, who was still sitting up now, propped against Thisby's backpack, talking to Mingus. Iphigenia smiled.

"One last one," said Thisby. "This one'll take you all the way back up to the Castle."

Moments ago, Thisby had gotten word that a rather angry General—leading a rather large army—had finally managed to break the Master's resolve when she insisted that she be let into Castle Grimstone. Undoubtedly, the Master was buying time at the moment, stammering and trying to find a way to say "We lost the royal twins" that wouldn't result with him losing his head in turn. The thought made Thisby want to stall a bit, but all things considered, the Master had come through and made the blackdoors for her when she really needed them.

"Can I stay here a moment?" asked Iphigenia.

"Is it your stomach?" asked Thisby.

Iphigenia laughed a little bit. Admittedly, it did hurt to laugh.

"No. I mean, it hurts, sure. But I'm all right. I just want to sit for a minute."

Thisby sat down beside Iphigenia, who stared straight ahead.

"Has anyone found Ingo yet?" Iphigenia asked after some time.

"I don't think so . . . but Catface is looking," said Thisby.

"It's okay. I don't think he made it."

"What makes you say that?"

"It's a twin thing. It feels a bit like losing your arm."

She paused.

"Well, losing a finger at least."

Thisby didn't know what to say. There wasn't really anything *to* say. She looked over at the Princess in her bloody dress, her hair disheveled, her face smeared with mud, and expected to find her crying. To look defeated. Yet somehow Iphigenia looked stronger than ever. It was the strength of a Queen. Maybe more than that.

Thisby felt the *Good Feeling*.

That was what she called it anyway. The *Good Feeling* always started somewhere in her chest—or maybe it was her back, it was hard to be sure—and it burst out racing through her entire body like a wave of energy, repeating in short tingly ripples until it faded away. It was a feeling that was more than happiness, more than joy, it was an elevation of spirit, it was her heart singing. She sometimes thought that it felt like the real her was trying to get out. Like her happy ghost was banging against the cage of her chest. Other times it felt almost like something was pulling her in a particular direction, like a magnet had spun around her internal compass and suddenly the needle was pointing her toward exactly where she needed to go. All she knew was that once she had the *Good Feeling*, she never wanted it to end.

Needless to say, Thisby smiled.

"What now?" she asked.

It was Iphigenia's turn to smile.

"I don't know. I suppose I go back to Lyra Castelis and continue to prepare to be Queen. It could be years until I ascend to the throne. Decades, even."

"And in the meantime?"

Thisby was wondering how to broach the subject. Iphigenia as well.

Neither of the girls had ever had a friend before—well, not a human one, anyhow—and watching them attempt to navigate the subtle and complex social bonds of friendship was a bit like watching a monkey trying on a hat. They shuffled in their seats, wondering what to do next; Thisby clutched the blackdoor bead tightly in her sweaty palm.

"Well . . . ," said Iphigenia, breaking the silence. For a moment it felt as if she wasn't going to finish her thought, but when Thisby didn't bail her out by speaking out of turn, she felt compelled to continue.

"I suppose I should be going," Iphigenia said as she stood, smoothing out the folds of her dress. The futile attempt at straightening her filthy and bloodstained dress would've made Thisby laugh if she hadn't felt an immense weight in her chest at Iphigenia's announcement.

"I suppose," mumbled Thisby in agreement, without sounding like she agreed at all.

Thisby handed Iphigenia the blackdoor. She briefly imagined herself running over to the Darkwell and dropping the bead in through the holes of the temporary grate. "Now you can't go! You've gotta stay!" she'd yell. It was a stupid thought, and it embarrassed her.

Iphigenia threw the blackdoor bead at the ground and it burst open, the portal crackling to life before them. Through the doorway was an empty room in Castle Grimstone, looking strangely lifeless, like a dusty oil painting. There was no noise, no heat from the other side. Just stale air and some dust motes drifting through a grayish sunbeam that formed a cross on the black marble tile.

Iphigenia took a deep breath, but did not step forward.

"Iphigenia . . . ," said Thisby.

The Princess turned.

"I think I'd really like to write you once in a while," she continued. "Do you think that would be okay?"

Iphigenia nodded.

"And I'd like you to write me, too."

Iphigenia nodded again.

Iphigenia stepped through the blackdoor and turned back toward the gamekeeper. They watched each other for some time. From a distance it almost appeared as if the girls were looking into a mirror, yet their reflections couldn't be more disparate. On one side was the mousy gamekeeper standing on the edge of the Darkwell, and on the other, a princess, standing in an empty castle. They both waved good-bye in unison.

"Thisby, I . . . I'm happy that we met," said the Princess.

But before the poor girl on the other side of the mirror could respond, the blackdoor snapped shut, and Thisby was alone.

How long she stood there, she wasn't certain. But after some time, Thisby walked over to Mingus and her backpack, hefted the enormous bag up onto her shoulders, and began the long walk back.

As they walked, she hooked Mingus back to his usual spot on her backpack, where he dangled just over her shoulder, glowing a soft, comforting blue.

"Are you okay?" he asked after some time.

Thisby smiled. She'd been doing more of that lately than she would've expected, given the circumstances.

"I'm fine, you?"

"Tired."

"Me too."

On the walk back, Thisby hummed a mindless tune and thought about everything she'd have to add to her notebooks over the next few days. It was going to be hard to keep track of it all. But she'd try her best. She always did.

CHAPTER 29

Thisby Thestoop climbed the same ladder she climbed every day, up three hundred and four rungs back to her bedroom. She set down her bag and unhooked Mingus's jar, carried him over to her desk, and locked the jar into its dedicated spot.

Mingus slid out and into a large glass enclosure that sat atop her desk. Attached to the enclosure were a series of clear glass tubes supported by brass rings that wrapped around the entire room. It was one of the many gifts the Master had given her since she'd refused to take his job and agreed to stay on as gamekeeper. It was also one of the only ones she hadn't sent back.

After the incident at the Darkwell, many of the dungeon's residents had pushed for Thisby to ascend to the Master's role, but she'd rejected their offer, as flattering as it might have been. She preferred to stay down in the dungeon where she felt she belonged, much to the delight of the current Master. Of course, Thisby had a few changes in mind that went along with her refusal, but the Master was happy to meet her demands if it meant he could keep his job—and his head, as was customary when relinquishing the position.

There was a knock at her door.

"Come in!" said Thisby.

The door swung open to reveal Grunda standing there, smiling. Of Thisby's few demands, one of them was the instant and permanent appointment of Grunda to Roquat's old position as liaison to the castle. It went without saying, perhaps, but she was doing a much better job than her predecessor.

"It's time . . . Master," she said politely with a wink.

"Don't call me that!" chided Thisby.

Despite her refusal to formally accept the role of Master of the Black Mountain, many residents of the dungeon wouldn't let it go, much to her annoyance.

Thisby preferred being gamekeeper. It was what she knew, what she'd trained her whole life for, where she could do the most good. She didn't want to live in the castle and deal with the local lords and ladies whose foolish children went adventuring down into the dungeon and never returned.

She liked her life as gamekeeper and didn't want anything to change . . . well, almost anything.

"It's time to put the book away, we have to go!" she called to Mingus, who'd taken to using the little mechanical arms the Master had installed on Thisby's desk for him. Since his experience in the Deep Down, he'd even begun adding to her notebooks himself at times, using his knowledge of growing up in the Deep Down to round out some of her notes on the subject. She even caught him doing little cartoons in the margins.

As she passed out of her bedroom, Thisby slid the notebook back into its proper spot on her shelf. Over the past couple of months while she was waiting for the repairs on the Darkwell to be finished, she'd lovingly copied each book by hand into nice leather-bound volumes. It was a treat for herself after surviving the ordeal. She'd donated her originals to a small library that Grunda had organized for future generations of gamekeepers—not that anybody was in a hurry to replace her; it was just that after all these years, it felt like time to share some of the things she'd learned.

The repairs to the Darkwell had gone about as well as Thisby could've hoped. They managed to source some of the extra blackweave needed for the repairs from the City of Night, and by the time the work was finished, you'd hardly have known it was ever broken in the first place. Combined with Grunda's and the other goblins' magic, as well as the newly restored gate, the Darkwell was as secure as it had ever been. Restoring order to the dungeon after the invasion was a lot of work, but it was good work, and Thisby was happy to do it.

Thisby had told Grunda about her encounter with the Eyes in the Dark, at least what she could remember of it. She'd felt so disoriented after their encounter that she often felt as if the whole thing were a terrible dream. It made Grunda nervous, and for a few weeks she'd insisted that Thisby wear a good luck necklace until the next full moon, but truth be told, there wasn't a whole lot that could be done about it—except for making a trip into the Deep Down to confront him—and so life soon returned to normal.

Thisby made her way up to the castle and knocked on the door. She and Grunda were escorted inside by two polite ghouls in leather jerkins bearing the newly designed sigil of Castle Grimstone—the design had been Thisby's suggestion as well. The sigil was shaped like the Black Mountain and inside it there were four symbols that Thisby thought best represented the dungeon; a claw, a skull, a sword, and a door. Mingus insisted that the symbols had to mean something, but Thisby wasn't convinced. In the end, he'd suggested that maybe the claw represented the monsters, the skull represented the Master, the sword represented the adventurers, and the door represented either the Deep Down or magic in general, but Thisby didn't really care what they meant. For her, it was what they stood for that mattered, and what they stood for was a new beginning.

For as much as had stayed the same in the Black Mountain, a lot had changed as well. Access to the castle was no longer strictly forbidden to creatures who dwelled in the dungeon, and the Master had to personally hear the complaints of any creature, no matter how big or small, if they wished for their complaints to be heard. The Master hated this, of course, but he made do since it was still preferable to the alternative of "gruesome death." Just barely.

A small crowd was already waiting at the gates of the castle when Thisby and Grunda walked out onto the grounds. Thisby was feeling anxious about this whole thing and started to wonder if it was too late to back out. She wiggled her pinky toe over the top of the toe-which-comes-next-to-the-pinky-toe and fidgeted with her well-starched tunic, smoothing out the folds.

"Psst! Thisby!" whispered Mingus.

She looked over at Mingus's jar and saw that he'd put in his "surprised eyes," which were big white circles with tiny little black dots for pupils. Thisby laughed and felt a little better. It was a new joke that he'd added to his repertoire last month, and somehow, she hadn't gotten sick of it yet.

Thisby was wearing her best dress clothes, which doubled as her only dress clothes. They weren't exactly comfortable, but she figured she could make do for now. She had a pair of new, nonpatchwork leggings decorated with little embroidered T's for Thisby that some of the goblins had made for her as a gift for the special occasion.

She'd even managed to get her hair to lay flat by combing it through with some dire slug ooze, which had been quite the ordeal, as Thisby had an awfully hard time sitting still and Grunda wasn't exactly practiced at combing hair gently.

The gates to the castle opened, and an extravagant carriage decorated with ornate gold scrollwork rolled in. Two well-dressed servants hopped down and rushed over to the doors, taking little bouncy steps. The carriage doors opened.

Iphigenia took the coachman's hand and stepped down to the ground, although she might as well have been floating above it. Her dress was green and gold, with little stones that lit up, reflecting the sunlight and created the aura of a sunrise breaking over a field on a spring morning. It was fit for a queen . . . well, a future queen, at least.

"Thisby!" she called.

The air of formality and ceremony deflated at once as Iphigenia rushed over to Thisby and wrapped her arms around her. Thisby's anxiety melted away. It was as if nothing had changed since the last time they'd seen each other. They'd sent letters back and forth for months, but there was no easy way for the Princess to come visit, as busy as she was, and as far as Thisby visiting her, well, that had been out of the question . . . until now.

"Are you ready?" Iphigenia asked.

"I guess so," said Thisby.

One of Iphigenia's servants attempted to take Thisby's

backpack from her, but Iphigenia just laughed and waved him off.

"I think she'll keep it! I'm not sure you could lift it anyway!"

They climbed aboard the carriage, and Thisby looked back at Grunda as the door swung closed. It was Thisby's first time leaving the dungeon, and it was almost as frightening as walking into the Deep Down had been. She was only going to be gone for a few weeks, but she was already terrified thinking about the state the dungeon would be in when she got back. At least she had Grunda there now to keep an eye on things.

Iphigenia looked at Thisby from across the carriage and beamed at her.

"So, what's the castle like?" asked Thisby.

"Oh, you know . . . it's full of monsters trying to kill you and people trying to steal your gold. You should feel right at home."

Thisby smiled and the carriage rolled on.

Life in Nth was far from perfect—just visit Three Fingers one day and ask how the town got its name, ugh—but based on the voices coming from that carriage, nobody would have ever known. High atop the Black Mountain, the Master sulked in his chambers, dreaming of how things used to be, and far, far below, in the place where light cannot touch, the Eyes in the Dark waited, dreaming of the same. But there, in that carriage, two girls were dreaming of how things would be from this day forward.

Iphigenia looked at Thisby from across the carriage and beamed at her.

The adventure continues with

Thisby Thestoop

AND THE

Wretched Scrattle.

Take a sneak peek!

Chapter 1

It was raining, because of course it was. Never before in the history of rain had a downpour been colder, grayer, or drearier than it was that night, and honestly, it was all getting to be a bit much. Even the ravens who were normally game for the whole "dark and stormy" bit felt uneasy with the excessive use of clichés, and so, as the hearse-black carriage rumbled past, they decided to flap from their regular perch atop a gnarled yew tree to what they considered to be a far less derivative spot on the roof of a nearby cobbler's shop.

The coachman blinked his hooded lantern several times at the gatekeepers in a series of dots and dashes, which in turn caused the large wrought iron gates to yawn open with the loud squeal of metal rubbing metal. Beyond the gates was a sparkling white castle, or at least what should have been a sparkling white castle had it not been for the gloomy overcast sky of that particular night, which instead shrouded the building in a sort of bilious green pall. Even the lights which flickered from inside the castle windows—normally so happy and inviting—looked downright macabre, like two candles placed inside the vacant eye sockets of a giant's skull. Out in the distance two ravens cawed derisively.

The gates slammed shut behind the carriage as it rattled onward toward the Castle, slick cobblestones shining like black marble in the advancing torchlight. It trundled along until it came to rest in front of the towering drawbridge of Lyra Castelis. The attendants who'd been traveling alongside the carriage climbed down off their horses and opened the carriage door, allowing a very tall, very elegant shadow to exit the vehicle.

The shadow's face was indiscernible beneath the upturned collar of a dark, fur-lined cloak and wide-brimmed hat, but whoever it was moved like a ballet dancer. At first glance, it seemed as if the figure was untouched by the rain, simply stepping in between the drops with such ease that it seemed curious as to why everyone else didn't just do the same. Upon closer inspection, however, raindrops could definitely be seen pattering gently on the shadow's wide hat, collecting in small pools before choosing an edge from which to run off in a thin trickle. It was something of a relief to see the figure touched by rain, proof that it was at least corporeal.

Shaking themselves awake from the spell caused by watching the figure, the carriage attendants remembered their mission and ran after the shadow, their mostly-decorative swords rattling in their hilts. The castle guards, looking much more professional than those two struggling to keep up, swung open a set of small wooden guest doors nested within the gargantuan drawbridge and bowed ever so slightly as the shadow whooshed by them without so much as acknowledging their presence.

Inside the castle, the world transformed. The earthy smell of rain was instantly replaced by the scent of warm baked bread and stale floral arrangements, the light transitioned from its uneasy, rainstorm green to the pleasant orange glow of a crackling hearth on the first cold night of autumn, and the rush of rain becoming a gentle pitter-patter accompanied by the distant twinkling of harp strings. In other words, it was nice. What wasn't nice, however, was the shadowy figure, who suddenly looked extraordinarily out of place where only moments ago it'd looked perfectly at home.

The shadow strode down the hall on long, bowed legs, the dark cloak trailing behind, flapping like an angry bird. Castle guards stared but did not make any motion to interfere as the figure walked right down the vaulted hallway, past the marble statues, the priceless paintings, and the brightly polished suits of armor, through the large oak double doors inlaid with jewels and twirling, decorative golden bands, and right up the dark red carpet to where Parlo Larkspur, the King of Nth, sat upon his throne. Beside the King was a young girl, seated in her own—albeit significantly smaller—throne. They both watched the shadow approaching with rigidly fixed smiles that barely concealed their displeasure at its arrival.

"Welcome to Lyra Castelis, my dear Marl." The King beamed. "I trust that your journey to Oryzia was as comfortable as could be expected given the weather?"

Marl removed her hat and bowed. "Yes, m'lord."

The shadow was suddenly no longer a shadow but a regular human woman, tall and thin and fairly androgynous. If she'd been a man, you would've called her pretty, as a woman you might call her handsome. Either way, it was fair to say that she was striking. Much more than what would've been expected from her entrance. Her green hair cascaded down past her shoulders, her nose was long but pleasantly sloped, and her eyes tilted down gently at the outer corners a bit, creating a sort of charming, sleepy countenance. All these factors combined to create a face which was not so much traditionally beautiful as it was a challenge to ignore. The only things off-putting about the stranger were the dark purple circles under her eyes, which made them look deeply bruised and tired. They were the eyes of someone who read far more often than they slept.

Marl smiled gently. One of the guards came up to take her cloak.

"Please," boomed King Larkspur, who boomed more often than not even when he didn't intend to, "allow me to introduce . . ."

"Your daughter," said Marl with a soft lilt.

With a flick of her wrist, Marl politely waved away the guard that carried off her sopping wet cloak and hat.

The King did not look perturbed by the interruption, as perhaps he should have. Rather he simply beamed proudly at his daughter and then back toward his rather unusual guest.

Beneath her cloak, Marl was wearing expensive robes as black as the night sky; the cloth was black, the trim was black, even the stitching was black. In fact, the only thing that Marl wore which was not black was a golden bracelet that dangled off her right wrist. It was in the shape of a dragon biting its own tail.

Marl smiled again, this time a bit apologetically.

"Forgive my interruption, m'lord, I only meant that of course I'm familiar with the lovely, brave, and famous Iphigenia Larkspur, Crown Princess of Nth, Chosen Heir to the Throne."

Iphigenia sat absolutely still as she studied the stranger. At last, with great effort spent to show no emotion whatsoever, she nodded curtly in Marl's direction, who returned the nod graciously before continuing.

"I suppose you would like the news, m'lord."

King Larkspur nodded. With a wave of his royal hand, several guards, including those who had arrived with Marl, excused themselves from the chamber and closed the door behind them with an ominous *ka-chunk!* that resonated throughout the throne room. When at last they were down to the minimum number of necessary and trusted guards—which it turned out was exactly four, for some reason—Marl proceeded.

"In Umberfall, they're plotting against you and your kingdom every day, m'lord. I hear the whispers in the capital, both in the streets and inside the palace walls. But what they have in ambition, they lack in numbers. Their army is sturdy enough to defend a fortified position but far too small to make the journey south through the mountains. They'd lose too many soldiers in the process, exhaust their resources, and by the time they were on the doorstep of your kingdom, they'd be as good as dead. As long as the Umberfalians are trapped north of the mountains, we can rest easy."

Iphigenia looked over to her father, who seemed pensive as he stroked his salt-and-pepper beard that, as of late, had become more salt than pepper. Her father was a robust man but Iphigenia had seen him begin to wear around the edges since last year. Since Ingo's death.

The death of her brother had sent shockwaves through the kingdom but nowhere had it been worse than inside Lyra Castelis itself. Not only her father but everyone who lived within the castle had loved Ingo—*wonderful, brave, charming Ingo!*—and the fact that he'd died a traitor was more than the royal family could bear. For months, her father had lived in outright denial, refusing to admit what Ingo had done, but over time, in the face of no other options, he came to accept the truth. At least, that's what he said publicly, officially denouncing his son and having his name stricken from the Larkspur family history—a punishment reserved exclusively for traitors.

Between Iphigenia and her father however, things had yet to return to normal. It was likely that they never would. Although it was awful to admit, Iphigenia couldn't shake the feeling that somewhere deep down inside there was some small part of her father that blamed her for what happened in the Black Mountain. After all, if she'd never been born, things would've worked out just fine. Ingo would've been King, and everybody would have lived happily ever after. But she was born. Much to the displeasure of seemingly everybody.

"Of course, we must consider all possibilities . . ." Marl said, letting her words hang ominously in the air. The chamber felt oddly colder.

The King leaned forward in his great throne so that it creaked beneath his not insubstantial weight. Along with showing his age, his diet had begun to catch up with him as well. The King's brow furrowed and his eyes widened in a pantomime of worried confusion. Iphigenia was embarrassed for him, that he was playing so easily into Marl's game, letting himself show his emotions like a child. Marl seemed to be reveling in it.

"What do you mean?" asked the King.

Iphigenia rolled her eyes.

Since being back in the castle—and having everyone treat her as if she was somehow responsible for her brother's death—Iphigenia had felt a bit more like her old self again, whatever that meant. All that she knew was that she'd been growing more impatient with people in the castle and their absurd political games lately, particularly since Thisby's visit.

The visit had been wonderful. So wonderful, in fact, that the residual happiness had lasted for weeks even after Thisby's carriage pulled away from the gates of the castle. It was like eating slices of leftover birthday cake; the memories of her visit had sustained Iphigenia for some time but by now whatever scraps remained had long since gone stale. She'd even gotten to the point where it made her feel slightly sick to her stomach to even think about their time together, not knowing how long it would be until she could see her friend again. Her only friend. Iphigenia chased the thought from her mind.

"There is a chance, however slim, that the Umberfalians could make it through the mountains and into Nth."

The King was eating out of Marl's hands now. His brow was fully knitted and he tugged at his beard as if in deep contemplation.

"But how?" he asked.

"There is one path in that we haven't considered. One shortcut into Nth. Through the Black Mountain."

The emphasis Marl placed on the words *"Black Mountain"*

made it seem as if she'd expected the King to gasp, but he didn't. Instead, his face just sank, and Iphigenia saw the same defeat in his eyes that she'd seen over and over again since she'd returned home from the dungeon. When her father learned about Ingo's death, she saw that look on his face for the first time. Now, it happened too often to count. Something about it made her sick. She wanted to feel empathy for her father's suffering but she had no pity for Ingo, and to see that pity in another, especially her father . . . it was unbearable. A king was meant to be strong, to punish the wicked. And here was her own brother, his own son, more wicked than any, and yet he pitied him. He pitied himself.

Iphigenia couldn't stand to look at him and so she turned to Marl. She'd had enough of sitting quietly now.

"The Black Mountain wouldn't sit idly by and watch an army pass through. Especially not an Umberfalian army," she said with what might've passed for a sneer. "Anyone stupid enough to try to pass through the dungeon would be dead before they reached the halfway point . . ."

Iphigenia hesitated.

" . . . I should know," she finished.

Books by
ZAC GORMAN!

HARPER
An Imprint of HarperCollinsPublishers

www.harpercollinschildrens.com • www.shelfstuff.com